THE DEVIL
MAY CARE

Center Point
Large Print

**This Large Print Book carries the
Seal of Approval of N.A.V.H.**

THE DEVIL
MAY CARE

David
Housewright

CENTER POINT LARGE PRINT
THORNDIKE, MAINE

This Center Point Large Print edition is published
in the year 2014 by arrangement with St. Martin's Press.

The text of this Large Print edition is unabridged.
In other aspects, this book may vary from the original edition.
Printed in the United States of America on permanent paper.
Set in 16-point Times New Roman type.

ISBN: 978-1-62899-231-1

Library of Congress Cataloging-in-Publication Data

Housewright, David, 1955–
  The devil may care / David Housewright. —
    Center Point Large Print edition.
  pages ; cm
  Summary: "The search for a suddenly missing man entangles unlicensed
P.I. Rushmore McKenzie with one of the most powerful-and-ruthless
local families"—Provided by publisher.
  ISBN 978-1-62899-231-1 (library binding : alk. paper)
  1. McKenzie, Mac (Fictitious character)—Fiction.
    2. Private investigators—Minnesota—Fiction.
    3. Large type books. I. Title.
  PS3558.O8668D48 2014b
  813′.54—dc23
                                                2014019451

For Renée,
the best is yet to be

.................Acknowledgments

I wish to acknowledge my debt to India Cooper, Pat Donnelly, Tammi Fredrickson, Maggie Hood, Keith Kahla, Mark MacDonald, James McDonald, Anita Muldoon, Alison Picard, Dan Polachek, and Renée Valois.

...................................One

The last time an attractive woman tried to pick me up in a bar was never, so when the young lady climbed the stool next to mine, flashed a 100-megawatt smile, and said, "Are you McKenzie?" my first thought was "Is this a trick question?"

"Yes, I am," I said aloud. "And you are . . . ?"

"Riley Brodin."

Usually when people introduce themselves they offer you their hand. She didn't. I tried to place her in my memory. She was not a classic beauty. So many attractive women tend to look like so many other attractive women, each of them borrowing heavily from the same magazines, TV shows, movies, and whatever else drives what we consider fashion these days. Yet Riley's face, liberally sprinkled with freckles, was as unique as her name, and startling ivory-colored hair cut close to her scalp emphasized the individuality of her looks. I suspected that half the people she met thought she was pretty; the other half not so much. I was in the first camp. On the other hand, she was maybe twenty years younger than me, so I immediately deposited her into the look-but-don't-touch category despite the way her skirt slid up to there. If a man knows what's good for him, he'll limit his lust to women who are roughly the same age as he is.

"How do you know me?" I asked.

"My grandfather. He speaks of you often, although I'm not sure he likes you very much."

"Okay . . ."

"McKenzie, how brave are you?"

"How brave do I need to be?"

"That doesn't answer my question."

"What exactly do you want, Ms. Brodin?"

Nina saw the exchange from where she was standing at the far end of the bar. She had never seen an attractive woman try to pick me up, either. I've known her long enough that I could read the expression on her face as she approached. "Now what?" it said.

"Hi," she spoke aloud when she reached the end of the bar where we were sitting. I took a deep breath. Her perfume tinged the air with the faint scent of vanilla, and I was reminded of the eclairs you can get at Wuollet Bakery down on Grand Avenue in St. Paul. I love eclairs.

Riley smiled brightly. "You're the lovely Ms. Truhler, aren't you?" she said.

Nina's eyes flitted to my face and then back to the girl's. I was curious as to what her response would be, but Riley cut her off before she could speak.

"I apologize," she said. "That was rude of me."

"I wouldn't say that," Nina told her.

"That's how my grandfather refers to you. The lovely Ms. Truhler. He likes to hang labels on people, using adjectives to describe them. I'm his clever granddaughter. My father is that dead-beat son-in-law. My mother is—well, that doesn't matter."

"Who is your grandfather?" I asked.

"Walter Muehlenhaus."

I stopped breathing. Nina did, too, but not before gasping a mouthful of air to tide her over while we digested the news. Walter Muehlenhaus —I knew him as *Mr.* Muehlenhaus—was rich, powerful, and connected in the way you'd expect the old robber barons like J. P. Morgan and James J. Hill to be connected. Those conspiracy movies Hollywood makes where the hero follows the clues all the way to the top? That's where Muehlenhaus sat. He's the reason the state legislature voted to build a billion-dollar football stadium for the Minnesota Vikings on the exact location of the old stadium even though it would have been cheaper and far more convenient to move it to any of the other sites that were proposed.

After regaining my composure, I said, "Mr. Muehlenhaus sent you?"

"Oh, no," Riley said. "He'd be furious if he knew I was here."

"Why are you here, then?" Nina asked.

"I'm embarrassed that I've never been to

Rickie's before." Riley turned on her stool to examine the neighborhood bar-slash-restaurant-slash-jazz-club that Nina had named after her daughter, Erica. Most of the tables, booths, comfy chairs, and sofas arranged downstairs were filled, as was usually the case on a Tuesday evening, and half of the tables in the upstairs dining room/performance area were occupied as well, even though the music wouldn't begin for another two hours yet. "I don't get across the river very often," she added.

That didn't surprise me. Folks in St. Paul and the eastern suburbs, if you gave them a good enough reason they might be induced to cross the Mississippi into Minneapolis. However, the people who live there rarely, if ever, travel to this side of the river. Most natives will tell you that whoever invented the label "Twin Cities" was being ironic. We aren't twins. We aren't brothers. Hell, most of the time we aren't even friends. Which made the question that more imperative.

"What do you want, Ms. Brodin?" I asked again.

"My BFFs call me Riles."

"Ms. Brodin . . ."

"I need a favor. My grandfather says that's what you do. Ever since you quit the St. Paul Police Department to collect the reward on that embezzler you tracked down, you do favors for friends."

"We're not friends."

"I know, but—"

"And your grandfather—the last time I saw him he was trying to frame me for murder."

"He could have tried harder, McKenzie. He didn't because he respects you. Still, you did cause him a great deal of embarrassment giving out the names of the politicians and businessmen involved in that online prostitution ring."

"He wasn't on the list, and he didn't like the men who were any more than I did."

"Grandpa's strength comes from the perception that whatever it is, he can fix it, break it, build it, or make it go away. People came to him for help, and he was unable to provide it because of you, and those men remember; they remember that he was unable to help. It diminished him. Anyway, that's why I'm here. I need someone who can stand up to my family."

"You mean your grandfather," I said.

"If necessary."

"That's not something I'd like to make a habit of."

Riley nodded as if I had spoken a truth universally accepted and began glancing around the club again. I liked her face despite the freckles—or maybe because of them. Her eyes glistened with intelligence, and her mouth seemed capable of warm and generous smiles. Yet there was something sad about it, too, as if it were well acquainted with sorrow. I had the uncomfortable feeling she wanted to share the sorrow with me and didn't know quite how to go about it.

"I met him, you know," Riley said. "Mr. Teachwell. The embezzler you caught. He came to the Pointe when I was a little girl. Some party or something. That's what we call the house on Lake Minnetonka. The Pointe."

"Riley," Nina said. She spoke in a voice I've heard her use only when speaking to her daughter. "Do you want a drink? Something to eat? We have a fine bar menu."

"No, I . . ."

"You can talk to us when you're ready."

"I need McKenzie . . ."

"Do you want me to leave?"

"I need you to find my boyfriend." Riley was staring into Nina's silver-blue eyes when she spoke. She spun on her stool to face me. "I need you to find Juan Carlos."

I don't know what Nina was expecting, but she said "your boyfriend" the way some people say "bubonic plague" and stepped back from the bar.

"How long has he been missing?" I asked.

"Three days," Riley said.

"That doesn't seem like a very long time."

"You don't understand."

"Nina and I have often gone more than three days without seeing or speaking to each other."

"Yes, but we always knew where the other person was," Nina said.

She had me there.

"You don't understand," Riley repeated. "He's not at his house. He doesn't answer his cell. I can't find him anywhere."

"Maybe he doesn't want you to find him," I said.

Her brow knotted, and her lips formed a thin line that plunged downward at the ends. For a moment she looked ugly.

"I'm not a starry-eyed teenager, McKenzie. I know what it's like to be dumped by a guy who doesn't even have the courtesy to call. This is different. Something is terribly wrong."

"Have you contacted the police?"

"You know who I am. You know I can't call the police without provoking a scandal."

"The cops out where you live aim to please. They're trained to keep secrets of the rich and famous."

"No," she said.

"Why would there be a scandal?"

"Not scandal, exactly."

"What, then?"

"You make every question sound like an accusation."

"I don't think so."

"Listen to yourself."

I was starting to lose patience. I glanced up at

Nina to see if she had an opinion. She shrugged her indifference.

"Ms. Brodin," I said. "You're a member of one of the wealthiest families in Minnesota, if not the nation. You have plenty of resources to draw on, and not just the police. Yet you come to a complete stranger for help. Stop hemming and hawing. Tell me what and tell me why or go away."

She stood, although I don't think she meant to. It was as if the tension in her body caused it to levitate off the stool.

"People don't talk to me that way," Riley said.

"Let me guess—you don't like it."

"No, I don't."

"Do you get a lot of that—people telling you what to do?"

"Yes. At least I did before my trust fund kicked in. Now my family only makes strong suggestions."

"Strong suggestions involving your boy-friend?"

"He's intelligent and handsome and charming and good and I know he loves me." She chanted the words as if they were an incantation that would make him miraculously materialize out of a wisp of smoke. When that didn't work, she spoke in a weak voice. "Will you help me?"

"Tell me something, Ms. Brodin. You said your grandfather likes to label people. Just out of curiosity, what does he call your boyfriend?"

"The immigrant."

"What does he call me?"

Riley hesitated. "He says . . ."

"Yes?"

"When he uses your name, he always calls you 'that fucking McKenzie.' "

"Okay," I said. "I'll help you."

Riley looked at Nina and smiled. Nina smiled back. I gestured at the stool. Riley reseated herself, smoothing her skirt over her thighs. She took Nina up on her offer and ordered a Cape Codder—cranberry juice and vodka with a twist of lime. She made no effort to pay for the drink after it was served. She sipped the beverage and started talking. She became more animated as she spoke; her breath came out in gusts between her words. Nina wanted to listen, but the responsibilities of owning a high-class saloon started pulling at her. She'd leave to deal with a patron or an employee and then return to hear a bit more of Riley's story before being drawn away again. She paid an assistant manager to take care of these problems for her, but Nina had given her the evening off. Foolish girl. 'Course, she knew I would tell her what she missed, later. I always told Nina everything. Well, not *everything*.

"His name is Juan Carlos Navarre," Riley said.

That made me lean back and say, "Huh."

"I know what you're thinking," Riley told me.

"There's a sleepy little village called Navarre on a spit of land between the upper and lower parts of Lake Minnetonka, pretty much at the center of the lake. Juan Carlos said he looked into it and couldn't find a connection to his family or even the region called Navarre in northern Spain. It's just a coincidence."

Actually, that's not what I was thinking. I was thinking that Navarre's name was very similar to Juan Carlos Navarro, the captain of the Spanish Olympic basketball team that the USA beat for the gold medal in London, yet I nodded my head in agreement just the same.

"What does he do?" I asked.

"He's an entrepreneur. Like his father."

Felipe Navarre had owned several businesses in Spain, most of them headquartered in Madrid. Riley read the names carefully to me from a document that she had stored on her smartphone. She had compiled all the information she had on her boyfriend, which I found telling—although I didn't tell her that.

According to Riley, Juan Carlos was the only child of Felipe and Susan Kowitz, an American who grew up in Prior Lake, Minnesota. Sadly— and Riley sounded sad when she told me this— Felipe and Susan were killed in an automobile accident seven years ago while Juan Carlos was away at college. The boy inherited everything, but he didn't want to run his father's businesses as much as he wanted to build his own, so when the debt crisis hit Spain, he sold off his holdings and decided to try his luck in the United States. He had dual citizenship because he was his mother's son, so there wasn't an issue with him immigrating to America.

"Juan Carlos speaks perfect English with the cutest accent," Riley said. "He came to Minnesota because he wanted to be close to his roots, his mother's roots. He settled on Lake Minnetonka because, well, because he fell in love with the place just like the Europeans who used it as a summer vacation home did back in the 1850s."

They met—Riley and Navarre—at Club Versailles, also located on Lake Minnetonka. The club had a swimming pool, a diving pool, hot tubs, saunas, a private beach, and a pier with slips for dozens of boats both big and small. It had tennis courts, an executive golf course, a driving range, walking and bike trails, locker rooms, a fitness center, a ballroom, banquet facilities, a restaurant and bar with live music on the week-ends, hotel rooms for rent and condos for sale, and a long waiting list. It was one of those places that sold shares instead of memberships, and if you had to ask how much it cost you couldn't afford to join. I had heard about it but have never been inside the place.

"It was love at first sight," Riley said. Nina had returned to our spot at the bar just as Riley spoke those words, and she smiled. "During the Fourth of July weekend. There was a dance at the club after the fireworks. I was standing on one side of the dance floor and Juan Carlos was at the other and our eyes met and I—I don't even remember who I was with, who I was talking to. I just walked toward him and he walked toward me and we met in the center and—have you ever seen *West Side Story*, the part where Maria met Tony? It was like that. It was like—it was like we had known each other before and we were being reunited after many years. Have you ever had that feeling? I told Juan Carlos about the feeling, and he told me that we had met before. In our dreams."

The way Riley smiled, I got the impression she liked the dream.

"Let me guess—the Sharks and Jets are against it," I said.

"My family hates him, if that's what you mean. My father especially hates him. He claims Juan Carlos is nothing but a con man who's only after my money. Why else would he be interested in me, my father says. I'm not pretty, he says, so why else would a man care about me except for my money. I'm smart, though. McKenzie, I might not be pretty, but I know things."

Not pretty? my inner voice asked. I raised my hand like a cop trying to stop traffic. "Wait," I said. Nina caught my eye. She shook her head in a way that Riley couldn't see. "Never mind. What about the rest of your family?"

"My grandmother, grandfather, they keep asking what do I know about the boy, the imm-i-grant. My mother—I don't want to talk about my mother."

"When was the last time you saw him?"

"Saturday. No, I saw him Friday night. But I spoke to him on Saturday at eleven thirty. Eleven thirty a.m. We were supposed to meet for lunch."

"At Club Versailles?"

"No, at Casa del Lago. It's a Mexican restaurant in Excelsior. Which is another thing. Juan Carlos owns the place. He bought it after he first came to Minnesota, after he moved to his house on Lake Minnetonka. It was run-down and I heard it was going bankrupt and he took it over and turned it into a real hot spot in just a few months. Would a con man do that?"

"Tell me about the lunch."

"He didn't show," Riley said. "He called and said something came up and he couldn't make it. He was very apologetic. He said he would call me and we would do something later. He said something else. He said, 'I'll never give you up.' He didn't say it in a creepy way, though. He said it . . ."

"Like someone was trying to keep him from seeing you," Nina said. "And he wasn't going to let them."

"Yes."

"You said Navarre has a house on Lake Minnetonka," I reminded her.

"He does." Riley dove into her bag, produced a key, and slid it across the bar. I did the math quickly in my head and thought, They've known each other for just a breath over three months, yet she has Navarre's key.

When did you give Nina your key? my inner voice asked, but I didn't answer.

"Have you been there?" I asked. "To his house?"

"I went this morning," Riley answered. "I knocked, rang the doorbell. There was no answer. I didn't go inside."

"Why not?"

For a moment her eyes lost their color.

"I understand," I said.

I took the key and slipped it into my pocket.

"Thank you," Riley said.

I hesitated for a moment before I had her send all the information she'd gathered on Navarre to my smartphone. In the beginning I had zealously guarded my cell number from all but a few close friends, yet slowly it escaped my grasp. Now it seemed as if everyone knew how to reach me, including a few nonprofits and political organizations seeking financial support.

I also had her send me a photo of Navarre.

"This is the best one I have," Riley told me. "He

gets upset when people take his photo. I don't know why."

Some people might have found that suspicious. Not me. I don't like to have my photo taken, either. I have pretty much bought into the belief held by some primitive civilizations that a camera has the ability to steal your soul.

The photo Riley sent displayed a handsome young man wearing a pink polo shirt and standing in front of a cabin cruiser emblazoned with the name *Soñadora*. His dark hair was tousled by the wind, his dark eyes half closed against the bright sun, and he was grinning sheepishly as if he were caught doing something that embarrassed him. He didn't look like an immigrant, Hispanic or otherwise. He looked like a kid who worked for Goldman Sachs. Maybe that's why he was embarrassed.

"If I find Navarre, what do you want me to tell him?" I asked.

"That I love him," Riley said. "That I want to see him. That he should call me."

"What if he says no?"

"Then I'll be wrong about him. And my family will be right."

The way she said it, I got the impression that she was more fearful of the latter than the former.

A few moments later she left Rickie's. Nina and I watched as she crossed the floor and passed through the doorway. Riley was an accident of family and wealth, and I wondered briefly if she would be able to survive it.

"Do you think she's pretty?" I asked.

"She's an interesting-looking girl," Nina said.

"Is she pretty, though? She doesn't seem to think so."

"If you're told something long enough, you start to believe it. I've been told, for example, that I'm the lovely Ms. Truhler."

"That's what I heard, too."

"Do you think Riley was telling the truth?"

"About you being lovely?"

"About Juan Carlos. About her family."

"No. Not all of it, anyway. But then people seldom tell you *all* the truth."

"She loves him. I think that's true."

"Maybe."

"Tell me—was it love at first sight when you met me?"

"No."

Nina's downcast eyes told me she was disappointed in my answer.

"No, it was a few days later when I saw you at the Minnesota Club," I added. "You were wearing a long, sleek, searing-red evening gown. Remember?"

"I remember."

"You pushed that thug down a flight of stairs."

"I remember."

"That's when I knew you were the woman for me."

"You're such a romantic. That's why you're going to help Riley, isn't it? Because you're a romantic."

"That and to annoy Mr. Muehlenhaus."

That fucking McKenzie, my inner voice said.

"You think that's a good idea? Before when you messed up his plans it was kind of an accident. It wasn't personal. They just got in the way of what you had set out to do. This time, though, it's his family."

"I know."

"It's something to think about."

Two ....

The glacier that carved out the 11,842 lakes located in Minnesota was particularly kind to Lake Minnetonka—or "big water" if you speak Dakota. Actually, it's less a lake than it is a sprawling maze of interconnected bays, inlets, channels, peninsulas, and islands. The water surface covers about 23 square miles, yet its shoreline stretches for 125 to 150 miles depending on whom you talk to. It takes two hours to drive all the way around it by car—assuming you push the traffic laws—and when you do, you'll be passing through some of the most affluent zip codes in Minnesota. Half a million bucks might buy you a shack with a view of the water. Not that I saw any for sale the next morning while I was searching for Navarre's house.

Navarre lived on the northeastern shore of Crystal Bay. To reach it, I had to drive west a third of the way around the lake and then follow North Shore Drive east through the village of Saga Hill, down along West Arm Bay, and past a cobweb of narrow and poorly marked roads. I won't bore you with the details. Suffice to say I got lost. Twice. The first time was my fault. I turned left when I should have gone right. The second time I was thrown off by the sign planted at the mouth of the cobblestone driveway—FOR SALE REHMANN LAKE PLACE REAL ESTATE. I drove past it, realized my mistake, and worked my way back. I parked illegally on the main road across from the driveway while I checked the GPS app on the instrument panel of my Audi S5 against the directions Riley had sent to my smartphone. Yep, this was the place.

A young man watched intently from a ten-year-old red Nissan Sentra that he had parked—quite legally—on the other side of the road. I couldn't make out the details of his face. He seemed to be scowling, though. I gave him a smile. He took a long last pull on a cigarette and flicked the butt out the window toward me. You drive a $65,000 car, you get that sometimes.

I crossed the main road and followed the long driveway to a huge two-story house with white cedar shakes and blue wood shingles. It sat in the middle of an equally immense emerald lawn that sloped gently to the lake. I remained in the Audi for a few beats, just staring at the structure. I had seen high schools smaller than this. I went to the door and rang the bell. When that failed to rouse anyone, I knocked. There was no answer. I circled the house, moving clockwise around the attached three-car garage. A porch ran along the entire length of the rear of the house. I mounted the stairs and followed it from one end to the other, dodging white wicker chairs with brilliant blue cushions and white wicker tables with glass tops as I peered through the windows. Nothing moved inside the house or out.

A gazebo painted white with chairs and tables that matched those on the porch stood between the house and the shoreline, and I crossed the neatly trimmed lawn to reach it. Four speakers were mounted in the rafters, and for a moment I pictured myself and Nina sitting there with a bottle of wine, listening to some tunes, and watching the sun dip across the lake.

"Nice," I said aloud.

I walked the rest of the way to the lake; the morning sun made the waves on Crystal Bay sparkle like diamonds. The shoreline was braced with a wall of enormous boulders that stretched for a hundred feet. It was divided in half by a wide wooden dock; its planks were covered with water-resistant polyurethane. I stepped out onto the dock. It was equipped with both electricity and fresh-water hookups, although no boat was moored there.

There were plenty of boats dotting the huge bay, though, yet not nearly as many as during the summer, and I was reminded that it was the first day of October. It seems half of the people in Minnesota launch their boats—and ready their golf clubs, for that matter—on Memorial Day and then begin storing them away again right after Labor Day as if they can't wait for winter to begin. Meanwhile, given the length of our notoriously merciless winters, the rest of us strive tirelessly to stretch summer out until the very first snowfall, and sometimes longer. The folks still out on the lake were my kind of people.

I didn't see any bodies floating facedown in the lake, so I went back to the house. I made my way to the front door and used Riley's key to open it. I called Navarre's name when I stepped inside. A house gives off a certain vibe when it's unoccupied. I felt it as I closed the door behind me and stepped deeper into the foyer. "Navarre," I called again, but I was thinking "Wow." It's not often you see your face reflected in white marble when you enter a house. I called out yet again. When Navarre didn't answer, I stepped past the foyer into a living room. This time I actually spoke the word aloud. "Wow."

The living room was filled with white furniture; white rugs were strategically positioned on the gleaming hardwood floor. I walked around the rugs for fear of soiling them. Even the baby grand piano in the corner was white. The lid was open, and the way sheet music was arrayed above the keyboard suggested that it had been played recently.

The living room flanked a formal dining room, where I found a table that could easily seat two dozen beneath an honest-to-God crystal chandelier. The dining room opened onto an immense kitchen that was so opulent and so clean that I would have feared to cook anything in it. There was a door next to the refrigerator. The three-car garage was on the other side of it. A BMW 328i convertible was parked there, and nothing else—no rakes, no shovels, no lawn mowers, and no snow blowers; nothing that you might expect to find in a garage in Minnesota. I checked the Beamer. It was this year's model; there couldn't have been more than a few hundred miles on the odometer.

On the far side of the kitchen I found an informal dining room—it sat only eight—which led to a sunroom filled with more wicker furniture. Thick panes of tinted glass stretching from floor to ceiling served as walls and faced south and west. A family room lay beyond and featured both leather and upholstered furniture arranged in front of an HDTV just slightly smaller than the scoreboard at the Xcel Center.

Every surface in the house was fastidiously cleaned, dusted, vacuumed, or polished; every pillow, tapestry, quilt, comforter, and rug was artfully arranged; every collectible, antique, arti-fact, and work of art was displayed to maximum effect. There were no newspapers, magazines, or books littering sofa cushions or tabletops; no jackets, sweaters, or sweatshirts draped over the back of chairs; no mail, umbrellas, shoes, or keys discarded near doorways—nothing to suggest that someone actually lived there. The waste-baskets were empty, and so was the dishwasher. Even the food in the refrigerator looked as if it had been meticulously organized by an art director guiding a photo shoot.

I wandered up to the second floor. The staircase divided the upstairs more or less in half. I went to my right and discovered four bedrooms and three baths, each so pristine that at first glance you would have doubted that they had ever been used. I looked closer, however, and discovered that the bathroom off of what I assumed was the master bedroom contained a toothbrush, toothpaste, dental floss, mouthwash, shaving cream, a razor, extra blades, shampoo, conditioner, hair spray, deodorant, cologne, and other articles needful to a man who prized personal hygiene. Yet it all felt new and was so neatly arranged on shelves and in drawers that I suspected the owner suffered from an obsessive-compulsive disorder.

That theory was reinforced when I examined the bedroom. The king-sized canopied bed was perfectly made; the coverlet was so smooth it looked as if it had been ironed. Across from the bed was a polished bureau. Eight watches with brand names like Hublot, Omega, Glashütte, and Breguet were carefully arranged across the top according to the color of their wristbands. The drawers contained mostly socks, boxers, hand-kerchiefs, and short-sleeve polo shirts made by

Ralph Lauren, Brooks Brothers, and Fight Club, all immaculately folded. In the bottom drawer there was an orange sweatshirt with the name Macalester College emblazoned in fading blue letters across the front; its cuffs and neckline were frayed. It looked as if it had been worn every day for the past ten years, and if it hadn't been so neatly stored away I might have thought there was hope for Mr. Navarre yet.

The walk-in closet had more of the same. High-end suits, costly sports jackets, dress slacks, casual pants, jeans, dress shirts—all on wooden hangers, all arranged by color, and all with approximately two inches of space between them as if Navarre were frightened that they would somehow contaminate each other if they should ever touch. Dress shoes, boots, sneakers, and Top-Siders were just as precisely organized and set on the floor against the far wall of the closet, the back heel of each hard against the molding. Above the shoes were shelves filled with dozens of folded dress shirts; the shirts were also arranged by color. None of them looked as if they had ever been worn before. In fact, the only thing I discovered that seemed to have any age to it at all was a creased and scuffed gray leather satchel with the silver initials CBE riveted to the side. I assumed the initials indicated the name of the manufacturer, yet I wrote them down in a small spiral notebook I carried just the same.

I moved to the rooms to the left of the staircase. There I found a fourth bathroom. This one featured a large walk-in shower and a whirlpool bath. Fluffy white towels, each impeccably folded and smelling as if it had been washed with lemon-scented soap five minutes ago, were stacked on a white shelf. A door between the shower and bath led to a fully equipped exercise room that smelled of applewood. There was another white shelf with more white towels.

I left the exercise room and followed the corridor to an office. Riley Brodin had said that Navarre was an entrepreneur. If so, he conducted all of this business without the use of paper. Or computers either, for that matter, although I did find a couple of cable outlets in the walls and a router. I searched the room and discovered only two things that interested me. The first was an empty silver—and I mean *real* silver—picture frame lying facedown on the desktop. It was the only thing in the room that seemed askew. The second was a seven-year-old yearbook. Like the sweatshirt, it was from Macalester College, an expensive, private liberal arts school in St. Paul.

I tried the trick of opening the book and letting it fall to see what page it landed on. That didn't work unless Navarre spent a lot of time reliving a speech Walter Mondale had delivered to the student body. I searched for his name and came up empty. I tried Riley Brodin and discovered her name and photo listed under "Freshmen." Her hair was longer then and dark brown, and her expression was so damned serious it made me smile.

Just for giggles, I checked for a name that fit the initials CBE, but there were no matches to either students or teachers.

I left the book as I found it and continued down the corridor until I discovered a room that was empty except for a Celestron NexStar telescope set near a large window. Careful not to jostle it, I peered through the eyepiece. The telescope was trained on a large estate on the far side of Crystal Bay. Like Navarre's place, the estate was predominantly white and built to recall the architecture of the antebellum South; there were six Greek-like columns flanking the front door. The house commanded a bluff that overlooked a couple hundred feet of shoreline. There was a dock with slips for four boats; one of them had to be at least sixty feet long. A purple flag flew from a high pole at the end of the dock, and I thought it might carry the emblem of the Minnesota Vikings or maybe even Northwestern University, but no, it was just a purple flag.

I studied the estate the way Navarre must have. All in all, it made his place look like a starter home in the suburbs. It was because I was so occupied that I didn't hear her until she shouted, "What are you doing here?"

I must have leapt three feet into the air. When I came back down, I spun to face the woman. I took two steps backward and one to the side. My hand went to the spot behind my right hip where I would have holstered my gun if I had thought to bring it.

She stood in the doorway. Her fists were pressed against her hips. Her hair was reddish blond, her eyes were hazel, and she had an ample bosom that she accentuated beneath a crisp white shirt and dark blue blazer. Her skirt matched her jacket and ended a tasteful half inch above her knees. Her face was artfully made up to look younger than it actually was. I might not have noticed except she was trying awfully hard to appear assertive if not downright stern. Still, I could detect just a hint of alarm behind her eyes.

"I'm a friend of Navarre's," I said. "Who are you?"

"What are you doing here?" she repeated.

"Looking for Navarre."

"He's not here."

"I can see that. Who are you?"

"How did you get in?"

I reached into my jacket pocket. The woman's body tensed and then visibly relaxed when I withdrew the key and held it up for her to see. "Juan Carlos gave me a key." The use of Navarre's first name seemed to mollify her a bit.

"He gave you a key?"

"Actually, Riles gave me the key. Riley Brodin, Navarre's girlfriend." The woman didn't speak, but her eyes widened with recognition, so I kept on. "Do you know Riles?"

"I know of her."

"She's Walter Muehlenhaus's granddaughter." She looked away for a moment, and I wondered if the name Muehlenhaus had that effect on everyone. "Navarre gave the key to her, and she gave it to me because Navarre didn't have any other extras. I was supposed to meet him here."

"Did Juan Carlos give you the code to the alarm system?"

That slowed me down. I hadn't actually thought of that—I had a security system at my house; surely Navarre must have had one, too. Yet I didn't see a console when I entered the house. I wondered briefly if I had tripped a silent alarm when I unlocked the door, then dismissed the idea. I had been in the house far too long without being shot at for that to be true.

"He never said anything about an alarm system," I said.

"I checked when I arrived. It's been turned off."

"Not by me."

"By whom, then?"

"I don't know. Ask Navarre."

"He's not here."

"I know he's not. Who are you, lady?"

"Anne Rehmann."

I flashed on the sign at the end of the drive-way. "Rehmann Real Estate?"

"That's right."

"What's that about?" I asked. "Navarre didn't say anything about moving."

"When did you talk to him last?"

"He called Saturday. He was supposed to meet Riles and me for lunch at Casa del Lago. He called and said he couldn't make it."

Anne sighed, and with the sigh I saw the anxiety draining from her body. Everything I told her seemed to fit what she already knew—which is a trick they teach you at the police academy when it comes to conducting interrogations. Tell suspects what little you know in just the right manner, and they'll come to believe that you know everything.

"I don't know what Juan Carlos told you, but he doesn't own this house," Anne said. "He's leasing with an option to buy. The house actually belongs to Mrs. Irene Rogers. After her husband died, she decided it was too big for her, so she bought a condo at Club Versailles. Somehow she met Juan Carlos and agreed to let him stay here until I could find a buyer. I came over because I wanted to ask if he decided to make an offer. If not, I wanted to arrange a time to show the estate to a couple of prospects."

"So you don't know where Navarre is, either," I said.

She shook her head.

"That's odd," I said.

Anne snorted at the remark.

"A lot of people on Lake Minnetonka live according to their own private calendars," she said. "Screw the rest of us."

Dissatisfaction, my inner voice reminded me. *You can use that.*

"You'd think people would show a little consideration," I said. "I don't care how much money they have."

"The rich are different from the rest of us," she said, repeating a line often attributed to F. Scott Fitzgerald. "Haven't you heard?"

"Yes, they have more money," I said, quoting Ernest Hemingway's famous reply.

Anne snorted again and asked, "The Audi in the driveway, is that yours?"

"Yep."

Anne nodded her head. I knew exactly what she was thinking: You drive an Audi S5 coupe; you must have plenty of dough lying around. I waited for the question I knew was coming.

"Are you in the market for a home on Lake Minnetonka?" Anne asked.

"I am. In fact, the more Navarre talks about it, the more I like the idea. Tell me, how much are you asking for this place?"

"Five-point-four million."

I made a hissing sound. "That's a little out of my price range."

"What is your price range?"

"One and a half."

Anne nodded her head as if she knew it all along. "I have a few properties you might be interested in. Do you have a card?"

I didn't, but I gave her my name and cell number, and she dutifully jotted both down. I was sure that before sundown she'd know my net worth down to the last nickel—which would be a helluva lot more than I knew.

Anne gave me her card.

"Perhaps we can talk later this week, Mr. McKenzie," she said.

"Perhaps we can have lunch or dinner or drinks or all of the above." I gave her my best George Clooney smile, the one that suggested I was talking about more than business. "But only if you drop the mister. McKenzie is fine."

I smiled again. She smiled back.

Anne asked more questions along the lines of where I was living and what I did for money. Her interest seemed professional rather than personal, though, so I figured the smile wasn't working and decided to give it up. We made some noises about getting together later and said our good-byes with the promise that if either of us came across Navarre, we'd inform the other. I drove the Audi down the driveway and stopped at the main road. I waited for the traffic to clear while I contemplated my next move.

I had intended to visit Navarre's restaurant. It was located on Gideon Bay on the south side of the lake, which was easy to get to by boat, not so much if you drove. Yet I also wanted to chat with Mrs. Rogers, who apparently had a place at Club Versailles. According to my GPS, the club was just as hard to reach by car as the restaurant. It was more or less in the same direction though, so I decided to stop there first.

I checked for traffic. That's when I noticed that the red Sentra was gone, replaced by a black Cadillac DTS with silver wheels. The young driver stared straight ahead as I maneuvered onto the main road, but I saw him tilt his head to check me out in his rearview when I drove past.

When I was police, I was briefly partnered with a fabulous female homicide investigator named Anita Pollack. Nine out of ten times she could ID the killer immediately when we arrived at the crime scene—most of the time it was that obvious to her—and then it would be just a matter of connecting the dots. On the rare occasion when we would actually have to do some detecting, she would stroke her chin and speak the way you might expect Sherlock Holmes to. Her words came to me as I watched the Caddy receding in the mirror.

"There's fuckery afoot."

Three

Club Versailles took up a large chunk of a peninsula more or less in the center of Lake Minnetonka, not far from the town of Navarre, with Crystal Bay to the north and Lafayette Bay to the south. Signs warned that I was traveling a private road and that trespassers would not be tolerated. Yet I wasn't stopped on the road, nor when I pulled into the large parking lot. There were no guards at the door, either. Just a sign that declared nonmembers must report to the front desk. The lack of security surprised me. Given that the place looked like it had been built by someone who wanted to reproduce King Louis XIV's Sun Palace—only nicer—I half expected to see a troop of musketeers patrolling the grounds.

The carefully groomed woman at the desk was about thirty, although the pleated black skirt and white knit shirt with CLUB VERSAILLES printed in gold over her left breast made her seem younger. There was a name tag over her right breast. SARAH NEAMY, it read. I'm embarrassed to admit I would have noticed her breasts even if there hadn't been names hanging on them.

"May I help you?" she asked. Her entire body smiled at me.

"Good morning, Sarah," I said. "I'd like to see Mrs. Rogers if she's available."

She pondered my request for a moment and pointed vaguely at a wall to her left. "Her condo is over there," she said.

When I arrived I noticed two buildings, a main building with more wings than a shopping mall and a smaller building that looked like it was competing for a spot in Guinness World Records for most balconies. So I knew what she meant.

"I'm sorry," I said. "This is my first time here. I don't know the rules."

"They're pretty simple," Sarah said. "If you're a member you walk around like you own the place, because technically you do. If you're not a member, you walk around like you own the place until someone notices and says, 'Hey.' Mrs. Rogers, did you say?"

"Yes."

"It's nearly noon on a Wednesday, so she's probably on the patio playing poker with who-ever she's fleecing this week."

"Poker?"

"Mrs. Rogers told me once that she was a dealer in Reno when she was young. I've seen her play. I believe her."

I had no idea where the patio was or how to get to it. I pointed more or less toward the interior of the club. "May I . . . ?"

"Does Mrs. Rogers know you're coming?" Sarah asked.

"We've never met."

Sarah smiled some more, this time only with her face. "I'll tell her that you're here," she said. "You are?"

"McKenzie. Tell her it's regarding her estate."

"Wait."

While I waited, I examined the furnishings. Very plush. Very rich. I eventually ended up in a horseshoe-shaped Queen Anne chair with a view of the parking lot. Yet, as comfortable as the chair was, I felt uncomfortable sitting in it. I stood. I'm not easily intimidated by money. After all, I'm worth nearly five million bucks. Something about Club Versailles, though, conjured up memories of my blue-collar roots. I felt a little like a Visigoth just before he sacked Rome. Gazing out at the parking lot, I was glad I drove the Audi. I would have been embarrassed if anyone there had seen me in my old Jeep Cherokee, which was a new experience for me—being self-conscious about what other people thought.

What the hell is wrong with you? my inner voice asked.

Damn if I know, I told it.

You could whip out your checkbook and buy a membership right now!

Still . . .

"Mr. McKenzie?"

I turned toward Sarah's voice. A woman stood next to her. She was handsome in the way a well-cared-for antique was handsome. I guessed that she had probably been carded well into her forties.

"Mr. McKenzie," Sarah repeated. "Mrs. Rogers."

I offered the older woman my hand. She refused to take it.

"Are you my birthday present?" she asked.

"Your what?"

Mrs. Rogers looked me up and down as if she wanted to redress me in something closer to her taste.

"My birthday is tomorrow," she said. "My friends always chip in to give me a gift." She circled me as she spoke. "Nice ass."

Sarah's hand flew to her mouth, and she turned her head as she tried to suppress a laugh. "I need to get back to the desk," she said behind her hand and rushed away.

"I like that you're thin," Mrs. Rogers said.

"I didn't know that I was."

"Look around. We've become a nation of fat people. I, on the other hand, am not fat."

"No, ma'am, you are not."

"I have the same figure that I had my senior year in high school."

"I can see that."

Mrs. Rogers stopped in front of me. "Yes,

you'll do fine. Although . . ." She consulted a wristwatch that sparkled with diamonds. "It'd be better if you came back later when I have more time."

"I'd be happy to," I said. "Except I'm not your birthday gift."

"You're not?"

"No, ma'am."

"What that silly girl said about wanting to talk about my property, that's true?"

" 'Fraid so."

She swung her fist up over her head and down again like a desperate gambler who just lost his last dollar by a nose.

"Dammit," she said.

"You're putting me on, aren't you, Mrs. Rogers?"

"I can't imagine what gave you that idea. Do you drink, McKenzie?"

"Yes, I do."

"Come with me."

Mrs. Rogers walked briskly into the interior of the club, down a corridor, through a well-appointed card room, and into the bar. I followed like a small child afraid of being left behind.

"Steven," she called to the bartender.

"Mrs. R," he called back.

She replied by holding up two fingers and then slipped through a glass door onto a sprawling terrace with a stunning view of Lake Minnetonka.

She moved to the railing and turned, competing with the view.

"I have a slip of a girl taking care of my properties for me," Mrs. Rogers said.

"Anne Rehmann," I said. "Hardly a slip of a girl."

"Anyone half my age is a slip of a girl. She should exercise more, though, Annie should. Keep those perky breasts of hers from sagging." I didn't have anything to say to that. "Do I shock you, McKenzie?"

"Not particularly."

Mrs. Rogers swung her hand up and down again. "Dammit, I was trying so hard."

I decided then and there that I liked her. She possessed a natural aggressiveness that I found engaging, although I didn't tell her that.

Steven arrived carrying a tray with two martinis on top. He set the drinks on a small table near the railing. I held a chair for Mrs. Rogers. She nodded her head at me and sat.

"Old World manners," she said. "Don't see that anymore."

I took the chair across from her. She drank half of her martini in one gulp. I took just a sip. The alcohol sent a charge of electricity through me that curled my toes.

"Ho, ho, ho," I chanted.

"Gin martini," Mrs. Rogers said. "Picked up the recipe in London. I used to fly the New York to

London to Paris route for Pan Am. That was when we were called stewardesses instead of flight attendants."

"Sarah at the desk told me you were a dealer in Reno."

"Did that, too. And some acting, mostly bit parts. I lied about my age and got a job working for MGM when I was a kid. Danced in a Gene Kelly movie once, although you can hardly see me I'm so far in the back. Worked for an advertising agency. Have you ever seen the TV series *Mad Men*? It was very much like that. I was what Frank Sinatra used to call a broad, which might have been less respectable than a lady but a whole helluva lot better than a bitch. Do you gamble, McKenzie?"

"Occasionally. Not often."

"Why not?"

"I don't like to lose."

"Most people love to lose. Rich, poor, it makes no difference. Even when they win, people keep playing until they go bust. Look around. More people are gambling today than in the entire history of the world, and sooner or later they always lose."

"What about you?"

"Oh, I never lose."

"How is that possible?"

"I cheat. Just this morning I made eleven twenty-eight."

"Eleven hundred and twenty-eight dollars?"

"Eleven dollars and twenty-eight cents. What do you take me for?"

A woman, I thought, who somehow managed the most wonderful trick of growing old without ever growing up. But again, I didn't say it.

Mrs. Rogers took another pull of her martini.

"So, McKenzie," she said. "If you came here to dicker, don't bother. My price is firm. Five-point-four million. I'm not what you would call a motivated seller, so don't try to wait me out, either."

"I'm not interested in buying your home, although I have to admit it's ungodly beautiful."

"What, then?"

"I'm looking for your tenant."

"Juan Carlos? I didn't know he was lost."

"Disappeared Saturday morning."

"Who says?"

"His girlfriend."

"Riley Brodin?"

"Yes."

"You're a detective, then."

"In a manner of speaking."

"I can see why Riley would hire one. She'd be anxious if Juan Carlos up and left her."

"Did he up and leave her?"

"How should I know?"

"Mrs. Rogers, when was the last time—"

"If we're going to continue this conversation, McKenzie, two things need to happen. First, you have to call me Irene. Better yet. My close friends call me Reney. Call me Reney."

"Reney," I said.

"Second . . ." Reney held the empty martini glass straight above her head, not unlike the way Lady Liberty held her torch. A passing waitress took it from her and a few minutes later returned with two fresh drinks. I hadn't finished my first martini yet, and Reney watched with intense curiosity until I downed it. Damn thing nearly killed me, and I told her so.

"Lightweight," she said. "Where were we? Riley Brodin. I've been a member of this club since before Riley was born, and gossip is such that I pretty much know everything about her. She's spoiled."

"I hadn't noticed."

"Spoiled children aren't always malicious. Sometimes they can be very sweet. But she wants what she wants when she wants it. At the same time she's—what shall I say? When it comes to dealing with people of the opposite sex, she's an innocent. I think Riley's had a grand total of three boyfriends in her entire life, and her grandparents arranged all of them. Partly it's the fault of her screwed-up family."

"Her family is screwed up?" I said.

An expression crossed Reney's face suggesting that the number of fools she'd met in her lifetime had just increased by one.

"Are you really that uninformed?" she asked.

Yes, my inner voice said.

"I like to get a different perspective," I spoke aloud.

"You have Walter, who's the Prince of frickin' Darkness. That would be Walter Muehlenhaus."

"Yes, I know him."

"Although his wife, Maggie, is a sweetheart. She's an old broad, like me."

"Heady praise, indeed."

"You have her mother, who's the Whore of Babylon, and then you have Riley's father, who is, to be generous, a dumb ass. A girl like Riley, she must feel isolated both because of her family and because of her looks. Don't get me wrong, McKenzie. I think she's adorable. She reminds me of a tabby cat. Other people—the people on Lake Minnetonka, they all try so hard to fit in with everyone else, so naturally they reject those that don't fit in with them."

"That's probably true of most people no matter where they live," I said.

"Then along comes Juan Carlos, who can play Prince Charming with the best of them. He batted those baby browns at her . . . McKenzie, the girl didn't stand a chance."

"Are you sure that's what happened? Could be she chased him with the idea of breaking away from her screwed-up family and making a life of her own. I only say that because I met the girl and she doesn't strike me as a pushover."

Reney wagged her finger at me.

"You might be onto something there," she said.

"What can you tell me about Navarre?" I asked.

"I like him. Most people do. I invited him to the club; kinda gave him the run of the place as my guest, and he's settled in quite nicely. There's no question that's he's a cultivated young man of independent means. The question, of course, is how cultivated and how independent."

"What do you mean?" I asked.

"He dances superbly."

"I don't understand."

"I'm always suspicious of men who dance well. It requires a great deal of practice. Tell me, McKenzie—why would a man practice his dancing?"

"To impress his partner."

"Exactly. He wants so much to impress—with his manners, with his wealth. Of course, that's true of just about every member of the club."

"Do you think Navarre is after Riley's money?"

"I wouldn't say that. God knows the girl has more to offer than a healthy bank account. On the other hand, you know what they said about Lord Tennyson, the poet."

"Hmm?"

"He married where money was. 'Course, along with money, there's status. This club is filled with social climbers. Why else would you join except to say that you're a member?"

"People like to hang with people who are like them," I said.

"You're saying that money attracts money? I suppose there's some truth to the theory. Beyond that, though, I'm not sure what the members have in common with each other. You have the children and grandchildren of bankers and railroad tycoons who have never labored a day in their lives rubbing shoulders with the offspring of teachers and plumbers who earned their way here with the sweat of their own brows. You have people who create and build eating dinner across from those who only buy and sell. In this environment, almost anything can happen. Almost everything has. Money has a way of making people careless, of making them think they can live their lives without consequences. McKenzie —there are always consequences."

"I believe you."

"In that context, Juan Carlos is not all that unusual. Compared to some of our members, he's quite mundane."

"How did Navarre come to live in your house?"

"It seemed like a good idea to have someone stay there; keep an eye on the place while it's on the market."

"Why Navarre?"

"Why not? He pays rent. Seventy-eight hundred

a month. Covers the property taxes, utilities, maintenance . . ."

"Reney," I said. "Why Navarre?"

She stared at me for a couple of beats while her face went through the motions of remembering. "I . . ." She stopped and took a sip of her drink. "If I'm not mistaken, it was Anne Rehmann's idea. McKenzie, you don't think I'd let just anybody sleep in my house, do you? I met Juan Carlos here at the club. Actually, at my condominium. He came specifically to meet me. Told me who he was; told me that he was thinking of settling in Minnesota. He had a letter of introduction, which was an old-fashioned touch that I liked very much. Turned out we have friends in common."

"Here in Minnesota?"

"No. In Chevy Chase, Maryland. I used to live there with my husband back in the day. We were neighbors with a man who later became the counselor for economic affairs at our embassy in Madrid. He and his wife knew his family—Juan Carlos's family back in Spain. When he decided to come to Minnesota, they told him to look me up."

"Did you speak to your friends about Navarre?"

"Not"—another hesitation—"exactly."

"E-mail? Facebook?"

"Do I look like someone who spends time on Facebook?"

"You didn't check his references, did you, Reney?"

"Dammit, McKenzie. No, I didn't." Reney drained the rest of her martini and cast a coveting eye at mine. "Are you going to finish that?" I gestured for her to take the glass, and she did, drinking half of its contents before she spoke again. "Juan Carlos talked freely about my friends as if he had known them for years. Everything he said, too, it all rang true. Do you think he's an impostor?"

"I have no idea. I've never even met the man. All I know is that he's missing."

"I hope he's all right. I like him, McKenzie. I really do. He's a rogue, and I have a soft spot for rogues. My husband was one. I think you might be one, too."

"Will you ask your friends about him? Tell me what they say?"

"Yes."

We exchanged phone numbers.

"Just the other day I saw them together," Reney said. "Juan Carlos and Riley. They were holding hands, and I said to myself if I were Riley's age I could have plucked him out of her grasp just like that."

"I have a feeling you could still change a man's life."

"For better or worse, I wonder."

I kissed the back of Reney's hand.

"That which does not kill us only makes us stronger," I told her.

"McKenzie, that just might be the best compliment I've ever received."

Before returning to my Audi, I stopped off at the front desk, where I scanned a wine list that I stole while passing through the bar. Sarah watched me expectantly.

"Here," I said when I found something I liked—a French Bordeaux from Château Pontet-Canet. "Could you do me a favor?"

She shrugged noncommittally.

"Does Irene Rogers take her meals at the club?" I asked.

"Usually."

I reached into my pocket and pulled out a wad of folded bills. I had enough to cover the two-hundred-dollar tab plus a few dollars more. I gave two hundred to Sarah.

"Could you send a bottle of this wine to Mrs. Rogers's table tonight along with this note?"

I scribbled a message on Club Versailles stationery—*Happy Birthday to an old broad from McKenzie.*

Sarah read the note.

"You know, it's not really her birthday," she told me.

"I never thought that it was."

Sarah decided it was a good joke and agreed to help me out.

"Also, is Juan Carlos Navarre a member of the club?" I asked the woman.

"No. I understand that he's applied for membership. The board of directors hasn't voted on it yet. Why?"

"Does he spend a lot of time here?"

"More than a nonmember should, but—well, between Mrs. R and Ms. Riley Muehlenhaus Brodin"—she emphasized the name Muehlenhaus—"no one is going to say anything."

"Has Navarre been around lately?"

"I haven't seen him since Friday evening. He had dinner with Riley. I think they hit balls on the driving range, too."

"Are you open to a bribe, Sarah?"

Her body tensed and her eyes glazed with hostility at my words, yet her smile remained unchanged.

"No, Mr. McKenzie, I am not," she said. "Please don't offer me one. I won't like you if you do."

"I apologize, Sarah." I was speaking quickly because her good favor was suddenly very dear to me. "I meant no disrespect. Please forgive me."

She tilted her head in a way that suggested she was willing but needed more incentive.

"Navarre has disappeared, and I need to find him," I added. "I was hoping you would call if he shows up."

Sarah took a deep breath and answered with the exhale. "I suppose I could do that. Navarre isn't a member yet, so technically I wouldn't be breaking any rules of confidentiality."

"Are there rules of confidentiality?"

"A lot of people ask questions about our members; a lot of people would like to get the goods on them."

"What people?"

"Mostly other members. Why are you looking for Navarre? Is it because he's a phony?"

"What makes you say that?"

"Some of the richest people in Minnesota pass my desk. Many of them are friendly, many are kind and generous like Mrs. Rogers, and a lot of them aren't. Yet none of them, not even Mrs. R, has ever tried to impress me. McKenzie, I'm a salaried employee. No one cares what I think, only that I do my job—for which I am handsomely compensated, I might add. Juan Carlos, though—from the very beginning he wanted me to know that he was wealthy, that he was connected, that he was worthy of my respect."

"Could be he's nouveau riche and doesn't know how to handle it yet."

"Except that doesn't fit the story he tells everyone. Besides, like a man once said, it's not the nouveau that matters, it's the riche. If Juan Carlos has money, he got it yesterday."

Four..

I drove only 4.7 miles, yet it took me nearly twenty minutes to reach Casa del Lago—such are the driving conditions on the narrow roads surrounding Lake Minnetonka. The restaurant had a large patio overlooking Gideon Bay with a low railing that kept patrons from falling over the edge into the water. A couple of dozen tables were strategically placed across the colorful bricks, each with a large blue and white umbrella that promoted Corona Extra when opened. The lunch crowd sitting at the tables was divided into two groups. Half were dressed like they had just stepped off the deck of one of the cabin cruisers and speedboats tied at the pier jutting into the lake. Half were dressed as if they had arrived in one of the luxury cars parked in the asphalt lot. There were a few cars that looked like they were driven by what my old man would have called "just folks." Most of those were parked in the back of the lot, though, so I figured they belonged to the worker bees that managed the restaurant. I parked in the front row because, well, what did I have to be embarrassed about?

I stepped inside the restaurant. Someone had tried hard to make it appear like a Hollywood version of a Mexican hacienda, yet the all-white clientele and the neon Miller Lite and Dos Equis signs gave it away. The only thing that seemed authentic was the young woman who intercepted me at the door. She had long black hair and dark eyes and spoke with the soft accent of a woman who learned English in a house filled with people who spoke Spanish. Her name tag read MARIA.

"Table for one, or will you be joining other guests?" she asked.

"I'd like to speak to the owner, if he's available," I answered. She cocked her head at me as if unsure what to make of my question. "It's a personal matter," I added.

"If you care to wait at the bar," she said.

Maria directed me toward the stick. I crawled up onto the stool while she disappeared behind a door marked AUTHORIZED PERSONNEL ONLY. The bartender hurried over, and I ordered a Summit Pale Ale. He was quick in drawing it for me.

A few moments later, an older man dressed for yachting—not boating, yachting—joined me. He climbed the stool two down from mine and nodded. "Hey," I said, just to be polite. He ordered Glenlivet with one *nice* ice cube, whatever that meant. After he was served, he rolled up his sleeves as if drinking were serious work.

"Not many warm days left like this one," he said.

"No, not many," I agreed. In Minnesota,

September and October are the best months of the year. Unfortunately, November and December soon follow.

"Yeah, that's why I gotta start thinkin' about gettin' my boat outta the water. Once it gets cold it can be such a bitch."

"I suppose."

"You have a boat?"

"Used to. I took it out only twice in the past three years, so I sold it."

"I hear ya. I think I took mine out three, four times, and that includes when I put 'er in the water. Only brought 'er out t'day to burn some gas outta the tanks. She's just a money pit, but what are you going to do? Gotta have a boat."

"Where do you keep it?"

"I got a slip right on the edge of Tonka Bay Marina. Easy in, easy out. Hadda pay a pretty penny extra for it, too, that slip. It's worth the rent, though, sure it is. People forever maneuverin' in and out of the marina, always riskin' collisions, they see my spot, they gotta be jealous, gotta say, 'Damn, ain't that sweet.' How 'bout you? Where did you keep your boat?"

"In my garage."

He didn't say another word. Didn't even look at me as he picked up his Glenlivet and retreated across the restaurant, putting as much distance between him and me as possible without actually leaving the building.

Damn, my inner voice told me. *The rich really are different.*

A few minutes later I was joined by a pretty woman with a thin face, pale eyes, and fine blond hair with auburn highlights. She was older than Riley yet still below my lust threshold, although she was close enough to it that I was willing to make an exception.

"May I help you?" she asked.

"No, thank you. I'm waiting for the owner."

"I'm the owner."

Her response caught me by surprise, and I hesitated for a few beats. "I'm looking for Juan Carlos Navarre," I said at last.

"I'll tell you what I told the other guy. He's not the owner. He's not here. I haven't heard from him in a week. Is there anything else?"

She looked as if she were going to walk away whether I had anything more to say or not, so I thrust my paw toward her.

"My name's McKenzie," I said.

She hesitated for a moment before shaking my hand.

"Mary Pat Mulally," she replied.

I considered making a clever remark about a woman with an Irish surname owning a Spanish-style restaurant but thought better of it. Instead, I asked, "May I have a minute of your time, Ms. Mulally?"

I continued to hold her hand so she couldn't slip

away. She looked at my hand holding hers and then into my eyes. She sighed heavily and said, "Only a minute."

I released her hand, and Mary Pat led me through the restaurant, moving vigilantly as if she wanted to make sure that no one tried to steal it from her. Instead of a table overlooking Lake Minnetonka, she brought me to a booth with a splendid view of the parking lot, and I thought, smart businesswoman, she's leaving the best tables for her paying customers. I sat across from her. She waited for me to speak.

"Apparently I've been misinformed," I told her.

"Did Juan Carlos tell you he owned Casa del Lago?"

"No. It was Riley Brodin."

The way her eyes narrowed, I got the impression that she recognized the name and hearing it made her sad. Still, Mary Pat nodded her head as if it made perfect sense.

"Juan Carlos isn't the first man who tried to impress a woman with . . . let's just say it's not the entire truth," she said.

"What is the entire truth?"

"Whom do you work for?"

"Do I need to be working for someone?"

"Don't fence with me, McKenzie. I'm not in the mood."

"Riley Brodin. Her boyfriend disappeared. She's anxious that I find him."

"She's the granddaughter of Mr. Muehlenhaus."

"That's what I've been told."

"Technically, you work for him, then."

"No. Not even a little bit."

Mary Pat must have heard the outrage I purposely put in my voice, because she smiled slightly.

"Not Mr. Muehlenhaus?" she said.

"No, not Mr. Muehlenhaus. Why do you ask?"

"I think he's looking for Juan Carlos, too."

"What makes you think that?"

"A private investigator came by the other day. He flashed his ID at me like it was a badge and started asking all kinds of questions that were none of his business. I'm from the north side of Minneapolis, McKenzie. Real cops don't bother me any; I'm sure not going to be intimidated by a PI. When I refused to answer, he said his employer could make life on Lake Minnetonka impossible for me. I threw him out. I've been waiting for someone to knock on my door with bad news ever since. I thought that someone might be you."

"No."

Mary Pat shrugged her shoulders as if she were willing to take my word for it—for now.

"Then you have nothing to do with the Chevy Impala in the back row of the parking lot," she said.

"What Impala?"

She tilted her head at the window, and I took a look.

"See it?" she asked.

"Yeah."

"Inside is a man who has been watching my restaurant all day. Yesterday there was a different man in a Sentra."

"A red Sentra?"

"How did you know?"

"For what it's worth, Mary Pat, I don't think they're interested in you or your restaurant. I think they're waiting for Navarre."

"Why?"

"The PI. Did he tell you why he was looking for him?"

"No."

"Did you get his name?"

"No. That's one reason why I threw him out. He was acting all big and emphatic, but he wouldn't tell me who he was or whom he was working for."

"You're only guessing that Mr. Muehlenhaus sent him."

"Do you think I'm wrong?"

"No, I think it's a pretty good guess. Although . . . I've had dealings with Mr. Muehlenhaus in the past. He's usually more subtle than this."

"If you say so."

"What is your relationship with Navarre?"

"Juan Carlos is an investor. He lent the restaurant a sizable amount of money, for which he now receives a percentage of the profits until principal and interest are paid."

"I don't understand."

"It's simple. I was undercapitalized. The business was failing. The infusion of money allowed me to enlarge the patio, expand the pier, improve my menu, and provide my clientele with the kind of service it demanded. Truth be told, I was fortunate that Juan Carlos came along when he did. It's like I said, though—he is not an owner. Nor is he involved in the day-to-day operation of the restaurant."

"What I meant was, why did he invest in Casa del Lago? Did you advertise for investors?"

Mary Pat spoke carefully, weighing each word on her tongue like a politician—or someone else with plenty of secrets.

"What I was told," she said, "Juan Carlos began looking for business opportunities immediately after he settled on Lake Minnetonka. A banker suggested that I might be interested in a silent partner. Juan Carlos turned out to be less silent than I would have preferred. Other than that, I have no complaints."

"When was the last time you saw him?"

"Last Thursday during the dinner rush. Dinner and lunch is when he usually comes by. Juan Carlos will walk through the restaurant, hang out on the patio, meet and greet customers. He's very good at making friends. Sometimes he'll pick up a tab. It's never on the house, though. He always pays it out of his own pocket. He likes to be seen here. He likes to play the *patrón*. I don't mind too much because the customers seem to love the guy. Seatings are higher than ever. So are check averages. I was surprised when he didn't show up Friday and Saturday."

That started me thinking devious thoughts about the criminal behavior of unscrupulous characters. I zoned out for a few moments, forgetting completely that Mary Pat was sitting in the booth with me. She called me back.

"Hey," she said.

"Sorry. I was just . . . How much did Navarre invest in your restaurant?"

"I don't see how that's any of your business, McKenzie."

"You're right, you're right . . . I was just wondering, did he give you cash?"

"Of course not. Who makes loans like that in cash? Drug dealers, maybe. Gangsters. Do you think I'd be involved with someone like that?"

"No, no, I was just—"

"The transaction was handled through my bank. Lake Minnetonka Community."

"I was just wondering—"

"The paperwork was all properly signed, notarized and filed."

"Did anything seem out of whack to you?"

The question slowed her down. Mary Pat's mouth twisted into a kind of confused smile when she answered. "The interest rate on the loan. Juan Carlos could have done better with a government-backed CD."

I flashed on something Sarah Neamy told me earlier.

"Except then he wouldn't be able to walk around like he owned the place," I said.

"I suppose. Look, McKenzie. Whatever Juan Carlos is into has nothing to do with me. All I want is to be left alone. I have a good month or so left before the weather starts to turn nasty and I lose my lake traffic. When you find him, you might want to tell him that. This is a business."

I thanked Mary Pat for her time. I hadn't paid for the Summit Ale, but when I reached into my pocket, she told me it was on the house. I thanked her again and said I would be in touch. She didn't seem to care one way or the other.

I left the restaurant and walked toward the Audi, decided what the hell, it's such a pleasant autumn day in Minnesota, seventy-three degrees and sunny with the wind not blowing, why not risk my life frivolously? I passed the Audi and kept going until I reached the back row of the parking lot. I stopped in front of the Impala, took the smartphone from my pocket, and made a big production of taking a photo of the car's license plate.

A young man—he couldn't have been more than eighteen—poked his head out the window.

"What the fuck you doing?" he asked. "You don't fuckin' take no pictures."

I ignored him and took a few more.

"Asshole, I'll fuck you up."

He opened the car door and slid out. He wore his jeans low on his hips so that the top three inches of his boxer shorts were visible. Yet it was the image on the front of his tight T-shirt that caused me to rethink my actions—a large black handprint. In the palm of the hand were the numbers 937 resting on top of the letters *eMe*. The Black Hand of Death, an image usually associated with Sicilian gangsters, had long ago been appropriated by the Mexican Mafia—*eMe* spelled out the Spanish pronunciation of the letter *M*.

"Say cheese," I said and took his photograph just the same.

"Give that back," he demanded, as if my camera had stolen something precious from him.

He took a step toward me. When he did, I slipped the phone back into my pocket and took a step toward him, clenching my fists like I was ready to rumble. While he was sitting in the car, he was a machine yelling at a man. When he got out the situation changed. Now he was a man shouting at another man—a man who was bigger than he was. Doubt crept into his voice.

"Who d' fuck you think y'are?" he asked.

"Who the fuck do you think you are?" I asked in return.

He didn't answer. I gave it a beat and began edging away slowly. After a few steps, I turned my back to him and returned to the Audi. I gave him another look before sliding behind the steering wheel. He was talking on his own cell phone. It didn't look like the conversation was going well.

I drove out of the restaurant's parking lot and worked my way along a couple of narrow streets to County Road 19. The Impala caught up to me at the intersection. A thrill of fear rippled through my body as I watched the driver in my rearview while waiting for the light. I guessed that he was following someone's orders—he didn't look smart enough to be giving them himself. Whose, though? To do what?

Three possibilities came to mind. The first was to shoot me, but c'mon, I told myself, that's a little melodramatic, don't you think? Even the Mexican Mafia doesn't kill without a reason, and I hadn't done anything to anyone yet. The second was to find out who I was, except the driver could have accomplished that task the same way I intended to learn who he was—by running the license plate number of his car. There was a handful of Web sites more than willing to help for a fee. If they couldn't, you could always hustle down to the Minnesota Department of Public Safety building in St. Paul and fill out a DVS Records Request Form. It cost all of $9.50.

The third possibility seemed more likely—the driver was told to follow me with the expectation that I might lead him to Navarre.

The light changed and I took a left, heading east along the section of the county highway that was called Smithtown Road into the City of Excelsior. Excelsior was approximately one square mile in size with a population of about 2,400. It was founded in 1853 to serve wealthy visitors from New York and Europe, and its numerous antique shops, specialty stores, restaurants, theaters, and B&Bs suggested that it hadn't strayed far from its roots.

I stayed on Smithtown until it became Oak Street and hung a left at the Excelsior Elementary School to see if the Impala would follow. It did. *So you're not just being paranoid after all,* my inner voice told me. Still, by the time I passed the Bird House Inn I had reached a conclusion. Either the kid was told not to lose me at any cost, which meant he didn't care that I knew he was following, or he honestly didn't realize I was onto him, which made him a pitiful amateur.

Either way, you cannot encourage or condone such sinister behavior, my inner voice said.

I turned right and worked my way back to the county road. I eased the Audi out of Excelsior, caught Highway 7, and drove east between St. Albans Bay and Christmas Lake. I found KBEM-FM on the radio, only they were playing a jazz version of Paul McCartney's "Blackbird." That would not do at all, I decided, so I fiddled with the MP3 player until I found Billy Idol's cover of "Mony Mony."

Now that's traveling music.

I checked the rearview. The Chevy Impala had fallen back, allowing two other vehicles to come between us. I downshifted and stepped hard on the gas. "Shoot 'em down turn around come on Mony," I sang aloud. The Audi accelerated so effortlessly that I didn't know I was topping 90 mph until I glanced down at the speedometer. I checked the rearview again. The Impala had disappeared, yet I kept accelerating anyway, weaving in and around traffic just the way the skills instructor had taught me at the police academy.

I could have slowed down, but why would you own a $65,000 sports car if you can't wring it out every once in a while? Besides, I was carrying my St. Paul Police Department ID; the word RETIRED was stamped across the face. In case I was stopped, I had it positioned in my

I-394 splits at the edge of downtown Minneapolis. Go right and you'll merge with east I-94, which eventually leads to St. Paul. Go left and you'll end up on the doorstep of Target Field, where the Twins play baseball. I went left, worked my way around the ballpark, and drove north until I reached the city's North Loop, also known as the Warehouse District because of the number of old warehouses that had been converted into condos, apartments, boutiques, art galleries, and restaurants. As well as being listed on the National Register of Historic Places, the district was also ranked twelfth on *Forbes* magazine's list of America's Best Hipster Neighborhoods. Which meant that somewhere in the country there were eleven 'hoods where you were even more likely to see people wearing skinny jeans and Clark Kent glasses and saying things like "super sweet," "stylin'," and "let's bounce."

I found an open meter in front of Riley Brodin's building. Her address had been included in the packet of information she had sent me. Probably I should have called ahead. It's been my experience, though, that when asking questions sneak attacks nearly always work best.

I climbed the steps and rang her bell. She called

down, I identified myself, and Riley buzzed me in. Her condo was on the top floor. She met me at the door. Her makeup had been removed, her ivory hair was plastered to her skull, and she had a lemon-soap smell as if she had just stepped from the shower. It made her seem younger, but not more innocent.

"Did you find him?" she asked. "Did you find Juan Carlos?"

"Not yet."

Riley's shoulders sagged with the news.

"Then why are you here?" she wanted to know. "Why aren't you out looking for him?"

"We need to talk, Riles. I'm calling you Riles because you said it was the name your close friends use, and I think you're going to need a friend."

She found a chair and sat down, tucking her bare feet beneath her. I sat across from her.

"What is it?" Riley asked.

"I've been to Navarre's house. It's immaculate to the point that it looks more like a museum than a home."

"I know. He likes it that way. He said it's because he wants it to look perfect all the time."

"For who?"

"For me."

It took a few seconds for me to digest that bit of news. After I did, I said, "One thing about being neat, it makes it easier to notice the things that are

74

missing, and the only thing that's missing from Navarre's house is his computer. His clothes are still there, his toothbrush . . ."

"What does that mean?"

"It means he left in a helluva hurry. Except . . ."

"Except what?"

"His car is still there, too. A BMW 328i convertible."

Riley nodded her head as if she knew it all along.

"Does he own another car?" I asked.

"No, just the Beamer. Does that mean—do you think Juan Carlos was kidnapped?"

"I might have thought so if there weren't so many other people looking for him, too."

"I don't understand."

"Someone is watching his house, watching the restaurant. That's one." I hesitated, then decided there was no need to bring the Mexican Mafia into the conversation just yet. "There's another. Navarre's partner, his partner at Casa del Lago, Mary Pat Mulally, said that a private investigator came around asking questions and threatening her when she refused to answer them."

"Who? Who threatened Mary Pat? Who would dare?"

"Ms. Mulally thinks it's your grandfather."

Now it was Riley's turn to take a few moments.

"That doesn't make sense," she said at last.

"Not to us, maybe. The thing is, Riles, I don't

think Navarre is missing. I think he's hiding."

"Why?"

"Are you sure you really want to know?"

"What does that mean?"

"Navarre went poof for a reason. Finding him might not be to his advantage. More to the point, it might not be to your advantage."

Riley came out of the chair and moved to her window. From the window the city below looked like an intricate maze put together by an imaginative child, streets and lights and buildings and bridges all thrown together to create something both wonderful and bizarre. She stood there for what seemed like a long time yet was only a few moments. She turned abruptly, her back to the view as if it meant nothing to her.

"Find him for me," she said. "I can pay. I have plenty of money."

"I bet you do."

"You don't need money, do you, McKenzie?"

"No."

"You're probably the only person I know who can make that claim."

"Your grandfather."

She chuckled at the suggestion. "He needs it most of all," she said. "He needs it like the rest of us need oxygen. It's what keeps him alive, the source of all his power. Please, McKenzie, what can I do to convince you?"

It was against my better judgment, but I

answered her just the same. "All you need to do is ask."

"Will you find Juan Carlos for me?"

"I can try."

"Thank you."

"Don't thank me yet, Riles. I'm not promising you a happy ending."

"I know."

"Tell me about his friends. Someone who might have helped him."

"I don't know . . . he doesn't have—Juan Carlos is new to America. He's only been here . . . he hasn't had time to make any real friends except for . . . well, there's Mrs. R."

"And you."

"If he's in trouble, why doesn't he call?"

"Maybe to keep you out of trouble."

"Do you think?"

It seemed like a good time to change the subject, so I told Riley about coming across the yearbook from Macalester College at Navarre's house and suggested that he kept it because it contained a photograph of her.

"Really? Why would he . . . ?" She paused while she pondered the question and then shook her head as if she didn't like the answer. "I went to Macalester to please my mother. After my freshman year I transferred to the University of Minnesota and entered the Carlson School of Management to please my grandfather. No one wanted me to go to Harvard or Yale. It was like they didn't want me out of their sight."

"It must have been hard, must still be hard growing up Muehlenhaus."

"You have no idea. Although . . ."

"Hmm?"

"Juan Carlos seems to understand."

I decided that Riley was looking for a prince to rescue her and at that point in her life any prince would do, even an enigma like Juan Carlos Navarre. I also decided there was nothing to gain by discussing it.

"For what it's worth, Irene Rogers is on your side," I said.

That made the young woman smile for the first time since I entered her condominium. She was still smiling when I left.

Greg Schroeder was smiling, too. I found him sitting on the hood of the Audi when I exited Riley's building. His arms were folded across his chest. He unfolded them when I approached to let me see that his hands were empty, a show of professional courtesy I appreciated very much.

"That's a sixty-five-thousand-dollar, high-precision driving machine you're using for a park bench there, pal," I said.

"This piece of shit? I heard that the driver might be wanted for questioning concerning a pile-up on Highway 7."

"What are you talking about?"

Schroeder continued to smile as he explained it to me. "That kid you were racing, he clipped the back bumper of a car while trying to keep up with you. Spun it out. Caused a five-car melee. I nearly got caught in it myself."

"Was anyone hurt?"

"Couldn't say, although an ambulance was summoned to the scene."

"Dammit."

"If I were the county cops, I'd be tempted to take a look at the footage from the state's highway cameras, see if I could find someone to blame." He slid off the Audi and patted the quarter panel. "What comes from fast cars and loose women. Speaking of which—how's Nina these days?"

I closed my eyes and took a deep breath. Schroeder meant no disrespect to Nina. He was just trying to give me the business. I had known him for nearly four years. He was a trench-coat detective, one of those guys who wore white shirts and shoulder holsters under rumpled suit coats, a cigarette dangling from his lips while he asked for just the facts, ma'am. He drank his coffee black and his whisky neat and for all I knew he carried a photograph of Humphrey Bogart playing Sam Spade in his wallet. He had saved my life twice. The second time it cost me $10,000—in cash. The first time he had been working for Mr. Muehlenhaus.

I opened my eyes.

"Let me guess," I said. "You just happened to be in the neighborhood . . ."

"I was following the kid who was following you," Schroeder said.

"Why?"

Schroeder shrugged and smiled some more. You had to give it to him—few people enjoyed their work as much as he enjoyed his.

"You didn't pay Mary Pat Mulally a visit earlier, did you?" I asked. "You or one of your operatives?"

He shrugged again as if he were deliberately keeping secrets from me and didn't care if I knew it, although . . . When I first started out with the cops I actually believed that I could look into the eyes of a suspect—any suspect—while he answered my questions and tell if he was lying; that my gut instinct would take over and I would know the truth beyond a doubt. I soon learned different. Some people I can read, of course. Anyone can. Others are such gifted and experienced liars that even a polygraph can't find them out—which is why the test results are still inadmissible in a court of law. Yet I kept doing it; kept looking for the truth in their faces. Staring at Schroeder, I was able to detect a flinch, a tiny one, at the corners of his smile—if I hadn't been watching so intently, I would have missed it. Yet it told me that he had no idea what I was talking about and not knowing alarmed him as much as it did me.

"Why are you here, Greg?" I asked.

"Boss wants to chat with you," he said.

"Mr. Muehlenhaus?"

"Not this time."

Margaret Muehlenhaus floated on long dancer's legs and dancer's feet down the steps of the portico of her splendid house and across the front lawn. Sunlight reflected off the threads of her burgundy sundress and the lenses of the reading glasses that she wore on a silver chain around her neck. Her eyes were brown and flashed without help from the sun. The few streaks of gray in her otherwise chocolate hair were artfully arranged.

"Welcome to the Pointe," she said. After introducing herself she looked me over as if I might possibly be a salesman hawking encyclopedias door to door. Did people still do that? Probably not, but she was old enough to remember when they did.

"You are McKenzie, correct?" she said.

"Yes."

"Funny, you don't look like a syphilitic sonuvabitch."

"How is Mr. Muehlenhaus these days?" I asked.

"He doesn't want you setting foot inside his house."

"So, he's the same, then?"

She laughed at the question. "Come inside. I have fresh strawberry lemonade."

"Your husband said . . ."

"Oh, pooh."

Mrs. Muehlenhaus hooked her arm around mine and led me across the lawn, up the steps, and past the gleaming white columns that held up the porch. It was then that I realized this was the house that Juan Carlos Navarre had been watching through his telescope.

Once inside she shouted, "Agnes." A moment passed and she added, "Aggie."

"Ma'am," a voice called from another part of the house.

"We'll be in my room."

"Yes, ma'am."

Mrs. Muehlenhaus continued to hold on to my arm as she maneuvered me through the mansion. Despite her age, she carried herself with the erect authority of someone that had been both powerful and handsome and still remembered how it felt.

"The house has twenty-three rooms," she told me. "I haven't set foot in some of them for years. This room . . ." She paused in front of a large mahogany door, smiled more to herself than me, turned the knob, and pushed it open. "This is where I spend most of my time."

I stepped inside. Dozens of books had overflowed from the many bookshelves onto the furniture and floor. The walls not supporting bookshelves were filled with original paintings that seemed to have nothing in common except that the owner liked them. There were sweaters tossed here and there, and a white silk blouse that looked like it had been discarded quickly and then forgotten at the foot of a CD player. A cabinet next to it was filled with CDs ranging from Frank Sinatra, Tony Bennett, and Sarah Vaughan to U2, Rufus Wainwright, and Loreena McKennitt. Other CDs were stacked on the floor. There was also a 56-inch HDTV, a DVD player, and hundreds of movies, some of them in neat, alphabetical piles and some scattered haphazardly. Mrs. Muehlenhaus seemed particularly fond of Barbara Stanwyck.

I liked the room very much. It reminded me of my place on Hoyt. All it needed was a couple of hockey sticks and an equipment bag in the corner near the door. I turned to look and found a golf bag instead.

"In my world appearances carry great weight," she said. "I promise you, McKenzie, I am quite adept at playing the perfect wife of the powerful man. It is a role I both relish and enjoy. However, when I am not onstage, I prefer to retreat to this room. It's my secret lair. My girl cave. No one is allowed inside without my permission."

Mrs. Muehlenhaus sat on the leather sofa while I sat in a matching chair across from her.

"The staff is forbidden to clean in here." She reached down, picked a dirty dinner plate off the floor, and set it on the table in front of the sofa. "In case you're wondering."

There was a knock on the door. Mrs. Muehlenhaus said, "Enter," and a maid walked in carrying a silver tray with a crystal pitcher and two crystal goblets. She set the tray on the table and picked up the dirty plate. Her eyes cast about as if she expected to find others.

"Shoo shoo, shoo shoo," Mrs. Muehlenhaus said.

The maid left reluctantly. Her head swiveled back and forth as she made her way to the door until she found a dirty cup and saucer sitting on one of the bookshelves, dashed over to grab it, and hurried from the room before Mrs. Muehlenhaus could stop her.

"It's tough getting good help these days," I said.

"Tell me about it."

Mrs. Muehlenhaus poured the strawberry lemonade into the crystal goblets and handed one to me. It was delicious.

"I'd offer you something a little more robust," she said. "Only we don't know each other well enough to get sloshed in the middle of the afternoon."

"Here's looking at you, kid," I said before taking another sip.

"*Casablanca.* Good for you. My very first date

with a boy—I was thirteen—we went to see *Casablanca.* I wept at the end, and the boy laughed at me. I have not seen him since."

Mrs. Muehlenhaus waved at her piles of DVDs.

"I have a copy around here somewhere," she said. "Do you know that Riley has never seen *Casablanca*? I spoke to some of her friends when she was in college. They hadn't seen it, either. They didn't know who Ingrid Bergman was. Or Vivien Leigh. Or even Kate Hepburn. One of Riley's classmates told me she refused to watch black-and-white movies. How terribly sad.

"On the other hand, Riley reads an enormous amount. When she was younger, she'd sneak in here and sit for days at a time reading one book after another. She is a much more serious young woman than she pretends."

It's not possible for her to be more serious than she pretends, my inner voice said.

"Mrs. Muehlenhaus, why am I here?" I asked aloud.

"I want us to be friends."

"Okay."

"And because our mutual friend Greg Schroeder tells me that you're searching for Juan Carlos Navarre at the behest of my granddaughter."

"Mrs. Muehlenhaus, I am shocked by the company you keep."

"I like Mr. Schroeder. He reminds me of Dick Powell in *Murder, My Sweet.* Have you seen it?"

85

"I have," I said. I didn't see the resemblance between Schroeder and the actor, though, a thought I kept to myself.

"Do you know what Walter calls him? The dependable Mr. Schroeder."

"Ahh," I hummed.

"Do you know what he calls you?"

"Yes, I do."

Mrs. Muehlenhaus laughed as if it were all a great joke.

"I have taken a fancy to you, McKenzie," she said.

"Thank you."

"Don't thank me. It's not necessarily a compliment. I have appalling taste in men. Take my husband, please."

The way she spoke and laughed, I swear she was flirting with me just as Irene Rogers had.

It seems you have a knack with little old ladies, my inner voice told me. *I only hope you still have it when you're a little old man.*

When she finished laughing, Mrs. Muehlenhaus took a sip of her lemonade, smiled brightly, and asked, "McKenzie, why are you looking for Mr. Navarre?"

"Why are you?"

"You're not married . . ."

"No."

"Although you and the lovely Ms. Truhler seem

to be enjoying a long and extremely stable relationship."

"It bothers me, Mrs. Muehlenhaus, that you seem to know so much about my personal life. Scares me a little, too."

She reached across the table and patted my knee as if she expected me to think nothing of it and kept talking.

"Ms. Truhler has an equally lovely and extremely intelligent daughter to whom you have become quite attached. Rickie is her name."

"She prefers Erica," I said.

"What would you do, McKenzie, if you discovered that Erica was involved with a dangerous criminal? Would you intervene?"

"Is Navarre a dangerous criminal?"

"You didn't answer my question."

"You didn't answer mine."

Somewhere behind the closed mahogany door a voice boomed. "Margaret. Margaret, where are you?"

Mrs. Muehlenhaus smiled.

"He only calls me that when he's upset," she said.

The door flew open and Mr. Muehlenhaus stepped inside. He was a fairly tall man, and from the way he moved it was clear that he had no intention of ever surrendering to age.

"Dammit, Margaret. What did I tell you?"

Mrs. Muehlenhaus's eyes grew wide, her jaw

clenched, and she gestured with her head at the door. Swear to God, I thought I heard her growl.

"Oh, all right," Mr. Muehlenhaus said.

He spun around and left the room, closing the door behind him. A moment later, he knocked gently.

"Come in," Mrs. Muehlenhaus called.

Mr. Muehlenhaus reentered the room, moving quickly. He stepped in front of his wife yet pointed at me.

"Maggie, I left specific instructions," he told her.

"Yes, you did, dear."

Mrs. Muehlenhaus patted the empty cushion next to her, and Mr. Muehlenhaus sat. That was the end of the argument.

"Would you like some strawberry lemonade?" Mrs. Muehlenhaus asked.

"Actually, I would prefer some of your Scotch."

"You know where it is."

I watched Muehlenhaus rise from the sofa and move to one of the bookcases where a massive three-volume set of Shelby Foote's *The Civil War: A Narrative* was shelved. He pulled the books off the shelf, reached in, produced a bottle of Macallan thirty-year Highland single malt Scotch whisky, and returned the books.

"How 'bout you, McKenzie?" Mrs. Muehlenhaus asked. "Care for something a bit stronger?"

"No, I'm good," I said.

"You don't mind if I imbibe?"

"Not at all."

Muehlenhaus returned to the sofa. Somewhere he found an extra glass. He blew the dust out of it and poured a generous amount of liquor. He then poured an inch into Mrs. Muehlenhaus's now empty crystal goblet.

"I don't know why you hide this," he told her. "It's not even the good stuff."

"I'm eccentric. All I need is cats."

"You're allergic to cat hair."

"So I'm saved from the stereotype. Lucky me."

The crystal made a beautiful ringing sound when her goblet clinked against Muehlenhaus's glass. They drank while looking into each other's eyes, and I thought, They are genuinely in love. At their age and after all their years of marriage. For some reason, it made me less afraid of them.

"So, kids," I said. "Why exactly am I here, again?"

"Kids?" Muehlenhaus said. "Do I look like a child to you?"

"Here we go," Mrs. Muehlenhaus said softly before taking another sip of Scotch.

"Mr. Muehlenhaus, there are so many reasons for you to be pissed at me," I said. "A turn of a phrase, that's what's going to set you off?"

"Do you want me to tell you who you remind me of, McKenzie? I'll tell you. You remind me of those goddamned French bastards that guillotined

Louis and Marie Antoinette yet couldn't be bothered to burn down Versailles, that didn't so much as torch a single brick of the place."

"I'm a true Republican."

"No, that was a Democrat thing to do."

"Now you're just calling names."

"You resent people who are wealthy and who are in charge, yet you want to be wealthy and in charge yourself."

"I am wealthy."

"What have you done with your money? Tell me?"

"A couple days ago I bought a TV remote that looks like Dr. Who's sonic screwdriver. Does that count?"

"That'll make the world a better place, I'm sure."

"You know, dear," Mrs. Muehlenhaus said, "this is why I wanted to talk to McKenzie alone."

"It's not my fault," Muehlenhaus replied. "You can't have a civil conversation with fucking McKenzie."

"I heard that's what you call me," I said. "Do you want to know what I call you?"

"Oh, by all means, tell me."

"*Mr.* Muehlenhaus."

"Yes, well, that's what you should call me. I'm pretty sure I earned it."

"I'm pretty sure I've earned whatever you call me, too. That doesn't answer my question, though. Why am I here?"

"Riley." Mrs. Muehlenhaus caught her husband's eyes and held them. "You remember Riley, your granddaughter?"

"Yes. Of course. Please forgive my outburst," Muehlenhaus said, although he clearly didn't care if he was forgiven or not.

"McKenzie," Mrs. Muehlenhaus said, "we are concerned about Riley. We believe she is involved with the wrong people."

"Define wrong people," I said.

"Do we need to spell it out?" Muehlenhaus said.

"Please."

Mrs. Muehlenhaus glared at her husband some more.

"McKenzie," she said. "I do not concern myself with whether or not Juan Carlos is rich or poor. I don't care if he's Hispanic or white. I don't care if he's a Democrat or Republican, a member of the Tea Party or supports the ACLU—I really don't."

"Neither do I," Muehlenhaus said, but I didn't believe him.

"What I do care about is that we are unable to learn anything about the boy."

"He claims to be the son of wealthy parents," Muehlenhaus added. "Only his parents died seven years ago and he has no other family. Don't you think that's a little convenient?"

I was surprised at how suddenly the anger

formed in the pit of my stomach and shot up to my throat. Some other time and place I might have given it voice—being an orphan is no reason to denounce someone. But the Muehlenhauses weren't people you went off on, especially in their own home, so I fought it down and spoke as carefully as possible.

"Both my parents are dead, and no, I don't find it the least bit convenient."

"Yes, well," Muehlenhaus said.

"Despite what you think of us—or at least what my husband believes you think of us—we are concerned only with the child's welfare," Mrs. Muehlenhaus said. "My family has been hurt by deceivers before. My daughter, Sheila . . ."

Mrs. Muehlenhaus didn't finish the sentence. Her husband reached for her hand and gave it a squeeze.

"You aren't worried about social fallout from Riley's involvement with *that immigrant,*" I said.

"Hmmph," Muehlenhaus said.

Mrs. Muehlenhaus smiled, but not much.

"We don't concern ourselves with such matters," she said.

"Look, kids," I said, adding the "kids" to annoy Mr. Muehlenhaus some more. "The young lady asked me to find her boyfriend who's gone missing. When I do, I'm supposed to deliver a simple message. That's it. If along the way I find evidence that proves Navarre is a louse, I'll be happy to pass it along. I'll be telling her, though, not you."

The way he glowered, I knew that Mr. Muehlenhaus not only wanted what he wanted, he wanted it exactly his way—Mrs. R's definition of a spoiled child. Mrs. Muehlenhaus, on the other hand, seemed more interested in the end result than how it was achieved.

"That's fine," she said.

"Is it?"

"Riley is our granddaughter, and we love her so much. We're just trying to look out for her. If you'll be kind enough to do the same . . ."

"I will do the same."

"Thank you, McKenzie. That's all I ask."

Muehlenhaus's foot began tapping a quick rhythm on the carpet. I don't think it was impatience so much as restless energy. It was as if he were finished with me and now his body felt the need to be up and doing something else.

"I decided I don't want to have any more conversations with you unless your wife is present," I told him.

"Why is that?" Muehlenhaus asked.

"I think you're less likely to shoot me in front of her."

"Oh, McKenzie." Mrs. Muehlenhaus rose from the sofa and offered me her hand. "Many people have made that mistake."

A few minutes later, Muehlenhaus escorted me

to the front door of his house. He didn't offer to shake my hand, merely said, "I'll be in touch," as I passed through the doorway. He was smiling, though, like a magician with an endless supply of rabbits and hats.

I heard the floorboards creak when I stepped onto the old-fashioned wooden porch that ran the length of the front of the house, and it occurred to me that they had *always* creaked. They creaked when Bobby and I were at the University of Minnesota and before that at Central High School and even before that when we both attended St. Mark's Elementary School just a few blocks away. They creaked when we hung out at Merriam Park across the street and when we were rookies with the St. Paul Police Department and when Bobby bought the house from his parents after they retired to their lake home in Wisconsin. I found myself walking across the porch listening to the varying tones the floorboards gave off. Step in the right places in the correct order and I was sure you could play Beethoven's "Ode to Joy."

The door opened abruptly and Katie Dunston, Bobby's younger daughter, poked her head out. "What are you doing?" she asked.

I bounced up and down.

"Hear that?" I said. "Hear how the floorboards creak?"

"They always creak." Katie disappeared back into the house, leaving the door open for me. I heard her shout, "It's McKenzie."

I entered the house, closing the door behind me. Shelby Dunston called from the kitchen. "Are you hungry? I was just putting away the leftovers."

"I'm good, thank you," I called back.

A moment later she appeared, a dish towel in her hand.

"Hey," she said.

"Hey." I moved toward her. She lifted her cheek for a kiss, and I gave her one. "What's going on?"

The look she gave suggested that the question was in poor taste and she was disappointed in me for asking it. Shelby left the living room and returned to the kitchen without speaking. I glanced at Katie and mouthed the same question.

Katie pointed upstairs and mouthed back, "Victoria."

I moved toward the thirteen-year-old and whispered. "What about Victoria?"

"She got caught cheating in school."

"What? No way. Victoria doesn't cheat. She has a four-point-oh average, for God's sake."

"She wasn't actually cheating. What she did, she let a boy copy off of her paper."

"Uh-oh."

"Yeah. Mom is—she's freaking out. Yelling at Vic for letting a boy use her like that. I mean she said stuff you only hear on the FX Channel, you know?"

"Where is Vic?"

"Banished to her room until she's twenty-one and if she doesn't like it she can move out right now."

I heard Shelby's voice behind me. It was loud and clear.

"What are you doing, young lady?" she wanted to know. "Telling family secrets?"

Katie took a step backward.

"No, ma'am," she said. "I was just telling McKenzie that I'm an independent woman and no guy is ever going to make a damn fool out of me."

"Are you swearing in my house?"

Katie seemed confused. "You did."

"Go up to your room right now."

Katie glanced up at me. She was almost smiling. "See," she said.

Shelby watched while Katie retreated upstairs. She called to her, "And I don't want to see you again until you've done your homework."

Katie called back, "I've already done my homework."

"Don't you sass me, young lady."

Shelby turned and glared at me.

"Do you have something to say, McKenzie?" she asked.

Ever since she wed my best friend, it seemed as if Shelby's main goal in life was to see me married with children. It annoyed her to no end that Nina and I had been together for so long without benefit of matrimony. I was tempted to ask her what she thought of the institution now, only I didn't have the nerve.

"Is Bobby here?" I asked instead.

"He's downstairs watching a ball game, the coward. Tell me something. When did the woman become responsible for disciplining the children? When I grew up it was always the man. My mother, whenever we screwed up she would say, 'Wait until your father gets home,' and when he got home we would get it. You know what Bobby did when he came home? He hugged her. Hugged. Her. Asked Vic if she understood how big her mistake was and why we were so angry."

"He was being the good cop."

"Oh, and that makes me the bad cop?"

Shelby's lips became a thin line etched across a granite face. She brought her hand up and pointed at me, didn't say another word. Just pointed.

"I'm ahh, I'm going downstairs, now."

Shelby didn't answer. Just kept pointing. She was still pointing when I opened the door in the kitchen that led to the basement stairs. A moment later I was standing next to Bobby's sofa in the rec room that I helped him build. He was watching two National League teams trying to take an early lead in their best-of-five playoff series on his HDTV. I knew for a fact that he didn't care for either baseball team, didn't care who won or lost. We didn't speak until the batter hit a lazy fly ball to left.

"I don't know who I'm more concerned about," he said. "Victoria or Shelby."

"Think Shelby is overreacting?"

"I don't know. I only know that Victoria, and Katherine, too, for that matter, have never done anything wrong that you and I haven't done ten times worse when we were kids. Shelby, too, if the stories her friends and family tell are true. We turned out all right. Sorta. So, how upset do you allow yourself to get? How tough should the punishment be? It's hard being a good parent these days."

"I met your children. Someone is doing a pretty decent job."

Bobby gestured with his head toward the basement steps. "I think so, too, but Shelby isn't in the mood to hear it."

A few minutes later I had a Leinenkugel and a seat on the sofa.

"Are you just visiting or do you have something in mind?" Bobby asked.

I explained my involvement with Riley Brodin and the Muehlenhauses. That made him laugh. "You never learn, do you?" he said. Then I told him about the kid in the parking lot of Casa del Lago.

"Are you sure?" Bobby asked.

"Black handprint and in the palm the numbers

nine-thirty-seven resting on top of *eMe*." To confirm my claim, I showed him the photograph I had taken, along with a shot of the Chevy Impala's license plate.

"Nine-Thirty-Seven Mexican Mafia," Bobby said. "They've been gone for what? Seven years, now? Eight? They were located in West St. Paul; got their name from the address of a car wash on South Robert Street where the founders used to work. It's not even there anymore, the car wash. The DEA, the BCA, and the Westies—they hit them hard—you should remember that. You were still a cop, I think, when that happened. Apparently they had a CI, an inside man that set up the gang. Half of them went to prison; some were absorbed by other Hispanic street gangs—Norteños Fourteen, Latin Kings, BFL. The others got out of the life."

"Could the gang have been reformed?"

"Not that I heard. Even so, who wears gang sign on a T-shirt? Ink, sure, everyone does tats. Colors. I know of a gang that always wears tan slacks and white shirts with button-down collars. Motorcycle clubs like putting patches on their jackets, their vests. A T-shirt? That's new."

Bobby paused to drink some beer and watch a few more at-bats. All the while I could see the wheels spinning in his head, and I knew enough not to interrupt the process. Bobby was the best cop I knew—even better than I was. Certainly he was smarter at playing the game than me, not fighting the regs that seemed to be written to keep us from doing our jobs so much as caressing them, massaging them until they yielded exactly what he needed. We started together at the St. Paul Police Department nearly twenty years ago. He was now a commander in the Major Crimes Division.

"Why would anyone wear a T-shirt with the name of a defunct Mexican street gang?" he asked at last.

"Nostalgia?"

Bobby ignored the remark.

" 'Course, anyone can wear a T-shirt," he said. "I've seen you wearing a shirt that claimed you were property of the Minnesota Twins, and we both know that you sucked at baseball."

"I was a great baseball player."

Bobby stared straight ahead without answering until the half inning ended. He said, "No, you really weren't," so softly I barely heard him and then added, "Let me make a few calls," in a louder voice.

Which was exactly what I wanted to hear.

A short time later I left him and went upstairs. Shelby was sitting in her living room and reading a historical romance novel written by someone named Julie Klassen. The light from the floor lamp made her wheat-colored hair glow and her green eyes sparkle. I watched her for a couple of beats and not for the first time asked myself, What if I had been the one who spilled the drink on her dress way back in college instead of Bobby?

Her eyes lifted from the book and fell on me. She started to smile but fought it back down.

"Permission to speak to the prisoner?" I asked.

"Are you going to give Victoria a hug and tell her everything is going to be fine and dandy, too?"

"No. If it comes up in conversation, though, I might tell her she has the best mother in the world and should listen to her."

"I behaved like such a bitch, McKenzie."

"Isn't that part of the job description?"

"She really is a good kid. Isn't she?"

"I always thought so, but then I'm prejudiced."

"Did I ever thank you for making her and Katie your heirs?"

"Many times. You've also accused me of spoiling them rotten."

"Yes, and I wish you would stop."

"I was reminded today that I'm an orphan. That I have no family. I was surprised at how angry it made me after all this time."

Shelby stared at me for a beat. "At least you have us." She gave me a dismissive wave and returned to her book. "Go," she said. "Talk to Victoria. Don't let her think for a second that I'm not still angry."

I walked upstairs, found Victoria's bedroom door, and knocked. The fifteen-year-old was sitting at her desk, a laptop opened on top of it. She seemed happy to see me.

"Welcome to the gulag," Victoria said.

I glanced around the bedroom. It seemed to have been decorated by a young woman with plenty of interests and not too many worries. There was an abundance of books, posters of celebrities, and handwritten signs with slogans like "There's no sense arguing over every mistake, you just keep trying till you run out of cake" and "Do something brave every day and then run as fast as you can." The walls were painted blue. Her closet doors were open, and I could see her clothes suspended on light blue hangers alternating with dark blue hangers and arranged according to color—white, gray, pink, red, green, blue, purple, and black.

Victoria caught me examining her closet and said, "You have to admit, that looks cool."

"I'm guessing you've been grounded before," I said.

"Have you heard what I'm in for this time?"

"Yep."

"God, that was stupid. I was so stupid doing that for a guy. I don't even like him that much. Stupid. God. This could knock me off the honor roll. Do you know I haven't received a grade below an A since the third grade? Then I do this.

Mom was right. She said no one who cares about me would ever ask me to do something that put me at risk."

"Did you tell her that?"

"We're not speaking. She needs me to suffer in silence for a while. Besides, I'm not entirely sure how letting a guy cheat off my chemistry test will lead to sexual abuse, prostitution, or unwanted pregnancy. Still . . . Have you ever done anything that stupid, McKenzie?"

"Frequently."

My answer didn't seem to give her much comfort.

"What do you want, anyway?" Victoria asked.

"*¿Cómo es tu Español?*"

"*Mejor que la tuya.*"

"Everybody's Spanish is better than mine," I told her. "I need you to do some research for me."

"Why not? I'm not going anywhere."

"There's a hundred bucks in it."

"Even better."

I gave her the names Felipe Navarre and Susan Kowitz, as well as Juan Carlos Navarre, and told her that most of the information I wanted would probably be found on Spanish-language Web sites and that it would be at least seven years old.

"Didn't Juan Carlos Navarre play basketball in the Olympics for Spain?" Victoria asked.

"That was Navarro."

"Oh yeah. Anything specific that you're looking for?"

"Something that proves Juan Carlos is actually Felipe and Susan's son. I'll pay double for a photograph."

A few minutes later I excused myself from the Dunston household and started driving toward Rickie's. My cell phone played the Ella Fitzgerald–Louis Armstrong cover of "Summertime." As a rule, I would not have answered it—I don't like to talk on my cell and drive at the same time. The caller ID flashed the name Irene Rogers, though, so I made an exception.

"Reney," I said.

"McKenzie, thank you so much for the wine. That was very kind of you."

"It was my pleasure."

"It isn't my birthday, you know."

"I know."

She thought that was funny.

"I didn't open the bottle yet, but I will if you join me for dinner tomorrow night. Say, seven o'clock?"

"I'd like that."

"We can talk some more about Juan Carlos."

"Did you contact your friends?"

"I did. They said they met Juan Carlos in DC about two and a half months before he showed up at my condo, so the letter of introduction was legitimate. My friend, though, she told me that up until he knocked on their door, she had no idea that Felipe and Susan had a son."

"He just showed up out of the blue?"

"He did. Speaking of which, there's someone knocking on my door now. I need to go. Tomorrow at seven here at the club?"

"I'll be there."

Two blocks later, Ella sang to me again. This time the display read SHEILA BRODIN, and I wondered, Why do so many people have my cell number?

"This is McKenzie," I said.

"This is Sheila Brodin," the voice replied. "I wish to speak to you about my daughter."

"Ma'am—"

"Don't call me ma'am. Do you know where Porterhouse is?"

"The steak house in Little Canada?"

"Meet me."

I had questions, such as when and how would I recognize her. Sheila hung up before I could ask them.

I arrived ten minutes later. Porterhouse was crowded and noisy. All of the dining room tables and booths were occupied and the maître d' was surrounded by unseated customers clamoring for attention. The small bar was just as packed by men and women who drank expensive cocktails while waiting for their names to be called. I had no idea how I was going to locate Sheila Brodin in that busy throng, and then I did. She was the only person sitting alone—at a small table in the corner. I made my way to her side. She was wearing a sheer black blouse that revealed shadows of what lay beneath and a tan linen skirt with a high slit on the side. She glanced up at me as if she had expected a man to be looking down her shirt.

"McKenzie?" she asked.

"Mrs. Brodin."

"Call me Sheila."

She gestured at the chair opposite her. She squirmed in her seat and drew the fingers of both hands through her shoulder-length hair as I sat. Her hair was the dark red that you see in very old furniture, and her face combined the pleasant features of a Mrs. America contestant with the expression of an executioner. I figured she perfected the look by studying the models in *Vogue.* Even with the table between us I could feel the heat radiating from her body.

"Drink?" she asked.

"Later."

The smile came and went so quickly that I almost didn't see it. She might have thought I was suggesting a relationship beyond the moment. I wasn't, though. She reminded me of a cat, and not one of those domestic breeds, either. Something big enough to bring down a full-grown man. I suspected she had many kills in her time. I wasn't going to be one of them.

"What do you think of me, McKenzie?" she asked.

It was an awkward question, especially considering what I *was* thinking of her, and I didn't answer it.

"You know of me, don't you?" she said. "You know what they say."

"I really don't."

"Whore. Slut. Adulterous. Depraved bitch."

"I hadn't even heard your name until your mother mentioned it a couple of hours ago."

"My mother? That paragon of chastity and goodness?"

"Mrs. Brodin, what do you want of me?"

"I'm a mother, too. Are you sure you don't want a drink?"

I shook my head. She finished hers in one gulp and stood.

"The service is iffy when it's this crowded," she said. "I'll be right back."

I watched her as she moved to the bar. Others watched her as well. She knew it, too—her walk was meant to catch the eye. When she returned with a fresh drink, she said, "How is Riley?"

"Confused," I said. "Worried."

"About Juan Carlos?"

"You're aware of him, then?"

"Of course. Riley brought him over to the house, which she's never done with any man. That's the reason I asked to speak to you. I want you to do something for me, McKenzie. I'll pay for it any way you like."

Any way? my inner voice said.

"What?" I asked.

"Let Riley have her chance."

"Her chance for what?"

"Happiness. Don't ruin it for her the way they ruined it for me. Riley is a brilliant girl and beautiful, and she's been put through so much, not just by me, but by all of them. She deserves her chance. I don't want you fouling it up."

"Why would I do that?"

"If you take Muehlenhaus money, you do as Muehlenhaus says."

"Okay, now I get it," I said. "Now I understand why you called. You have spies at the Pointe."

"It's the only way I have of keeping track of my family."

"Your spies told you I was there this afternoon, that I spoke to Maggie and Mr. Muehlenhaus. They were mistaken, though, if they told you that I'm working for Mr. Muehlenhaus. I'm not. I'm working for Riley."

"Is that the truth?"

"What exactly do you think is going on?"

"I think Riley found a man to love. A good man.

A strong man. Only he doesn't meet with their approval. He doesn't fit the Muehlenhaus plan. And they'll do whatever they can to get rid of him."

"You're not suggesting . . ."

"You know my father," Sheila said. "You know what he's capable of. Do you honestly believe he'd allow Riley to marry just anybody? She's the girl now. The Muehlenhaus Girl. There are nieces and nephews and cousins. They don't count. The old man has decided that the family's legacy rests with her."

I glanced about for a waitress. Suddenly a drink didn't seem like a bad idea.

"Your parents claim they're concerned for Riley's welfare just like any good grandparents would be," I said.

"Her welfare? McKenzie, have you ever heard of Rosemary Kennedy, JFK's sister? She was considered a wild girl like me, someone with erratic mood swings, who liked to sneak out at night and party. Her father, Joseph Kennedy, was an extremely ambitious man who wanted his son to be president. He couldn't tolerate that kind of behavior from his daughter because it conflicted with his ambitions, his welfare. So he had her lobotomized, had them shove a needle through her eye and scramble her brain. He turned her into a zombie. My father would have done the same thing to me, if he could have.

"See, I was supposed to be the Muehlenhaus Girl. Yet as hard as they tried to shove me into their round hole, that was how hard I fought against it. I make no claims to virtue, McKenzie. I am well aware that I caused most of my own problems. I was not *a good girl*. I married Alex Brodin for no other reason than he was gorgeous—that was two hundred pounds ago—and then I cheated on him. But I didn't deserve what happened to me.

"After Riley was born, I was exiled from the Pointe. Banished. I was allowed to return only on special occasions. I could see my daughter only during supervised visits. I was told if I tried to challenge this arrangement, my father would see to it that the courts declared me to be an unfit mother and forbid me forever from having any contact with Riley. He would have done it, too. You and I both know it. Then there was money. I had none of my own. My parents paid me an allowance—one hundred and twenty thousand dollars a year—to stay away. If my name were printed in the newspaper, they would dock my allowance. They made the same arrangement with Alex except, instead of giving him money, they allowed him to have a bank.

"Not once did they say they were doing this to protect Riley from her irresponsible parents. No, they always said they were doing it to protect the Muehlenhaus legacy. If you ask me, it's the

Muehlenhaus legacy that Riley needs to be protected from."

I didn't know what to say. I found it fascinating the way we find all screwed-up families to be fascinating. I just didn't know what it had to do with me, and I told Sheila so.

"You can be a man and look out for her," Sheila said.

"I already promised your parents I would do that."

"I can't pay you what they're paying you."

"They're not paying me anything."

"I have other assets."

Sheila leaned back in her chair to give me a good look at them. They were impressive, I must admit. Yet I had learned long ago that temptation exists everywhere and it comes at you from the strangest places at the oddest times. If a man isn't careful, he could fall all the way down the staircase and not even know it until he hit the bottom step.

"Navarre is missing," I said. "Riley asked me to find him. I said I would. For what it's worth, I also intend to look out for her."

God knows someone needs to, my inner voice said.

I left without looking back.

Seven

I had a dream that I'd been dreaming in various forms ever since I graduated from the University of Minnesota. In the dream I was back in school, in my senior year, going for my BS degree in criminal justice. It was finals week and I needed to pass an exam in order to graduate, but I couldn't find the classroom where the test was being held no matter how hard I searched. Not only that, I hadn't studied. I had signed up for the course, yet for reasons that seemed vague to me, I had never bothered to attend a single lecture. Now my entire future was at stake. Yet the dream ended before I learned what happened—it always did.

This time I was awakened by the sound of my telephone. It rang and kept ringing, always a bad sign. Despite the fact that I carry an expensive smartphone, I still maintain a landline at my home. None of my friends call that number, though. Only tradesmen, political groups, and charities, and they usually give up after five rings. It became clear after the seventh that whoever was calling wasn't going to give up without an answer. I rolled out of bed and picked up the receiver.

"McKenzie," I said.

"Rushmore McKenzie?"

"Who's calling please?"

"This is Chief John Rock of the South Lake Minnetonka Police Department."

Oh, crap, my inner voice said. I had been on the job for over eleven and a half years. It didn't matter. Whenever a cop approached me I still asked the same question—what did I do? This time I flashed on what Greg Schroeder had said about an accident on Highway 7 the day before. *Oh, crap.*

"Yes, Chief," I said. "What can I do for you?"

"You spoke yesterday afternoon with Ms. Mary Pat Mulally, owner of the Casa del Lago restaurant here in Excelsior."

I couldn't think of a reason to deny it, so I didn't.

"Ms. Mulally told you that her place of business was being watched by individuals unknown to her," the chief added.

"Yes," I said, drawing out the word slowly.

"She said you confronted one of these individuals in the parking lot."

Dammit, it is about the accident.

"In a manner of speaking," I said.

"I want to talk to you about that," the chief said. "Please meet me at Casa del Lago immediately. Or at least what's left of it."

"It'll take about forty minutes for me to—wait. What do you mean, what's left of it?"

"Someone set it on fire last night."

● ● ●

I dialed Bobby Dunston five seconds after I said good-bye to the chief. He identified me through caller ID.

"It's a little early for you, isn't McKenzie?" he asked. "It's barely nine a.m."

"I need help."

"That's what I've been saying since we were kids."

I told him about the call from Chief Rock.

"I didn't even know there was such a thing as a South Lake Minnetonka Police Department," I added.

"Small, maybe a dozen full-time officers. Created through a joint powers agreement between the cities of Excelsior, Greenwood, Shorewood, and Tonka Bay. Usually handles thefts, burglaries, property damage, driving offenses, disorderly conduct and public intoxication complaints—that sort of thing. Most of the heavy lifting is done by the Hennepin County Sheriff's Department."

"You're just a frickin' fount of information this morning, Bobby."

"Isn't that why you called me?"

"I called because I was hoping you had something on the Mexican Mafia and the kid I told you about."

"I haven't had a chance to look into it."

"I wish you would. It would be nice if when I

meet the chief I had something in my pocket to bargain with—you know, in case I'm in trouble."

"When aren't you in trouble?" Bobby sighed dramatically. "Haven't we had this discussion before about you not involving me and the St. Paul Police Department in your little escapades?"

"Yes, we have."

"As long as we're on the same page. I'll call you back."

He did, too. I took the call even though it meant driving with one hand through the narrow streets of Excelsior until I reached Casa del Lago. I parked in the back of the lot, putting plenty of space between the Audi and the official vehicles, a single fire truck and a couple of police cars.

I could see the front of the restaurant. It was deeply charred. A load-bearing wall must have collapsed, because the roof above the door was listing hard to the right. From the outside, the rear of the restaurant appeared more or less intact; the Excelsior Fire District had positioned huge fans in the windows and doorway that blew smoke out across Lake Minnetonka. The patio seemed unscathed. Mary Pat Mulally sat at one of the tables. She looked as if she were attending the funeral of someone she dearly loved. There were two women doing their best to comfort her. What made me hesitate before leaving the Audi was the identity of one of the women—Riley Brodin.

I left the car and walked toward them. Before I got halfway, a large man wearing a white shirt stretched tight across his ample stomach and an indifferently knotted black tie intercepted me. There was a gold badge pinned over his left breast and a triangular patch with the words SOUTH LAKE MINNETONKA POLICE DEPARTMENT sewn to his right shoulder. Two men standing behind him looked almost exactly the same except they were smaller and their shirts were blue.

"You McKenzie?" the man asked.

"Yes."

"I'm Chief John Rock. This is Officers Tschida and Lindberg." No one offered to shake my hand, so I didn't offer to shake theirs. "What do you know about this?"

You wouldn't think that someone who was a cop would have a problem with authority, yet I do, so my first inclination was to play the smartass with Rock. The anguish in Mary Pat's face made me reconsider.

"You're pretty sure it's arson, I take it," I said.

"Someone smashed the glass in the front door and tossed a Molotov cocktail inside," the chief said.

"They weren't trying to hide the crime. What about security footage? Cameras pick up anything?"

Tschida and Lindberg glanced at each other.

They seemed impressed that I knew about such things.

"Nothing we can use," the chief said.

"Where were you last night?" Tschida asked.

Chief Rock gave him a hard look yet said nothing.

"When last night?" I asked.

"Approximately four thirty a.m."

"So when you say last night, what you really mean is early this morning, right?"

"Where were—"

"I was in bed. No, there aren't any witnesses to confirm my alibi."

I reached for the smartphone in the left inside pocket of my sports jacket. The abrupt movement caused all three officers to flinch. I paused, said, "I'm reaching for my cell," then slowly pulled it out.

The chief and Lindberg relaxed. Tschida did not. "Are you armed, McKenzie?" he asked.

"I have a nine-millimeter SIG Sauer locked in the trunk of my car."

"Do you have a permit to carry?"

I stopped fiddling with my cell long enough to answer. "Yes. It's in my wallet. The wallet is in my right inside coat pocket. Do you want me to reach for it?"

He snorted at me.

Lindberg asked, "Why do you have a gun?"

I found the pic of the kid I met the day

before and handed the smartphone to the chief.

"This is why," I said.

Chief Rock held the phone up for the officers to see.

"The shirt—is that gang sign?" he asked.

"Nine-Thirty-Seven Mexican Mafia. That's why I have a gun in the trunk of my car. I'd be wearing it behind my right hip, only I didn't want to make you guys nervous."

"Why?" Tschida asked. "D'you think we'd be scared or something because we're just a small-town police department?"

I ignored the question. Instead, I gestured toward the restaurant's patio. "One of the young ladies with Ms. Mulally is Riley Brodin."

"Old man Muehlenhaus's granddaughter?" the chief asked. There was a sense of awe in his voice that I found disturbing.

"Turns out she has a boyfriend named Juan Carlos Navarre who's been missing since Saturday. She asked me to find him. Navarre is an investor in the restaurant. I came here yesterday afternoon to ask Ms. Mulally what she knew about Navarre's disappearance, which wasn't much. She told me that Casa del Lago was being watched. I asked the kid about it. He had nothing to say.

"The kid, by the way, is named Arnaldo Nunez. He's eighteen. The car is owned by his mother. The Nine-Thirty-Seven was a street gang in West

St. Paul that was crushed about eight years ago. The kid was way too young at the time to be involved. It turns out, though, that his older brother was a founding member. His name is Cesar Nunez, and he's currently doing time in Stillwater for a drug conviction stemming from his time with the gang."

"How do you know all this?" the chief asked.

I could have invoked Bobby's name; I knew he wouldn't approve, though. Instead, I said, "It's all public record."

"So you think Nunez is responsible for the fire," Tschida said. "What reason would he have?"

I had a thought, but I kept it to myself. Instead, I glanced around the area, looking for Navarre and anyone who might be doing the same. I saw no one that appeared even remotely suspicious. 'Course, by then I was late to the party.

"All I know about Nunez is what I told you," I said.

Chief Rock returned my smartphone.

"He couldn't have been involved," he said.

"Why not?" Tschida asked.

The chief spoke to his officer like a teacher lecturing a student who hadn't been paying attention in class. "Because he's currently in Two Twelve Medical Center with a shattered leg and a concussion, the result of a car accident on Highway 7."

I might have told the chief that Nunez had

plenty of help—the drivers of the red Sentra and black Cadillac DTS I saw at Navarre's house came to mind. I became distracted when he pressed a beefy index finger against my shoulder and said, "You wouldn't know anything about that, would you, McKenzie? A pile-up on Highway 7?"

"No, why would I?"

The chief stared at me as if he expected the steely glare in his eyes and the scowl on his face would be enough to cause me to break down and confess. When that didn't work, he said, "I think we'll have a talk with Mr. Nunez."

"I'd like to be there," I said.

"This is police business," Tschida told me. "You police?"

I returned the phone to my pocket. "See you guys around," I said and resumed my walk to the patio. I half expected the cops to call me back. They didn't.

The three women were sitting so that they faced the burnt-out restaurant, their backs to the patio table. Mary Pat Mulally sensed my approach. She turned her head expectantly, yet when she saw that it was I her expression became disappointed. Riley Brodin recognized Mary Pat's frustration and rubbed the back of her shoulder.

"He'll be here soon," she said.

The third women didn't speak, although she

clutched Mary Pat's hand as if she feared the consequences of letting go. Up close I recognized her as the young maître d' who greeted me when I came to Casa del Lago the day before—Maria.

"I'm so sorry about what happened," I said.

"Who would do such a thing?" Mary Pat wanted to know. "Why?"

I caught Riley's face. Her expression gave nothing away.

"I don't know," I said.

"Was it the people who were watching, the kid in the Chevy Impala you talked to?" Mary Pat asked.

"The police are checking it out."

"I told the police about the people watching the restaurant," Mary Pat said, "and the private investigator looking for Juan Carlos. I told them about you, McKenzie. They didn't believe me, the police. They wanted this to be an accident, a wire shorting out, a grease fire. When the fire marshal told them it was arson, they seemed disappointed, like it was a big inconvenience to them.

"McKenzie, I don't know what to do. What if the insurance company denies my claim because —I think they call it the arson defense. If they suspect the fire was deliberately set, they won't pay off even if I didn't set it."

"We don't know that yet," Riley said. "My father will be here any minute."

"If they don't pay . . ." Mary Pat ceased

speaking as if it were too painful to finish the sentence. After a few moments she said, "Look at my place."

It seemed like a really bad time to ask if anyone had seen Navarre, so I didn't. Instead, I waited. I tried to lure Riley away with head gestures so I could speak to her privately, only she would have none of it. Finally a man approached.

"He's here," Riley said.

Alex Brodin had a round face that didn't like the sun and a round body that was wrapped in a crisp blue suit expertly tailored to accommodate his girth. The suit dripped of money, and so did the platinum watch around his wrist. I didn't know what Sheila Brodin had seen in him. I suppose he might have been an athlete once; he might even have been handsome. Now he looked to me like a man who made his living selling tips at Canterbury Park racetrack.

"I'm sorry it took so long," he announced to the group.

"Good morning, Dad," Riley said.

The way Brodin looked at her—I should say the way he didn't look at her—there was something workmanlike about it. As if he were a painter and she were the side of a house. His feelings toward his daughter were all business.

"Good morning," he said. He moved to the table and stood in front of Mary Pat. "I spoke to the insurance company. There will be an investigation just as I told you over the phone. They will be looking for motive and what they call opportunity evidence that implicates you in setting the fire."

Mary Pat cried out in pain and sorrow. Brodin continued speaking as if she hadn't made a sound.

"You must be prepared to produce your business records and answer questions," he said. "And make your key employees available to answer questions as well."

"You mean me?" Maria asked. She released Mary Pat's hand as if she had suddenly learned it was radioactive.

"Everyone," Brodin said.

"How long will it take?" Mary Pat asked.

"The company refuses to commit to a timetable. You can expect that their investigators will be thorough. The company has a fiduciary responsibility to its shareholders, after all."

Mary Pat barely had enough voice to get the words out. "What about my place?"

Even the birds that flew in the clear blue sky above knew she was hanging by an emotional thread.

"This is why we insisted that you buy business interruption insurance." Brodin seemed pleased with himself when he said it. "You'll have enough money to make your mortgage payments and compensate your vital employees for six months."

"That won't fix my restaurant. I need the

money to rebuild before winter sets in, before my repeat customers forget about me, or I could lose everything."

"It's doubtful the insurance company will make a determination anytime soon. Nor can we be confident that its decision will go in your favor."

"What about you? You can loan me what I need to rebuild, and when I settle with the insurance company, I can pay you back."

"I'm afraid my hands are tied."

"What does that mean?" Riley asked.

Brodin didn't answer his daughter. Instead, he spoke directly to Mary Pat. "Minnetonka Community is already carrying a sizable loan on the business . . ."

"I was paying it off," Mary Pat insisted. "I was ahead of schedule. The restaurant was making good money."

"I appreciate that. Unfortunately, it's a matter of collateral." Brodin gestured toward the burnt-out restaurant. "You no longer have much."

"Are you saying you won't help me?"

"There's only so much that I can do."

"I'll sign for the loan," Riley said. "I have plenty of collateral."

Brodin studied his daughter the way a parent does when he feels his authority is being challenged.

"If that doesn't satisfy your . . . bank, then I'll make the loan myself," she added.

"You don't understand," Brodin said.

"If that doesn't work out, I'll loan Mary Pat the money she needs," I said.

Riley spun to face me, a surprised expression on her freckled face. Brodin stared as if he were estimating my income, subtracting my overhead, and coming up with a balance in the red.

"Who are you?" he asked.

"My name's McKenzie, and I have five million dollars that I can convert to cash in seventy-two hours."

"That fucking McKenzie," Brodin muttered in reply. He glared at Riley as if he couldn't believe that she would allow herself to be seen in public with such a disreputable character.

"I take it you've heard of me," I said.

"My father-in-law hates your guts."

"Now you know why."

"This is all moot." Brodin's voice became indignant. "First, we must wait to hear what the insurance company has to say. Of course, Ms. Mulally, one way or another Minnetonka Community Bank will find a way to accommodate you."

Mary Pat reached out and grabbed his hand as if Brodin had just done her a favor.

"Thank you," she said.

"We must get inspectors in here to provide a detailed analysis of the damage . . ."

"Yes."

"And, of course, reliable contractors to estimate the cost of repairs."

"Yes," Mary Pat repeated. She stood. The expression on her face went from despair to cheerful just like that. It was as if she could see the future. "I know people. I'll start making calls."

"I'll speak to my people as well."

"What people?" Riley asked. "You're president of the bank. You own the damn thing."

"Riley." Brodin was unable or unwilling to disguise his anger. "You have no idea how things work."

He left the patio and walked briskly to his car. Maria watched him go. She looked as if she were wrestling with the question of whether she should stay or leave as well. Mary Pat provided the solution when she took the young woman's arm.

"We must ask the firemen if it's okay to go inside now," Mary Pat said. "There is much work to be done."

Before she left the patio, though, Mary Pat turned to me.

"Why did you say what you did?" she asked. "We don't even know each other."

"Partly to help you and partly to annoy Brodin," I said. *Which is pretty much the reason you're assisting Riley,* my inner voice reminded me. "Partly because a man all but accused me the other day of doing nothing with my money except buying toys to play with. This was my chance to be a philanthropist."

She reached out and touched my arm. "Thank you," she said.

The touch and words somehow closed my throat. I couldn't speak. Instead, I nodded my reply and watched as Mary Pat and Maria left the patio and made their way to the fire truck.

Damn, McKenzie, my inner voice said.

"That was awfully kind of you," Riley said.

"I'm a helluva guy," I told her, and for half a second, I actually believed it. "Besides, it showed me something, the way you stood up for your friend. It made me want to stand up for her, too."

"I'm a helluva girl."

You're certainly an interesting girl, my inner voice said.

I took Riley's arm and gently led her to the railing, where we stood and looked out over Gideon Bay. There was a boat in the center of the bay just bobbing along.

"Have you seen Navarre?" I asked. "Have you heard from him?"

"No."

"How long have you been here?"

"A couple of hours. I came as soon as I heard."

"Navarre didn't show?"

"Why would he?"

"I didn't want to say anything in front of Mary Pat or the cops, but I think that's why the fire was set. A lot of people believe Navarre owns Casa del Lago. For some reason he wants them to believe that. I believe the fire was set to draw him out of hiding. Think about it. If someone torched your place, wouldn't you show up?"

"Why, though? Who? The kid in the parking lot that Mary Pat mentioned?"

I figured it was a good time to come clean, so I showed Riley the photos I took with my smartphone and told her what I had learned.

"Mexican Mafia?" she said.

"Not the *actual* Mexican Mafia. A street gang in West St. Paul."

"What has that to do with Juan Carlos? He's not from Mexico. He's from Spain. He's only been in the U.S. for six months. How could he have anything to do with a gang that doesn't even exist anymore?"

"I don't know."

"You don't know or you don't want to tell me?"

"I've told you everything." The expression on her face suggested she didn't believe me. "Have you told me everything you know?"

"What's that supposed to mean?" Riley asked.

"Mary Pat said it was a banker who told Juan Carlos that she was looking for a silent partner to invest in her restaurant. It wasn't a banker. It was you."

"My father—"

"It was you."

"Through my father. Juan Carlos said he was looking for business opportunities, and I knew that Mary Pat was looking for investors, so I had my father hook them up. What's wrong with that?"

"Nothing. I'm just trying to put all the pieces together."

"Mary Pat is my friend."

"How did you two meet?"

"What difference does it make?"

"She's a decade older than you are."

"No, only six and a half years. Besides, what has that to do with anything? You're worse than my family, prying into my life."

"Is that what I'm doing?"

"What would you call it?"

"Trying really hard to do what you asked me to do—find your boyfriend. You are a moody young lady, you know that?"

She chuckled and said, "I've been called worse."

"By who?"

"My family. Who else would have the nerve?"

"Tell me about your family."

"You're prying again."

"Tell me about your father."

"Look—we don't get along, simple as that, okay?"

"That was my impression. Why don't you get along?"

"Why, why, why—I don't know. Because I'm a Muehlenhaus and he's not. I mean—my father owns a bank. Lake Minnetonka Community. Well, you know that. It's a small bank, caters mostly to the lake crowd. At least that's where his biggest depositors come from. He wouldn't have any depositors at all, though, if he hadn't married into my family, and he knows it. I think he resents it."

"Your grandfather supports him?"

"His name does. Without it, there would have been no organizing group, no state charter, no shareholders. As for money, I don't think Grandpa has a dime in the bank himself."

"What about your mother?"

"She doesn't have any money in the bank, either, which shouldn't come as a shock since she and my father separated when I was a child."

"Separated—not divorced?"

"It's complicated. When it comes to money, everything is complicated."

"What about Navarre? Does he have cash in your father's bank?"

"Quite a bit, I think."

"Yet your father claims Navarre is a con man who's only after your money."

Riley twisted her head to look at me; it was almost as if she were surprised to see I was still standing there. Her full lips formed a tiny smile.

"I'm beginning to understand why my grandfather both likes and dislikes you so much," she said. "You have a way of sneaking up on people."

"It's a gift."

"You think my father is involved in Juan Carlos's disappearance, don't you?"

"I think nothing of the sort. I'm just—"

"Trying to put the pieces together. I get it now."

"Do you? I'm not so sure. See, I know why you came to me instead of involving the police when Navarre disappeared, and it wasn't because you were afraid of scandal. It was because you were afraid that your family was responsible, that they got rid of him somehow. Your mother believes it, too. I don't. Your grandmother and your grandfather hired a pretty good private investigator. They both want to find Navarre just as much as you do, although probably not for the same reasons."

"Is that what they told you? And you believed them? You're not investigating, McKenzie. You're taking sides."

"Oh, for—again, Riley? Again with the accusations?"

"What are you doing talking to my mother? My grandparents?"

"I didn't go to them, they came to me. We had conversations I could have done without, too. Look, I did pick a side. You're right about that. I picked yours. I'm trying to be your friend, but you make it so damn hard, honest to God."

Riley didn't have anything to say to that. She turned toward the lake, and I did the same. The boat was still drifting in the middle of the bay. After a while, it got under way. A few moments later, it disappeared from view, and I flashed on the empty dock in front of Irene Rogers's home, the one with electricity and fresh-water hookups.

What a nitwit you are, my inner voice told me. *How come you didn't think of that before?*

"Riley?" I said aloud.

"What?"

"Does Navarre own a boat?"

"Yes. A cabin cruiser. The *Soñadora*."

"Means 'dreamer.' "

"You speak Spanish."

"Enough for that. When was the last time you saw the boat?"

"Friday night. We used it when we went to dinner at the club."

"Where is it now, I wonder?"

Eight ....

Riley assured me that Navarre's boat had a comfortable sleeping compartment. She blushed when she said it, and for a moment I could imagine the two of them anchoring at night in one of the big bays until the morning sun. And all day long, too, for that matter.

The more I thought about it, the more convinced I became that the reason Navarre's security system was down and his BMW was still parked in the garage was because when the time came to run for it, he went by water, not by land. He simply dashed out the back door without bothering to set the alarm, hopped in his boat, and disappeared onto the vast and sprawling lake. He was probably out there now.

But where? Why was he hiding? From whom?

One question at a time, my inner voice told me.

Riley wasn't particularly helpful. The more I pressed her for information, the more curt and condescending her replies became. She insisted that Navarre didn't have any friends on the lake whose docks he could tie up to—because he's been in Minnesota for such a short time, you see. I told her that both Mrs. Rogers and Mary Pat Mulally said he was very good at making friends. She all but accused me of leading a Spanish

Inquisition. I couldn't remember meeting anyone as defensive as she was.

She did tell me where Navarre bought his boat, though. That was something at least.

McDonald's Marina was located on a strip of land that separated Lake Tanager from Brown's Bay in the upper northeast corner of Lake Minnetonka. I sat in the Audi and took it all in. Five piers and a chain of docks provided slips for at least 250 vessels, yet only half of them were filled. In fact, there seemed to be just as many boats resting side by side on wooden supports in a yard next to a massive warehouse as in the water, each of them shrink-wrapped in blue polyethylene film. They reminded me of toy boats still in their original packaging, assuming they were toys for giants. At the edge of the marina, a captain was trying to maneuver his cruiser into the waiting jaws of a huge boatlift and not making much progress. Apparently he wasn't very good at driving backward.

There were several buildings, all of them white. I walked to the building that looked most like an office while I adjusted the holster behind my right hip. I hadn't seen anything at the marina that frightened me, yet the gun wasn't doing me any good locked in the trunk. It was a 9 mm SIG Sauer P228. I had been a Beretta man most of my adult life. I had taken a SIG off of a disgruntled bartender in the tiny town of Krueger, Minnesota, a while back, though, and decided I liked it. When I got the holster the way I wanted, I hid it beneath my sports jacket. The sports jacket made me the best-dressed man in the marina.

The owner was occupied, so I wandered around, looking at the boats moored at their slips until he was free. I used to have a 28-footer with an eight-and-a-half-foot beam—the largest boat you can pull on a trailer in Minnesota. As I stopped to examine a pristine cabin cruiser I wondered why I sold it.

"The *Amante*," a voice said. I turned to see a middle-aged man dressed in cargo shorts and a polo shirt. He was reading the name painted on the boat's bow. "It means 'lover.' The previous owner, his wife named it. She said if a husband must have a mistress, it's best that she be made of fiberglass." He extended his hand. "I'm Jimmy. You were looking for me?"

I shook his hand and introduced myself.

"Are you in the market?" he asked. "We have some nice boats, new, used . . ."

"Actually," I said, "I wanted to ask about a boat called the *Soñadora*."

"I'm afraid you must have been reading one of our old flyers. I sold that boat seven, eight weeks ago. She was very similar to the *Amante* here. Thirty-eight feet LOA, thirty-six-inch draft, four-hundred-horsepower Volvo engine, three-hundred-gallon gas tank, sixty-four gallons of fresh water, sleeps five."

"How long could you keep a boat like that out on the lake?"

"How long can you go without a hot shower?"

"What do you mean?"

"You need shore power to run a hot water heater. Otherwise, it depends on your battery setup. With a good bank of storage batteries, and let's say you're frugal with your amp hours, running the refrigerator, microwave, blender, coffee-maker, TV, computer at the bare minimum, I'd say you might be able to keep this boat off the grid for three, four days. Five if you push it hard."

"How long would it take me to recharge the batteries?"

"You could do it overnight."

"Where?"

"Lots of places—Minnetonka Boat Club, Wayzata Marine, Howard's Point, Rockvam Boat Yards, Blue Lagoon, Excel. There are private docks, too, depending on who you know. Listen, if you want to live on the hook for a few days, I can show you several boats besides this one that would be damn comfortable. You need to understand, though, the Lake Minnetonka Conservation District rules won't allow you to use a watercraft as living quarters. You can't actually live on the lake."

"But I can take a boat out for a few days at a time with no problem, right? The lake police won't bother me."

McDonald's smile was a bit askew, as if he weren't sure whether I was naive or up to something.

"It's the Hennepin County Sheriff's Department Water Patrol," he said. "No, they won't bother you. Plenty of people go camping on their boats. Just remember to make sure you mount a white light that's visible from any direction between sunset and sunrise."

I pulled up a map of Lake Minnetonka on my smartphone. It was so damn big with so many miles of unbroken shoreline and so many places for a man to conceal a boat, not to mention just anchoring in the middle of a bay or inlet somewhere, hiding in plain sight. I didn't even know where to begin looking for Navarre, although I figured it might actually be easier to sneak up on him after dark when I could concentrate my search on any white lights I saw flickering across the water. That would require a boat, though, and a pilot who knew the lake, because if I could get lost just trying to drive around it . . .

'Course, Navarre might also be moored in a slip at one of the many marinas, paying dockage fees for the day while he recharged his batteries and took on fresh water. It had been nearly a week since he took the *Soñadora* out, and Jimmy McDonald said five days was the maximum. I could check on each and every marina in turn. Grunt work, I knew, but that's what private investigators do.

You should apply for a license one of these days, my inner voice told me.

Yeah, I'll get right on that.

What else?

Would Navarre have the balls to return to Irene Rogers's dock? How 'bout Club Versailles? They would accommodate him if Mrs. R said so. Would she say so? Would they even bother to ask her? I called Mrs. Rogers. There was no answer, so I left a message. I called Sarah Neamy. She assured me that the *Soñadora* was not currently tied up at one of the club's slips.

What else?

Anne Rehmann. Rehmann Lake Place Real Estate. Did she have a dock with fresh water and electrical hookups? It seemed unlikely a real estate agent could afford it, given the lake's exorbitant property values, although—taking prospects out on the water, I could see how that might be a powerful sales tool. Except she had been looking for Navarre, too. When I met her at Mrs. R's house . . .

Wait a minute. The first time I saw Anne, after she startled me, she asked what was I doing and

I said I was looking for Juan Carlos and she said he wasn't there. How could she have known that? She couldn't have known that unless . . . Maybe Anne already knew where he was. Maybe Navarre was at her place. Maybe he sent her to get some of the clothes and toilet gear that he left behind.

C'mon, McKenzie, my inner voice said.

Maybe, I told myself. Think about it. It was Anne's idea that Navarre occupy Mrs. R's house in the first place—isn't that what Mrs. R said? It's possible they have a relationship.

And wouldn't that make Riley happy.

I called. Anne's voice mail said she would be out of the office until early in the afternoon. However, my call was important to her, and if I left a message, she would return it as soon as possible. I hung up and found Anne's address on my GPS. Her office was in Deephaven. I could be there in twenty-one minutes if I skipped lunch.

I skipped lunch.

Rehmann Lake Place Real Estate did have a dock on Lake Minnetonka that it shared with a half-dozen other businesses. It was narrow, made of treated redwood planks, and could accommodate three boats on either side. Only one boat was tied up there, though, an 18-foot speedboat with a 75-horsepower Mercury engine.

Oh, well, I told myself.

The office was located at one of the few spots on the lake where the road actually hugged the shoreline. The dock was on one side of the road, and a modest office park was on the other. I waited for traffic to clear and pulled into the parking lot. There were three two-story buildings arranged in a semicircle, all of them designed to resemble a Cape Cod cottage. Anne's office was located on the top floor of the far-left cottage; there was an insurance office on the bottom. All of the cottages were painted white. It occurred to me that most of the structures I had seen on Lake Minnetonka were white, and I wondered if there was a lake association that dictated the color.

What if you wanted mauve? my inner voice asked.

There were several cars in the lot. I recognized Anne's from when we met at Mrs. Rogers's place and parked next to it. An outside staircase led to her office door. I climbed the staircase two steps at a time just to prove that I could even at my advanced years. The door was unlocked, and I stepped inside. A desk chair was lying on its side as if it had been thrown across the room, and I nearly tripped over it.

I looked up. There was a man standing behind the desk. I took him in all at once—six feet, 190 pounds, brown eyes, brown hair cut in a military style, wearing a white T-shirt beneath a black leather jacket and jeans. His left hand was gripping Anne's red-blond hair and yanking it backward so hard that her back was arched. Her white blouse had been torn open. The man's right hand was violently squeezing her breast through a pink bra trimmed with lace. His mouth was close to her ear as if he had been whispering to her. His entire face was twisted in a snarl. Her face revealed the fear and pain she was suffering.

They both looked at me.

I looked at them.

There was a balcony behind the desk. The sliding door was open, and I could hear the sound of traffic moving in the distance.

"McKenzie," Anne said.

She spoke in a harsh whimper, yet her voice echoed in the office like a starter's pistol.

Her attacker released Anne's breast and lunged for a knife that was lying on top of the desk. He continued to grip her hair with his other hand, and the sudden movement turned Anne's head savagely.

She screamed in pain.

I reached for the SIG Sauer.

He brought the blade of the knife against Anne's throat and spun her toward me.

I went into a Weaver stance, my feet shoulder-width apart, knees bent, weight slightly forward, my gun hand pushing outward while my support hand pulled inward.

"Don't move," he said.

I took two steps forward.

He positioned Anne's body so that it was between him and me and hid behind it.

"I told you not to move," he said.

The tip of the knife pressed against Anne's skin yet did not penetrate. Her breath came in shallow gasps. I stopped moving.

"Drop the gun," he said.

No, no, no, my inner voice screamed.

"Drop it."

You never give up your weapon, you never give up your weapon, you never give up your weapon . . . It was my inner voice chanting, yet it was the words of my skills instructor at the police academy. *Give up your weapon and everyone dies.*

"I'll kill her," he said.

I didn't answer. Instead, I deliberately centered the sights on his forehead, my hands perfectly still. It was unlikely I would miss from that distance. He seemed to understand and pulled his head behind Anne's.

"I mean it—I'll kill her." His voice was louder, yet his words weren't as certain as before. He was beginning to reconsider his position. His eyes darted around the office. It was as if he were searching for an option—any option.

"If she dies it'll be your fault," he said.

"Please," Anne said. Her voice was just above a whisper. "Please."

His eyes turned toward the open balcony door

and he began edging toward it, keeping Anne's body between him and my gun.

"No one else has to get hurt over this," he said. "We can make a deal."

My sights followed his movements.

"No one else needs to die."

He stopped in the doorway leading to the balcony and raised the knife blade as if he were preparing to plunge it into Anne's throat. My hands tightened around the gun.

"Don't," I said.

He lowered the knife tip even as his eyes fixed on mine.

He shoved Anne hard toward me.

I made no effort to catch her. Instead, I tried to step out of the way to make sure her body wasn't between me and her attacker. Only she flailed her arms toward me as she fell. It slowed me down. By then he was vaulting the second-story balcony railing. I reached the railing just in time to see him roll to his feet as if he had been jumping from second-story heights his entire life. I brought the SIG up and sighted on him. He was in full stride now, his back to me, sprinting toward the wooded area behind the cottages. I decided he was already beyond the gun's effective range and let him go. I should have shot at him anyway. I should have emptied the goddamn magazine.

I turned toward Anne. She was lying in a fetal position on the office floor. Tears stained her cheeks; the sound she made was a painful fusion of dry heaves and breathless shrieks. I recognized her reaction from when I was a cop responding to sexual assaults. Anne had ceased being a person and become something else. I tried to put my arms around her. She shouted "No" and rolled away from me. Her hands gripped the ends of her torn blouse and pulled the material close over her chest. Her blazer was lying on the floor next to her desk, yet I gave her my sports jacket just the same. She wrapped it around herself like a comforter. It was only then that she allowed me to take her in my arms. She rested her head against my chest, and I rocked her back and forth until her humanity returned. It took a long time.

"He was waiting for me," Anne said. I was still holding her; by then we had moved to the sofa against her wall. "I didn't see him at first. I came in after my appointments and went behind my desk. Before I could sit down he put his hands on me." She was watching the balcony while she spoke. The sliding door was still open. "I guess he was hiding out there."

"Have you seen him before?"

Anne shook her head.

"You try to be careful," she told me, although I think she was talking mostly to herself. "Never show a property to someone you don't know, never work an open house by yourself, get personal information you can verify—we should call the police. Should we call the police?"

"That's up to you."

"I want to call the police, McKenzie. I will not be afraid. I will not be embarrassed. I will not be upset with myself later because I was afraid and embarrassed."

I punched 9-1-1 into the keypad of my cell and told the operator that we needed assistance. I recited the address. Anne had calmed herself nicely, but I knew the pain and fear were residing just beneath the surface and could return in a moment, so instead of actually saying we wanted to report an incident of criminal sexual conduct, I used the code: 10-33.

"The police are on their way," I said after ending the call.

"I was so frightened," Anne said. "Then you arrived . . ." She turned her head to look at me. "McKenzie, why are you here?"

"Doesn't matter. It can wait."

"No, tell me."

"I was hoping you knew where Navarre was."

She came off the sofa in a hurry and looked down at me. Her face was flushed and her fists were clenched. She'd buttoned my sports jacket, but the ruined shirt beneath it fell open to reveal her breasts. I averted my eyes.

"Navarre," she said. "Navarre, Navarre. That's what he wanted. Navarre. He said . . . if I told him where Navarre was he said he would make it nice for me, otherwise . . . he put the knife to my throat and said, he said otherwise he'd make sure it hurt."

"It's okay, Anne." I was on my feet and reaching for her. "You're safe now. It's okay."

She pushed me away.

"It's not okay. It's not. Juan Carlos was here. He was hiding here. His boat—he tied up at our dock, the dock we all share. He asked me not to tell anyone. He asked me to get clothes for him. He asked me—he said men were after him."

"What men?"

"Terrorists. From Spain. ETA, he said. They were after him because of something his father did years ago. That's what Juan Carlos said. Then this man, this man . . . I told him Juan Carlos wasn't here. I told him that he left this morning. That's when he tore my clothes, that's when he tried . . . He was going to . . . Oh, God."

"How did he know to come to you?" I asked. "How did this man know that you even knew who Navarre was?"

She answered just as the cops came through the door.

"He said Mrs. R told him."

Nine ....

They put me in handcuffs and locked me into the back of a South Lake Minnetonka Police Department cruiser that was parked a couple of rows from the front of the building where Irene Rogers had lived. I didn't blame them.

From my seat, I was able to watch the comings and goings of deputies from the Hennepin County Sheriff's Department as they swarmed to the crime scene. The lead investigator, crime scene photographer, photographic log recorder, evidence man, and all the rest—some came in plainclothes, some carried equipment, all wore firm expressions. Soon the assistant county medical examiner appeared, with a face that seemed carved in granite. He was followed by a large man dressed in the tan-on-brown uniform of the sheriff's department, except that his shirt was white, which made him an administrator, and he had gold insignia on his collar, which made him a major. No one smiled except Officer Tschida, who was manning the door. An arson in the morning and a killing in the afternoon—he was having a helluva day.

Sarah Neamy sat on a bench outside the building with a deputy and stared at her hands. She had discovered the body just moments before the deputies arrived; I was the one who sent her to Mrs. R's condominium. I longed to speak to her, but my current situation forbade it. Served me right for losing my temper. While I watched, the deputy received a call on his radio. A moment later, he led Sarah inside the building. Her face was pale and tear-stained when she returned. She was having difficulty walking, and the deputy had to hold her upright as they moved toward the club's main entrance.

I didn't realize the building had a name until the media arrived, until a long-legged TV reporter named Kelly Bressandes did her standup in front of a sign—the Villas of Club Versailles. I had no doubt she would lead the evening news. Millionaire socialite raped and murdered in an exclusive playground of the rich—of course she would lead.

Would Kelly mention that wonderful old broad once danced with Gene Kelly? my inner voice wondered.

Probably not, I told myself. Her name no longer identified a living, breathing woman with a rich and exciting biography. Mrs. Irene Rogers—Reney to her friends—was a victim now. That is how she'll be catalogued in the big book. Her history, her accomplishments, her recipe for gin martinis, all of that would soon be replaced in the memories of the people who knew her. Instead, she would now and always be defined by one of the most terrible things that could happen to a woman. Worse, she would also be forever linked to her killer. People would say, "Remember poor Reney Rogers?" "Isn't it awful what happened to her?" "Did they ever get the guy who did it?" Murder does that.

Inevitably, Mrs. R's body was enclosed in a black vinyl body bag and hoisted onto a gurney. The gurney was rolled down the corridor from the door of her condo to the elevator, taken to the ground floor, rolled out into the parking lot, and loaded into an ambulance for transport to the Office of the Hennepin County Medical Examiner on Park Avenue in downtown Minneapolis. Right after the TV crews got the shot, they packed their equipment into sparkling vans with their logos painted on the doors and departed.

Bressandes was the last to leave. She had waited to get a comment from the major. When he declined, she turned to Chief John Rock of the South Lake Minnetonka Police Department, who took a moment to straighten his tie and wave Officer Tschida out of the shot before agreeing to be interviewed on camera. I knew Bressandes personally and liked her, yet I was glad she didn't notice me locked in the back of the squad car, glad I didn't have to speak to her.

I had spent enough time in harness to be leery of police department administrators. As I watched the major through the car window giving instructions to his deputies, though, it occurred to me that he didn't seem to be your run-of-the-mill politician. I used to have season tickets for the St. Paul Saints minor league baseball team. You could always tell which of the players had game, which of them had a chance to make the Show, simply by the way they moved, the way they carried themselves on the field. The major carried himself like a cop.

Soon he was moving toward me; a tall man wearing a suit and tie and carrying a notebook was at his side. When they reached the car they both opened a door and slid inside, the major on the rear passenger side and the plainclothes in the front. They left the doors open, which I appreciated. It was a pleasant seventy-one degrees outside, yet with the windows closed the inside of the car was starting to heat up.

"Rushmore McKenzie?" the major said. "Is that right? I'm Major Kampa. I'm in charge of the Investigative Division in Hennepin County." He pointed at the front seat. "Lieutenant Pelzer. He runs our detective unit."

Nothing but the best for Mrs. R, my inner voice said.

"Gentlemen," I said aloud. "Listen, can you do something about this?"

I leaned forward on the seat so they could get a good look at the cuffs that secured my hands behind my back.

"You punch a cop, you take your chances," Kampa said. There was no compromise in his voice.

"He's not a cop," I said. "He's a grade school hall monitor with delusions of grandeur."

When I spoke, they both looked toward Officer Tschida, still standing at the door of the Villas, still smiling as if this was the most fun he's ever had. I noticed that neither of them disagreed with me.

"Nothing we can do about it," Kampa said.

"I used to be police myself."

"We know who you are, McKenzie," Pelzer said.

"At least . . ." I leaned forward again. "Can you at least take the gun? It's kinda uncomfortable."

Kampa reached behind me and removed the SIG Sauer from the holster beneath my jacket. He showed it to Pelzer.

"That dumb ass didn't even . . ." The lieutenant never finished his thought. Instead, he closed his eyes and shook his head.

"Tell me you have a permit," Kampa said.

"I have a permit," I said.

Kampa balanced the gun on his thigh. "Nothing I can do."

"Don't worry about it, Major. My problem, not yours. Tell me how I can help."

Kampa gestured at Pelzer, and the detective

started asking questions. I liked that—the major deferring to his lieutenant.

It was clear from what Pelzer asked that they had already spoken at length with Anne Rehmann, as well as the deputies that had responded to her office. Now they wanted to hear my side. I told them everything, starting with Riley Brodin accosting me in Nina's bar. I had no doubt that Mr. Muehlenhaus and probably Riley, too, would be extremely upset that I spilled their secrets to the sheriff's department. I was past caring. The sight of Mrs. R . . .

After the deputies arrived at the real estate office in response to my 911 call, I told them that the man who attacked Anne might have also attacked Mrs. R, and I begged them to send deputies to her condominium. They did, too, without much prompting at all. At the same time, I called Sarah Neamy and told her to check on Mrs. R, told her that I was worried. The deputies wanted me to remain at the office and answer their questions. Anne wanted me to remain, too, even though she was also concerned about her employer. Yet I was desperate to get to Club Versailles, so I blew them off, after first telling the deputies how to get hold of me and then telling Anne I would call later.

Even so, from the moment the deputies had arrived at the real estate office to the instant I pulled into the parking lot of the club, at least forty-five minutes had passed. Members of the sheriff's department and the South Lake Minnetonka Police Department were already on the scene. Officer Tschida was at the door to Mrs. R's building. He tried to keep me from going inside, which was bad enough. Calling me an asshole and saying "The bitch is dead, there's nothing you can do"—I lost my temper, something I hardly ever do. I smacked him in the mouth and tossed him off the stoop.

I found Mrs. R's condominium on the fourth floor. The door was opened. I stepped across the threshold. Several investigators were already processing the crime scene. That's when I saw her. Mrs. Rogers was lying naked on the floor, her body bearing signs of terrible abuse. Her wrists were bound with an electrical cord and tied to the leg of a heavy chair. Her ankles were also lashed together and attached to her sofa. A clear plastic bag had been pulled over her head and fixed in place with a thick rubber band. Her eyes were open and so was her mouth—she had died fighting for breath.

Tschida caught up to me then. He cuffed my hands and dragged me outside—although I don't remember much about that.

Major Kampa didn't speak a word while I gave my account, and Lieutenant Pelzer only interrupted to ask a few pertinent questions.

"What do you know about this ETA that was supposedly stalking Navarre?"

"I never heard of it," I said.

"Do you think Navarre is a fraud?"

"I'm still working on it."

"Navarre's boat—the *Soñadora*—is it on the lake?"

"Anne Rehmann said he left her dock early that morning. Other than that . . ."

I had a few questions of my own, starting with how the killer managed to get inside a secured building.

"Suspect gained entry through an unlocked balcony door of an unoccupied condominium on the ground floor," Pelzer said. "After that he just walked up to her place. There was no forced entry, so she must have let him in."

"I was on the phone with Mrs. Rogers last night," I said. "She said she had to hang up because someone was knocking on her door."

"What time last night?"

"Nine."

Pelzer closed his notebook. "The ME gave us a preliminary estimate of the time of death. Set it at about nine this morning."

We both knew what that meant.

He had her for twelve hours, my inner voice said.

"Sonuvabitch," I said aloud.

"Where can we reach you if we have more questions?" Pelzer asked.

"South Lake Minnetonka jail, I guess.

Assuming it has a jail. They might transfer me to your pretrial lockup in downtown Minneapolis."

Kampa examined the SIG balanced on his thigh.

"Fuck that," he said.

I was surprised. The way his head whipped around to look at the major, Pelzer was downright astonished.

Kampa slid out of the car and walked purposely toward Tschida, my SIG Sauer still in his hand. He saw Chief John Rock and waved him over. They reached Tschida at the same time. Kampa showed my gun to both of them. I couldn't hear what he said, but his words prompted Chief Rock to reach behind Tschida and smack him on the back of the head—an idiot slap. More words were exchanged, and Tschida half walked, half ran to the squad car. He opened the car door, pulled me out, unlocked the cuffs, and said, "Please, McKenzie, would you just get the hell outta here and don't come back?"

A few minutes later, both Major Kampa and Lieutenant Pelzer joined me where I had parked my Audi. Kampa returned the SIG to me, handing it over butt first.

"What happened?" I asked.

"Without backup from the Hennepin County Sheriff's Department, the South Lake Minnetonka PD ceases to exist," Kampa said. "I don't work with screwups."

"Thank you."

"The book says you're all done, McKenzie. This is a capital offense, and you don't involve yourself in our investigation even a little bit or I'll toss your ass for obstruction, ex-cop or no—you're not even licensed. Understand?"

"Yes."

"My gut tells me, though, that you might be useful. You can talk to Mr. Muehlenhaus and his daughter, for one. I doubt I can get through the front door. So you keep looking for Navarre if you wish. Just stay away from the murder, and don't even think of doing anything illegal, not even spitting on the sidewalk if you know what's good for you, and 'specially don't go around telling people that you're working with us, and we should be okay."

"Thank you," I said again.

"Keep in touch, McKenzie."

I watched Major Kampa turn and walk away. Lieutenant Pelzer lingered to give me his contact information.

"He's a real cop, isn't he?" I said.

"Yep."

"You don't often see real cops rise up that high. Usually it's just the politicians."

"Sometimes you get lucky."

I didn't feel lucky, though. Or talkative. Yet there were debts to be paid, the first to Sarah Neamy. I had sent her to Mrs. Rogers's condo. She had seen what I had seen.

I found her in the office just behind the reception desk where I had first met her. The door was open, and I saw her sitting very still in a straight-back chair against the wall, her hands folded in her lap, looking down, a penitent schoolgirl in her uniform. She seemed to know who I was without looking up to see.

"How could someone do that to another human being?" Sarah asked. "McKenzie, do you know?"

In my time, I had heard that question answered in so many ways by so many people—psychologists, sociologists, criminologists, even stand-up comedians. Explanations included everything from a chemical imbalance in the brain to childhood abuse and neglect to environmental pressures to an overdose of Twinkies. For a long time, I went along with them. I used to pride myself, especially when I was a cop, on telling people, "I don't believe in evil, I believe in motive," as if that somehow proved I had an understanding of the human condition that the average citizen simply couldn't fathom. I had seen so much over the years, though, that the theories no longer satisfied. I discovered that I preferred the much simpler answer that I gave Sarah.

"Some people are evil."

She nodded her head as if she believed it, too.

"They're having an emergency meeting, the board of directors," Sarah said. "I don't know exactly what they hope to accomplish. Better security. Armed guards? They kept saying it wasn't my fault. 'It's not your fault, Sarah.' I don't know how it could be my fault. I'll probably be fired within the month, though."

"Why?"

"It's all about the morale of the members. Everyone will want to put this behind them as quickly as possible. If I stay, the members, every time they look at me they'll be reminded of poor Mrs. R because they'll know I was the one, the one . . . that I discovered . . . I saw . . ."

I rested a hand on her shoulder, and she covered it with her own hand. She looked up at me for the first time.

"I'm sorry I sent you there," I said.

"It's not your fault," she said.

I said, "I'm sorry," again, just the same.

"Juan Carlos didn't do this, did he?"

"No. It's someone looking for him."

"Where is he?"

"I don't know."

"If you find Juan Carlos, will that help you find out who . . . hurt Mrs. R?"

"I hope so."

"Juan Carlos had to fill out a questionnaire before he could be considered for membership in the club. I can get you the form. Will that help?"

"It might."

"Come back tomorrow."

"Sarah, just get me a copy. Keep the originals. The county deputies might want them, and I don't want to mess with those guys. They did me one favor, I don't expect another."

"I will."

"You should go home."

"Home?"

She looked at me as if it were the first time she had ever heard the word.

I returned to Anne Rehmann's office. It was locked up tight. I called her number and was sent to her voice mail. I told her she could return my call—even though I hoped she wouldn't— otherwise I would try to see her tomorrow. I didn't want to talk any more, didn't want to comfort anyone, didn't want to think. It was Thursday evening in early October, and there were any number of sporting events taking place that could distract me from the day. Baseball was in the first round of playoffs, college football was approaching midseason, the NHL was ramping up—there might even be a game on the NFL Channel. If that failed, I had access to a cabinet stocked with beer, wine, and other assorted alcoholic beverages. All things being equal, drinking myself silly didn't seem like a bad idea.

Halfway home, though, I broke my cell phone rule again and called Nina.

"Can I come over to your place?" I asked.

" 'Course you can, you know that. You don't have to call first."

"I thought this time maybe I should."

"Are you all right, McKenzie?"

"No. No, I'm really not."

Ten.................................

I woke in Nina's bed to the aroma of fresh-brewed coffee. Nina used to make lousy coffee—the EPA considered it a toxic substance—and I would invent excuses to avoid drinking it, until the head chef at Rickie's gave her a tutorial on how it was done. Now it was fabulous. Still, it wasn't enough to rouse me. I lay there instead, naked between the warm sheets, and listened to the sounds of morning outside the window. Even in the suburbs you can hear it, traffic like surf in the distance, a barking dog, a child's squeal, and for a moment I felt the icy hand of panic grip my heart. What the hell was I doing with my life? Where was I going? What did I hope to accomplish? They were questions I had been asking quite often lately, yet the events of the previous day made them seem more urgent. Questions without answers. Or did I simply refuse to give them answers for fear that I wouldn't like what they revealed?

Screw it, I told myself. I flung the top sheet aside and slid out of bed, determined to make the best I could of the day.

I had clothes in Nina's closet and bureau. I found them, and after taking a quick shower and shave—yes, I kept a razor there, too—I put them on. I paused briefly to check my cell. There were two messages from Riley Brodin, one from Mr. Muehlenhaus, and another from Greg Schroeder—nobody that I wanted to talk to at the moment. I ignored them all and sent a text message to Victoria Dunston.

"Well?" it read.

A few moments later she replied.

"OMG! U want 2 get me in trouble? I'll call 18er."

I went downstairs and found Nina in the kitchen. I would have paid real money to see her in the clinging silk number she had worn the previous evening. Instead, she was wearing gray sweatpants and a loose-fitting black T-shirt that proclaimed her affection for the Preservation Hall Jazz Band—a gift from Erica, who was attending Tulane University in New Orleans. The sweat at her temples and down the center of her back proved that she had already made her morning run. It did little to lessen my desire for her.

"Good morning," she said.

"Morning."

"Coffee?"

"Please." She went to her coffeemaker and retrieved the glass pot. I said, "You're up early."

"Actually, you're up late."

I glanced at the clock on the wall. Eight fifteen. That wasn't late for me, but then I was gainfully unemployed.

I sat at the table. She leaned across me and poured the coffee into a mug. "What are your plans for today?"

I pulled her down until she was sitting on my lap.

"I was toying with an idea," I said.

Nina kissed my cheek. "Besides that."

"I haven't decided."

"Yes, you have. You're going to find the man who killed your friend, who attacked the real estate agent."

"I am?"

Nina slid off my lap and returned the coffeepot to the maker.

"You decided that yesterday before you even called me, you know you did," she said. "I was just wondering how you were going to go about it."

"The key is Navarre. If I find him . . . I don't want to talk about that right now."

"All right, change of subject." She sat across from me. "I've been thinking."

I took a sip of coffee. Damn, it was good, and I wondered if Monica Meyer would share her formula with me. Probably not. She and I had been fencing with each other—sometimes playfully—ever since the chef was hired to manage Nina's kitchen.

"What have you been thinking?" I asked.

"Should we make this permanent?"

I took a deep breath the way you do just before you dive into a lake.

"What?" I asked.

"I was thinking . . ."

"Are you proposing, Nina? Because if you are . . ."

"No, no, God no."

"The answer is yes."

"What I meant, should we move in together?"

"Not marry?"

"You and I have no business getting married to anyone, much less to each other."

"I beg to differ."

"McKenzie, if we were married you'd want me to be Shelby Dunston, the perfect wife of the perfect policeman, keeping the perfect home, raising perfect children, providing you with a refuge from the troubles of your day, and let's face it—I'm not Shelby. I'm not the perfect wife. Ask my ex-husband if you don't believe me. I'm a girl who runs a saloon and likes it. I spend twice as much time there as I do here, and I wouldn't have it any other way.

"You—I'd want you to be the dutiful husband, mow the lawn, shovel the snow, open jars, and pretty much attend to my every desire. Only you're not that person, either. You're an adventurer. You do what you do for fun and because you think you're making the world a better place and because of some code of justice that you've never been able to articulate even to yourself, much less to me. Marriage would demand that we both make compromises for each other that would interfere with the lives we want to live. We'd end up making each other miserable. Look, we've had this conversation before."

"So we have."

"Well?"

"Would I be moving in with you or would you be moving in with me?"

"We could find a place that we both like. Somewhere in the city. Somewhere with a view of the river."

I liked that she said "the city." I'm a St. Paul boy, born and raised, and can't imagine living anywhere else, although . . . When I came into my money I moved my father and myself to a house on Hoyt Avenue. I thought I was moving to St. Anthony Park, a smart neighborhood near the St. Paul campus of the University of Minnesota. Unfortunately, I didn't realize until after I made an offer that the house was on the wrong side of the street; I had inadvertently relocated to the suburb of Falcon Heights—and Bobby Dunston and my other childhood friends have been teasing me about it ever since.

"Whose name would we put on the lease?" I asked.

"Mine, of course."

"Why of course?"

"If things go sour, I'll be the one throwing you out."

"Why can't I throw you out?"

She stood and spread her hands wide as if she were revealing herself to me.

"Yeah," I said. "You've got a point."

Despite my best lobbying efforts, Nina insisted on taking a shower and getting dressed alone. Apparently she needed to go early to her club, and I wondered if this was what she meant by compromises. It took me twenty-five minutes to drive from her place in Mahtomedi, a suburb northeast of St. Paul, to my home. That's something I won't miss, I told myself as I pulled into the driveway—the long commute. It wasn't until I put the Audi in park and turned off the engine that I noticed the back door to my house was standing wide open.

I started the Audi again, opened the garage door with my remote, and drove inside—I didn't want to be exposed to the open back door when I got out of the car. I exited through the side door of the garage, dashed across my lawn, and hugged the side of my house. I was carrying the SIG in both hands, the safety off, as I edged along the stucco wall until I reached the open door. I poked my head around the jamb, glanced inside, and quickly pulled it back again. I didn't see anyone, and no one threw a shot at me so I looked again, this time lingering for a moment. The house had a lot of windows, especially the kitchen. The morning sun shone through them, giving it a light, airy, and *empty* appearance. I eased myself inside.

The dining room was on the right; the "family room," as my father called it, was on the left. I went left because if I were waiting to ambush me, that's where I would be hiding. The room was cluttered with furniture, overflowing bookcases, vinyl records and CDs and the machines needed to play them, speakers, personal computer, flat-screen TV, and Blu-Ray player. Nothing seemed out of place. Even my Dr. Who sonic screw-driver had been left undisturbed.

Most people who find their homes broken into but nothing missing would be relieved. I was nervous with the realization that the intruder had not come to steal. Plus, he was savvy enough to bypass what I had been led to believe was a state-of-the art security system.

This is the second time someone got past your home defenses, my inner voice reminded me. *You'd be better off keeping geese.*

It was easier to search my house after I left the family room because there were so few places to hide. My dining room consisted of a matching table, buffet, and a half-dozen chairs. There was no furniture in my living room and two of the upstairs bedrooms at all. I bought the house for my father and myself. That's why I took the price on Teachwell—to buy the house and guarantee my father a comfortable retirement. My mother died when I was in the sixth grade, and it had just been the two of us. Unfortunately, he passed six months later, and I never got around to furnishing it properly.

A quick glance in my basement proved that the floor safe where I stowed a few guns, cash, and a couple of false IDs was unmolested. The safe and its contents got me thinking. If Navarre was from Spain, he must have a passport, right?

I returned to the kitchen. There were dishes on the table and a couple of empty Summit Ale bottles that I hadn't noticed before.

Really? my inner voice said. *The sonuvabitch raided my refrigerator?*

I looked closer. He had finished off my leftover beef stroganoff. Yet beyond that, he had done no damage whatsoever. I was convinced the intruder was the same man who killed Mrs. R and who attacked Anne Rehmann. Anne had used my name in her office. Learning more about me, including where I lived, probably hadn't been all that difficult for him. Which increased my anxiety. I imagined him sitting in the dark, eating my food, drinking my booze, waiting for someone to hurt. If Nina and I had been living together, it might have been her . . .

I tossed the SIG onto the tabletop. It bounced against a bottle and came to a rest. While I stared at it, the old questions returned—what was I doing with my life, where was I going—plus a new one. Nina's life had been endangered once before because of me; would I dare put it at risk again?

I lifted my eyes to the window. I could see the pond with the fountain at the center that my father had built in my backyard just before he died. At one time there were a dozen ducks nesting on its banks, plus a flock of wild turkeys that had taken up residence. I had actually tried to name them all. The turkeys were gone now, and the ducks—a few still paused on their flight south, attracted by the open water, yet not nearly as many as before, and none nested there.

You could move to someplace safer, my inner voice said.

Sure we could, I told myself. Sure we could.

I turned my back to the pond and the gun and the questions and went to the wall phone. I didn't know why I still maintained a landline. Just too lazy to cancel it, I guess. I called my security firm. I told the woman who answered that my home had been invaded yet the alarm had not sounded. At first she didn't believe me. Something in my voice convinced her not to argue the point, though. I told her I wanted the system repaired. She said she would send someone right out. I hung up. A moment later, my cell phone rang.

"What?" I said.

"Don't yell at me," Victoria Dunston said. "People keep yelling at me."

"I'm sorry, Vic. It's been a long morning so far."

"Tell me about it. We're not supposed to use our cells or iPods or anything else in class or the teachers will confiscate them. If the bell hadn't rung just as you texted me I'd be screwed."

"I didn't know that. I'm sorry."

"I'm just saying."

"Where are you now?"

"I'm hiding out in the band room, so it's okay. I have my laptop up. You want me to tell you what I know?"

"Please, except if it'll be safer for you to talk after school . . ."

"No, no, I got this. Umm, okay. Felipe Navarre. He was an interesting man. Made a lot of money, 'specially in the tech industry. He didn't invent anything, but he had this thing for being able to see stuff coming years before it arrived, you know? He was also politically active. About ten years ago, there was a group calling itself Euskadi Ta Askatasuna—which is Spanish for 'Basque Homeland and Freedom'—that the EU labeled as terrorists—"

"Wait," I said. "Is this ETA?"

"You heard of them?"

"Not till yesterday."

"Same here. ETA, they wanted independence for what they called the 'Greater Basque Country,' which consisted of pretty much all of northern Spain. There's an article that was printed in *Diario de Navarra*, a newspaper in the city of Pamplona in the region of Navarre, which is a part of northern Spain. This is where Felipe's family is from, by the way. Apparently they emigrated generations ago. Anyway, according to the article, ETA kidnapped someone close to Felipe and forced him to pay a ransom for the person's safe return, which he did. A couple weeks later, *El País*, a newspaper in Madrid, reported that the kidnappers were caught and executed, although the ransom money was never recovered. But here's the thing—the papers never identified who the victim was, male or female. I guess Felipe was notoriously protective of Susan, his wife, and the rest of his family. By the way, Susan Kowitz met Felipe when she went to Spain as part of the University of Minnesota's Learning Abroad Program. It must have been love at first sight, because she never came home."

"What about Juan Carlos?"

"Zippo. I mean, I looked everywhere for him. There were about a dozen obituaries printed when Felipe and Susan were killed, and not one mentioned a son. But here's the thing—I keep saying that, don't I? Here's the thing—the papers didn't mention anyone else in his family, either. I guess that means he didn't have a family or everyone in his family was keeping a low profile. Because of the kidnapping, maybe."

"What about the car accident?"

"Seems to be a straight-up accident. Felipe and Susan were at a party; he drank too much, rolled his car off a mountain. His blood-alcohol level was one-point-three something. That surprised me, by the way, that the police reported that. I didn't know foreign countries cared about drunk driving as much as we do."

"There was no suggestion that ETA was involved?"

"Nope, none. I looked into it because I knew it was the kind of thing you'd want me to look into. It's kinda moot, anyway."

"Why do you say that?"

"The accident was such a long time ago and because—McKenzie, there is no ETA, anymore. A few years after the kidnapping, it declared a cease-fire. The year after that ETA announced— wait, I have the quote here—it announced a 'definitive cessation of its armed activities.' A year after that it disbanded, so . . . I guess this means I don't get my bonus."

"The execution of the kidnappers—who did that? The Spanish government?"

"I don't know. Want me to find out?"

"See if you can. Probably won't amount to anything, but you never know. And don't worry about your bonus. I'll take care of you."

"You're the best, McKenzie."

"How are things at home?"

"Better. The guy who cheated off my paper told the principal that I didn't know he was doing it, so I'm off the hook. He took an F and a two-day suspension. It was kinda sweet, you know, him taking the bullet for me."

"Honey, it's sweet until he demands payment. Then it becomes something else."

"What are you saying?"

"Just be careful. This kid could be all right, just a guy who took a step out of line, and don't we all from time to time? Or he could be something else. You'll know when . . ."

"I'll know when he says he did something for me and now I should do something for him. I have a father, McKenzie. He talks to me all the time."

"I appreciate that."

"I appreciate that I also have a friend."

"Yes, you do."

"So when do I get my two hundred bucks?"

"One hundred. It's two hundred if you get a photo. Do you have a photo?"

"I'm working on it."

"That's my girl."

I mulled over what Victoria had to report until the security guys arrived. Nothing she told me supported Navarre's story. Unfortunately, it didn't entirely refute it, either. 'Course, Navarre could easily have learned everything Vic had discovered and shaped it to his advantage. She took all of a day and a half. Who knows how much time Navarre invested and what resources he employed besides the Internet to research his role? If it was a role.

"You sonuvabitch," I said aloud. "Who are you? Where are you? What are you doing here? Why are you hiding?"

Because of the lack of furniture, my house always had a kind of echo. "What the fuck?" I shouted and then listened as the words bounced from wall to wall. That's when the security guys chose to knock on my door. Talk about bad timing. I allowed my black mood to spill onto them. Probably it was unfair, although they discovered what the intruder had done to disable the alarm system quickly and with a minimum of chitchat. He was very clever, the intruder.

Don't you forget it, my inner voice warned.

The techs repaired the system at no charge and then upgraded it at a discount so no one could bypass it again the way the intruder had. They thanked me for my business. I apologized for being rude. They left. I set the alarm, locked the house, and climbed into the Audi. I adjusted my holster and at the same time remembered the cell phone in my jacket pocket. I listened to the messages left on my voice mail.

"McKenzie," Riley Brodin said, "the police want to talk to me about Juan Carlos. What should I do? Call me."

"You sonuvabitch," said Walter Muehlenhaus. "How dare you involve my family in a murder investigation? You and I are going to have a serious conversation and damn quick."

"McKenzie, it's Schroeder," the third call began. "You just can't help yourself, can you, pal? Give me a shout. We need to talk before Mr. Muehlenhaus has you whacked."

"Oh, McKenzie," said Riley. She was weeping as she spoke. "Is Juan Carlos responsible for all of this? Am I? Poor Reney . . ." She continued to cry until the voice mail cut her off.

I sat behind the wheel and waited for the courage to start the car and back it down the driveway. It was a long time in coming.

The Cities, or perhaps I should say "the Greater Twin Cities," although residents rarely call it that, actually consists of 188 communities scattered across seven counties. My place in Falcon Heights is more or less in the center of them. As a result, I'm not awfully far from anywhere. It took less than fifteen minutes using freeways and side streets to reach the Warehouse District in Minneapolis, and by then my mood had cheered considerably. There was something about being "up and doing, with a heart for any fate," as Henry Wadsworth Longfellow's "Psalm of Life" would have it. I wasn't even annoyed when I couldn't find an empty space on the street near where Riley Brodin lived. I hung a U-turn at the intersection and came back from the opposite direction, thinking I'd have to park farther away. Oh, well.

That's when I saw him.

Anne Rehmann's attacker.

Mrs. Irene Rogers's killer.

He was standing on the sidewalk directly in front of Riley Brodin's building and staring upward as if he were trying to figure out which windows were hers.

He was wearing the same black leather jacket.

The same white T-shirt and jeans. His hair didn't look as if it had grown at all.

Probably I should have called the police. Probably I should have parked somewhere out of sight and watched him until they arrived. The memory of Mrs. R's naked and abused body was too vivid, though. It drowned all reason.

I accelerated hard and maneuvered the Audi past a fire hydrant and onto the sidewalk. I drove straight toward him.

He saw me at the last possible moment and dove between two parked cars.

I foolishly—and I mean foolishly—cranked the wheel to the left and tried to follow him. There was no way the Audi could fit through the space. I smashed the back bumper of one car and sheared off the front end of the other. The alarm systems of both vehicles pierced the air. The Audi came to an abrupt halt. The engine stalled. Why the air bags didn't deploy I couldn't say.

I opened the car door and slipped out. The SIG was in my hands.

The killer was in the middle of the street. He had a gun in his hands, too. He held it like he knew exactly what it was for.

He fired at me.

I ducked. Bullets peppered the Audi like hail. Most of them were stopped by the engine block. A couple pierced the body as if it were made of tissue paper and flattened against the sidewalk and the brick building behind me.

I counted one-two-three and came up shooting.

I missed.

The killer sprinted across the street and hid behind a parked SUV.

The SUV offered no more protection than my Audi, yet I couldn't see my target, so I waited.

When his head came up, I shot at him again.

He took off running.

I tried to follow. The cars smashed together like that blocked my path. I had to dodge around them. By the time I did, the killer was out of sight.

I stood in a Weaver stance in the middle of the street and waited for movement. I heard a car start down the block. It drove off quickly in the opposite direction, too far away to read the license plate. I set my sights on the rear window. The shoot/don't shoot scenarios I studied while practicing with FATS, the police academy's firearms training system, kicked in and I removed my finger from the trigger and lowered the gun.

When the vehicle disappeared from view, I returned to the cars. The alarm of one died away, followed almost immediately by the other.

You are in so much trouble, my inner voice told me.

Movement to my right caused me to bring the SIG back up.

Riley Brodin emerged through the front door

of her building. She halted at the top step and looked down at me. I put the SIG back in its holster.

"What the hell happened?" she wanted to know.

"Believe it or not, I think I just saved your life."

"I never thought of you as a braggart, McKenzie."

She raised her eyebrows up and down when she said it. Clearly the young woman was under-estimating the situation.

I took my cell phone from my pocket.

"What are you doing?" Riley asked.

"Calling the police."

"Should we do that?"

"They'll resent it if we don't."

'Course, they're going to be pretty damn miffed anyway, I told myself.

"I don't want to get involved," Riley said.

"Sorry, sweetie," I told her.

"Dammit, McKenzie."

Riley fished her own cell out of her handbag. She dialed as I dialed. The 9-1-1 operator asked, "What is your emergency?" at the same time that Riley said, "Grandfather?"

The first thing I did when the Minneapolis cops arrived was surrender the SIG Sauer. The second thing was to inform them that I would answer no questions until Lieutenant Pelzer of the Hennepin County Sheriff's Department arrived. That caught the officers by surprise. Often they hear suspects screaming for their lawyers. But another cop? Still, they weren't so impressed that they neglected to slap the handcuffs on me.

They didn't cuff Riley, although they threatened to. Riley claimed she was late for an appointment, that she had nothing to do with the crashed cars and gunfight, that she had nothing to say anyway, and if they didn't like it they could take up the matter with her attorney. The cops weren't impressed with her, either.

I motioned for her to sit on the building steps next to me. When she did I told her to stop being so belligerent.

"It won't do you any good," I said. "Just go with the flow and everything will work out."

"I should never have contacted you, McKenzie."

"Too late now."

More officers arrived, and a lot of things started happening all at once. Techs and investigators, impressed by the bullet holes in my car, the sidewalk, and the wall of Riley's building, started shooting photographs, making measurements, collecting bullet fragments, and taking notes. A sergeant from the Violent Crimes Investigations Division was asking questions. I explained to him that this was all connected to yesterday's killing on Lake Minnetonka.

"The old woman at Club Versailles?" he asked.

I bristled at the word "old" yet let it slide. I informed him that when Lieutenant Pelzer arrived, the Hennepin County Sheriff's Department would probably claim jurisdiction, in which case he wouldn't have to deal with this mess. That didn't seem to cheer him up at all.

Meanwhile, another officer was making diagrams of the Audi and the cars I had piled into for a traffic report. Yet another wanted to see my driver's license. I asked Riley for help. She reached under my jacket, removed the wallet from my inside pocket, and gave it to the cop— either he didn't see my expired police ID or it didn't impress him at all. Next, the cop wanted to see my proof of insurance. I told him it was in the glove compartment of the Audi. The cop looked at Riley as if he expected her to retrieve it for him.

"I'm not your bitch," she told him.

"You got some mouth on you, honey," the cop said.

"I have a bad attitude, too. Want to do something about it?"

The cop shook his head as if he had heard it all before and moved to the Audi.

"You do have a bad attitude," I said.

"I called my grandfather. He's not happy."

"What else is new?"

"This is crazy, McKenzie. What were you thinking?"

"I was thinking that the man who murdered Reney and who attacked Anne Rehmann was standing outside your front door. If I had arrived just three minutes later, he would have taken you."

Riley shuddered at the thought of it. She took my arm, closed her eyes, and rested her head against my shoulder. I didn't know if she was feeling sorry for herself or Mrs. R until she said, "Reney was so kind to me."

"Me, too," I said.

"Mrs. Rogers was your friend?"

"Yes."

"Even though you only spoke to her twice?"

"I was her friend three minutes after I met her. It works that way, sometimes."

"It's never worked that way for me."

"Don't be so sure."

Riley tightened her grip on my arm.

There had been moments in our brief relationship when I was tempted to give Riley the spanking she so richly deserved. Other times—I would have hugged her if not for the handcuffs.

The sergeant seemed less charitable. He stood by listening to every word I spoke. I nearly shouted at him, "Yes, this is what's considered a *spontaneous utterance* and it can be used against me in a court of law whether you read me my Miranda rights or not, which you haven't by the way, you nitwit." I didn't, though.

By then the owners of the two vehicles had appeared. I had more trouble dealing with them than I did with the cops. How was it possible, they wondered loudly and angrily, that I had managed to crash into two parked cars, and what in the hell was I doing driving on the sidewalk in the first place? That, of course, was exactly what the cops wanted to know.

I knew I was going to get a ticket for either careless or reckless driving and wouldn't that make my insurance company happy? I was already paying an ungodly amount for coverage since they had me ranked as high-risk. The cops asked me to submit to a PBT, and I agreed. The preliminary Breathalyzer test came up negative, though, eliminating the possibility of a DWI charge—so I had that going for me. I had no doubt, though, that the cops were thinking I should be cited for DWHUA—driving with head up ass.

Lieutenant Pelzer finally arrived, trailed by a small army of deputies, and both he and the sergeant listened intently while I explained myself. It took a lot longer than I thought it would, what with the questions they both insisted on asking. They then asked the same questions of Riley, who was her usual ultradefensive self.

Eventually Pelzer took official charge of the investigation, and the Minneapolis cops handed over the evidence they had collected to the deputies, who promptly double-checked it all.

The cop who had caught the call in the first place reluctantly removed the handcuffs. He kept my gun, though; or rather the deputy he had given it to kept it. The owners of the two damaged cars were on their cells making travel arrangements and discussing lawsuits. No one seemed happy except for the tow truck operators who carted off the vehicles—oh, and my auto mechanic. 'Course, he was always delighted to hear from me, considering how much business I've thrown his way over the years.

It was when the tow truck operators were doing their thing that Greg Schroeder appeared, accompanied by a young man who was wearing a suit that looked like it had been given to him as a graduation gift. The young man announced that he was an attorney acting on behalf of Mr. Walter Muehlenhaus.

"Who?" Lieutenant Pelzer asked.

I didn't know if he was putting the lawyer on or not.

"I demand that my client, Ms. Riley Brodin, be released immediately," the lawyer said.

"Your client is not in custody," Pelzer told him.

"Then why is she being detained?"

"Give it a rest, Daniel," Riley told him.

"Ms. Brodin, you are not to answer any questions without an attorney present. Those are your grandfather's instructions as well as my own."

"Oh, shut up."

Riley started down the steps. Schroeder winked at me before following her. I was glad to see him. It meant that Muehlenhaus was taking Riley's safety seriously.

Daniel clearly wanted to go with them, yet was compelled to deliver a message first.

"You're McKenzie?" he wanted to know.

"I am."

"Mr. Muehlenhaus demands that you no longer involve yourself with any member of his family."

"Okay."

"What?"

"Tell Mr. Muehlenhaus that I will follow his instructions—as usual."

He didn't seem to like my answer, so he added, "Do you understand the implications of what I am telling you?"

"Yes, I do."

Daniel stared for a moment as if he were unsure what to make of me. He spun to look at Riley and Schroeder, who were now a half block away and walking briskly.

"Ms. Brodin," he called and raced after them.

By then the first two cars had been towed away and a wrecker was latching on to my Audi. I noticed that three kinds of fluid had pooled beneath it. Not a good sign.

"What a shitty morning this has been," I said.

"All of these expensive apartment buildings have security cameras," Pelzer told me. "Most of them look out onto the street. I'm going to check the footage. It had better support your story."

"It will."

"Then we should be okay."

"Have you searched Lake Minnetonka yet?"

"Up and down, over and around. We can't even find the damn boat, much less Navarre. We'll keep looking, though."

"How the hell do you hide a thirty-eight-foot cabin cruiser?"

"If I knew . . . We had Ms. Rehmann going through our mug books—well, our computerized imaging system. She sat through it yesterday and again this morning but didn't recognize the suspect. You might have better luck. After all, you're a trained observer."

"Who says?"

"I could arrest you right now and make it stick, shooting up the goddamn street. It wouldn't be any trouble at all. You realize that, right?"

"I do."

"Keep it in mind."

That's two favors you owe him, my inner voice reminded me as I watched him walk away.

No one offered to give me a ride home, and I didn't have the nerve to ask for one. Instead, I made my way the few blocks to Washington Avenue. J.D. Hoyt's was on the corner. They served the best grilled pork chops in the Cities. I had one for lunch—where had the morning gone?—while I waited for a cab. I took the cab to my house. It was locked up tight, yet I carefully searched it anyway. What was it that Jim Butcher wrote? "Just because you're paranoid doesn't mean there isn't an invisible demon about to eat your face."

My cell phone played "Summertime," and I jumped at the sound of it. It was my mechanic. He was first-generation Hmong, yet he spoke better English than I did—which wasn't that great an accomplishment. After all, for the most part I was educated in public schools. His voice was so serious it made my stomach feel queasy.

"Hang on to yourself, McKenzie," he said. I did while he carefully itemized the damage to my Audi. "I don't think your insurance is going to cover this," he added.

"It hadn't in the past," I reminded him.

"What do you want me to do?"

"Fix it."

"Are you sure? We're talking four grand just to replace the catalytic converter."

"It's a sixty-five-thousand-dollar car."

"Yes, and one of the most expensive to repair as it is."

"Fix it."

"You're the boss."

I noticed his tone had lightened considerably by the time he said good-bye.

I went to my basement, opened my safe, and retrieved a 9 mm Beretta. It felt like an old friend in my hand, which, I suppose, said something about the way I lived my life. I loaded it and was putting it in my holster when the cell rang again.

"I don't have much time," Riley said. "Grandpa's guard dog will be back in a second."

"He's a good man. Stay close to him."

"You think?"

"I'd feel better if you did. You shouldn't go back to your condo, either. Do you have somewhere else to stay? Friends who can put you up?"

"I don't know. I've always attracted a peculiar breed of fair-weather friends, people who are always up for a party or a road trip or some kind of outing as long as someone else is paying. A couple years ago on the Fourth, we rented a plane and flew in large circles around the Cities watching the fireworks. There were a lot of volunteers for that."

"Don't you have any real friends? Someone you can trust?"

"Do you?"

"Yes. Several."

"You're lucky. I can stay with my grandfather, I guess."

"Okay."

"McKenzie, will you keep searching for Juan Carlos?"

"Yes."

"No matter what my grandfather says?"

"No matter what."

"I'm afraid for him," Riley said.

She hung up, which was fine with me. Personally, I no longer gave a damn about Navarre. He could live or die or move to Iowa for all I cared. Just as long as he led me to Mrs. R's killer first.

I called Anne Rehmann. She said if I wanted to talk, I could visit her home in Deephaven, not far from her office. She met me at the door dressed in a thick blue robe over flannel pajamas, heavy socks, and fluffy slippers. I didn't know if she was cold or trying to make herself seem less like an attractive woman.

"Are you okay?" I asked.

"No, McKenzie, I'm not okay. How 'bout you?"

I didn't answer. Instead, I asked a question. "Will you help me?"

"You or Riley Brodin?"

I was surprised by the question.

"Mrs. R," I said.

"Come in."

Anne held the door open and I slipped inside. The house was small, some would say cozy, and tastefully decorated. Unlike my home, it looked as if someone actually lived there and enjoyed the experience.

Anne led me into her living room. There was a sofa against the wall, a blanket and bedroom pillow tossed casually on top of it. Anne sat on the sofa, gathered the blanket around her legs, fluffed the pillow, and leaned against it. A box of tissues was on the coffee table in front of the sofa; a dozen or so used tissues were scattered around it.

"I'm having trouble sleeping," she said. "I went to see the deputies this morning and afterward tried to take a nap, but . . ." She waved at a chair on the other side of the coffee table, and I sat. "They had me looking at pictures of criminals. So many pictures. I didn't see him, though, or maybe I did, I don't know. I'm tired, McKenzie. I can't sleep."

I was taught when I was a cop how to "chaperone" a sexual assault victim. I was taught about the feelings of fear, shame, anger, shock, and guilt they'll experience; taught about their inability to sleep and the nightmares they'll have when they do, the erratic mood swings, the sense of worthlessness that will come later. Yet all of it was in the context of keeping them composed enough to answer questions, to provide information that would help us catch their assailants. Listening to Anne, I knew there wasn't much I could do to console her or help her get past what had happened to Mrs. R, what had happened to her, what might have happened if I hadn't arrived at her office. Even capturing her attacker would do little to ease her pain.

"Tell me about Navarre," I said.

"It all comes back to Juan Carlos, doesn't it? I know the deputies are searching the lake for him.

That's what they said. I gather they've had no luck."

"None that I've heard of."

"I met Juan Carlos, it was early April."

That caught me by surprise—Riley said he arrived in June.

"He came to my office," Anne said. "He told me he was a Spanish national. He said he was interested in moving to Minnesota and wanted to see what properties were available on the lake. I'm not foolish, McKenzie. I understand the dangers of a woman working alone in real estate. At the conventions, that's something we always talk about. Protect yourself; always protect yourself. So I checked to make sure that he was registered at his hotel. I took his picture. I made a copy of his passport—"

"Wait. He had a passport?"

"Yes."

"Can I see the copy?"

"It's in my office. You'll excuse me if I don't go there anytime soon."

"I understand," I said.

"I took him out on the boat. I have a speedboat that I dock across the street from the office. We toured the lake. He was particularly interested in Crystal Bay. He asked about the big white house with the purple flag on the dock. The Muehlenhaus estate. I didn't think anything of it at the time. Why would I? Then there was Mrs.

Rogers's house across the bay. He was interested in that, too. I told him it was for sale. He asked if it was possible to lease the property. I told him I didn't think so, but we could ask Mrs. R to see if she was agreeable.

"We checked out a few more properties. He didn't seem to have any interest in anything outside of Crystal Bay, though. I took him back to the agency. He thanked me for my time and said he'd be in touch. Only I didn't hear from him again. That happens all the time. I didn't think anything of it.

"Then Juan Carlos reappeared in mid-June, and suddenly he and Mrs. R, they were the very best of friends. What's wrong with this picture, I asked myself. Juan Carlos told Reney that I suggested he move into her place to keep an eye on it while it was up for sale. It wasn't true, but Mrs. R was adamant that he do just that.

"I did my due diligence, McKenzie. I did my job. You need to know that. It's important that you know that because . . . I had Navarre checked out through a credit service. I demanded that he show me the money. His personal banker sent me a letterhead statement confirming that Juan Carlos had the liquid assets not only to lease the property but also to purchase it. Five-point-four million dollars, McKenzie."

"The letter? Did it come from Lake Minnetonka Community Bank?"

Anne nodded.

"I called him, too," she said. "The president. Brodin. I spoke to him to make sure the letter was legitimate. It was. Still, I shouldn't have signed off on it. I knew there was something wrong."

Anne closed her eyes. She was silent, and for a moment I was afraid she might have fallen asleep. I was wondering if I should wake her when her eyes snapped open.

"I did it because I liked the way he did me," she said.

"What?"

"I slept with him, McKenzie. I slept with Navarre. Many times. Does that shock you?"

"A little."

"Shocks me, too. I had sex with him that first day on the boat. I don't know what I was thinking. He was so . . . I fucked him again in my office when we got back. That's why I was so unhappy when I didn't hear from him again. When he showed up two and a half months later . . . I can't believe how stupid I was, selling out that way. I didn't even like him personally. Just the way he did me . . . When he returned, we started up where we left off. Then it ended."

"What ended it?"

"Ms. Riley Muehlenhaus Brodin. Juan Carlos met her at the club. Club Versailles, of which I am not now nor ever will be a member. He met her and completely forgot about me. Gave me up for a girl that looks like a character in Japanese anime."

I didn't get the allusion. I took it, though, that it wasn't meant to be flattering.

"Then he tied up at my dock on Saturday morning," Anne said. "He walked into my office like nothing had happened and asked for my help. He claimed a terrorist group called ETA was after him and he needed me."

"Did you believe him?"

"I wanted to believe him, McKenzie. I wanted to be needed."

"Why did he leave yesterday morning?"

"We heard that there was a fire at Casa del Lago. He wanted to check it out."

Maybe that was his boat you saw in Gideon Bay, my inner voice said.

"He didn't come back?" I asked aloud.

"No, he didn't."

I found Sarah Neamy behind the reception desk at Club Versailles. She looked as if she had aged three years since I had last seen her.

"The deputies were here," she told me. She spoke quickly, as if she wanted to get the words out before someone came along to stop her. "They were here all morning, asking questions about Mrs. R and Juan Carlos. The club's lawyer was here, too. I bet that comes as a surprise to you, Club Versailles has lawyers. He followed the detectives around, listening to the interviews. He was there to protect the club's interests, he said. The detectives wanted to see the questionnaire that Juan Carlos filled out. The lawyer wouldn't let them until he read it first. He claimed it was club property."

Sarah looked to her right and left before she bent down to a shelf behind the desk and retrieved a white envelope printed with the Club Versailles logo.

"I made a copy just before they arrived."

She gave me the envelope, and I said, "Thank you." I was desperate to take a look inside right then and there, yet didn't want to be seen doing so in the lobby. I slipped the envelope into my inside pocket, instead.

I asked the same question I had asked Anne Rehmann: "Are you okay?"

"I guess so," Sarah said. "Didn't get much sleep last night." She brought both her hands to her cheeks. "Do I look awful?"

"You look wonderful," I said.

"You're just saying that. Did you get any sleep?"

After I arrived at Nina's the evening before, I spent a half hour explaining myself, and the next two hours in her embrace. Afterward, I slept like a well-fed newborn. I couldn't tell Sarah that, though.

"A little bit of sleep, not much," I said. "What

about your job? Has anyone said anything?"

"Not yet, McKenzie. They'll wait until a mistake is made or someone complains. Club Versailles has lawyers, like I said. They won't risk a wrongful termination claim."

"It's so unfair."

"This is the rich and powerful, McKenzie. Fair is not a word they know."

"Ms. Neamy."

The voice came to us from the corner of the reception desk. We both turned to face it. A man stood there. He was handsome, in his late sixties, with the clouded-eyed expression of a man who has had to make too many decisions he didn't want to make.

"Mr. Curran," Sarah said. She had expected him to ask a question or bark an order. When he didn't, she gestured toward me.

"Mr. McKenzie, this is Mr. Curran. He's the president of the club. Mr. Curran, McKenzie is a friend—was a friend of Mrs. Rogers. He's also friends with Riley Brodin and the Muehlen-hauses."

I didn't know if she added that last part to protect her or me.

I disliked Curran immediately. He said, "Mr. McKenzie," in a conciliatory tone and shook my hand and added, "Mrs. Rogers was one of our great favorites." Yet I went on disliking him.

"Were you friends?" I asked.

"Not friends exactly. We knew each other for a long time. That's not the same thing, though, is it?"

"No, it isn't."

"I'm told that when we die, we regret the things we didn't do more than those we did. All day long I've been regretting . . ." Curran caught himself. He smiled at Sarah and said, "Thank you, Ms. Neamy." To me he said, "Mr. McKenzie, may I have a moment of your time?"

I said, "Sure," and followed him to an office not far from the reception area. It had a large desk and lots of chairs. The walls were filled with photographs of tennis matches, golf games, swimming meets, and all manner of social events. Curran was not in any of them.

He sat behind the desk and bade me take a chair across from him. He stared as if he wasn't sure how to approach our conversation and finally just blurted what he was thinking—"Did Juan Carlos Navarre have anything to do with Reney's murder?"

Wow, my inner voice said.

"Why ask me?" I said aloud.

"I'm told that you are . . . unofficially involved in the investigation."

"Unofficially then, Navarre had no hand in it that I'm aware of. It's possible, however, that the man who killed Mrs. Rogers was trying to get information about him. Why do you ask?"

Curran ignored my question and asked one of his own. "What kind of information?"

"I don't know."

The man stared at me some more before he said, "You're not actually a friend of Mr. Muehlenhaus, are you?"

"I've never lent him money, if that's what you mean."

"But you're working for him."

"I'm working for Riley Brodin."

"Ms. Brodin. I regret that I haven't been her friend, either. I was an economist, McKenzie. Very successful. Made a great deal of money. Retired young. I promptly became bored out of my mind and let them elect me president of Club Versailles. I think I've done a good job here—with the numbers, I mean. The people . . . There are members that I have seen at least once a week for years and yet I've never called them by name, shaken their hands, or had a drink with them. The only time I spoke to Mrs. Rogers was when a member complained about her poker playing on the terrace. You know what I did? I asked her to move her games to the card room. She asked me if I wanted to play. I declined. What an ass."

"Did you speak with Navarre?"

"Only concerning his application for membership in Club Versailles. He didn't impress me. No, that's not true. I was impressed by his bank account. The numbers. McKenzie, we've already told the sheriff deputies, so I don't see any reason to keep it from you—Navarre withdrew his application Friday afternoon."

"Why?"

"I think he knew I was onto him."

"What do you mean?"

"It happened earlier in the week. He—Navarre —was sitting on the patio with Ms. Brodin. They had ordered drinks. It was busy and the wait-staff was falling behind, so I brought the drinks out to them myself. As I approached, I could hear that they were conversing in Spanish. I speak Spanish. I addressed them in that language. Ms. Brodin seemed pleased by it. Navarre became angry, almost violent. He ordered me to stop interfering with them—in English."

"I don't understand."

"Spanish is like any other language; it has different dialects depending on where you're from. Take English. It's spoken differently in New England than it is in the South or the West or Minnesota or Canada, for that matter. I spent four and a half years in Spain, and Navarre's Spanish isn't Spanish Spanish, if that makes sense to you."

"What Spanish is it?" I asked.

"Mexican, I think."

"Are you sure?"

"I was sure enough that I nearly took steps to revoke his guest privileges. Navarre clearly did not belong here, and I have an obligation to protect the club."

"I'm sure you're very good at it."

"I didn't expel Navarre because he was Mrs. Rogers's protégé, for lack of a better word, and because of his relationship with Ms. Brodin and the Muehlenhauses. It was my intention to inform Mrs. Rogers of my suspicions, and perhaps Mr. Muehlenhaus as well, depending on how Mrs. Rogers reacted to the news. When Navarre withdrew his application, I decided it was better to forget about it. I've been regretting that decision all day as well."

"For what it's worth, I don't think it would have made any difference to what happened yesterday."

He raised his hand a few inches and let it fall back on top of his desk as if he weren't so sure.

"I don't know why you took the time to tell me all this," I said. "I appreciate it, though. I'd like to ask another favor, if I might. That young lady out there is convinced you're going to fire her. Something about club morale."

"No. I promise that will not happen. I've done enough things for this club that I've come to regret; I don't give a damn what the other members say. I will resign first. You can tell her I said so."

"It would be better if you did."

We rose together and filed out of the office.

When we reached the lobby, I went left toward the door and he went right toward the reception desk. "Ms. Neamy," I heard him say. I turned my head just in time to see Curran give her a hug.

I decided I was wrong before. I liked him just fine.

With the Audi in the shop, I was forced to drive my old Jeep Cherokee with the heavy-duty rock bumper and swing-away tire carrier mounted on the back. I had parked it in the rear of the lot, but not because I was self-conscious. Club Versailles had lost much of its awe for me. Seeing Mrs. R that way, I was reminded that the rich could die just as badly as the rest of us.

I opened the envelope Sarah had given me and examined its contents. Navarre had claimed Mrs. R's home as his address and Lake Minnetonka Community as his bank; there was a letterhead statement from Brodin confirming his accounts like the one Anne Rehmann had told me about. Navarre had also claimed ownership of Casa del Lago, which made me go "Hmm."

Felipe and Susan were listed as his parents, now deceased; Madrid was given as his home, and under "Education" Navarre wrote that he had a *titulo de máster* in business studies from the Universitat de Barcelona. That should be easy enough for Victoria to check, I told myself. Navarre also included a photocopy of his passport.

"That I can check myself," I said aloud.

I found my cell phone and used it to call U.S. Customs and Border Protection. After being put on hold for fifteen minutes—there were twelve callers ahead of me—I explained I wanted to determine the genuineness of a Spanish passport. A woman with a polite voice insisted that there was no way to authenticate a foreign passport number. I tried to argue with her. She asked if I wanted to report suspicious activity to Homeland Security. I thought about it, said no, I merely wanted to make sure the man using the passport for identification purposes was who he claimed to be. She suggested that I contact the Spanish embassy in Washington D.C., yet warned, "There's no way they will give that information to a third party." I called the embassy anyway. She was right.

"Well, dammit," I said aloud.

You had to give Mary Pat Mulally credit—she wasn't one to waste time. There was already a platoon of carpenters hard at work restoring Casa del Lago to its former glory by the time I arrived in Excelsior that afternoon. I had no idea exactly what they were doing, partly because it has long been established that I am hopeless when it comes to hammer and saw, and partly because of the CONSTRUCTION AREA DO NOT CROSS tape that surrounded the restaurant.

I walked up to the edge of the tape and peered through the open door. I could see Mary Pat and Maria. They were both dressed as if they were, well, tearing down and rebuilding a fire-scorched restaurant. Yet their clothes did little to disguise their generous curves, and I thought, one thing you have to say about Lake Minnetonka, the women are pretty.

I caught Mary Pat's eye and gave her a wave. She waved back. A moment later, she stepped outside, squinting against the bright sun. Her smile was glorious.

"Isn't this great?" she said.

"You're not one to let life's catastrophes get you down, are you?"

Mary Pat flung her hands up as if it were a silly question not worth answering.

"I bet you're still looking for Juan Carlos," she said.

"I am. Have you seen him?"

"Nope. You know what? Screw him. If he can't be bothered to even make a call when his business burns down, screw him. I'll buy him out."

"Can you afford to?"

"No, but my new partner can."

Maria moved to the door and leaned against the frame. Like her boss, she also shielded her eyes against the sun's rays. I knew she was eavesdropping on our conversation while pretending not to.

"Who's your new partner?" I asked.

"Riley."

"Riley Brodin is investing money in your restaurant so that you can get rid of her boyfriend? Wow."

"She was never happy that he was spending so much time here instead of with her, and besides—I doubt he's going to be her boyfriend for much longer. She's even more upset than I am that he hasn't contacted her, that he hasn't told her what's going on."

I flashed on Anne Rehmann's confession.

Yeah, there's a lot of things Navarre hasn't told her, my inner voice said.

"The only reason she was dating him in the first place was because of her family, because the people on Lake Minnetonka thought she should be dating somebody," Mary Pat added. "That's what she said, anyway."

"When was the partnership concluded?" I asked.

"This morning. During lunch, actually."

"Lunch?"

"Well, I was having lunch. Riley called and said let's do this. She seemed very excited. She said she should have invested in the restaurant from the very beginning."

"Why didn't she?"

"We were both afraid that it might get in the way of our friendship. Anyway, Alex Brodin already sent papers over to be signed. I'm waiting to have my lawyer review them first, though. I don't entirely trust Brodin. If it weren't for Riley, I probably would have taken my business elsewhere."

Riley didn't tell her what happened outside her building that morning, my inner voice said. *I wonder why not.*

"How long have you known Riley?" I asked.

"Couple years," Mary Pat said. "We met at the U. I was taking a noncredit business course at the Carlson School of Management." Her eyes took on a faraway look as she wrestled with her memory. "Riley was earning extra credit or something, working as a TA for the professor. She reviewed a paper with me that I wrote for class. I remember the dress she wore. It was blue, and I thought it was a little too revealing. For a while I was convinced she was involved with her professor, that she was more than just his teaching assistant. We went for coffee together and I found out it wasn't true. Oh, here . . ." Mary Pat reached into her pocket and produced a business card. "Take this."

On one side of the card was a photograph of Casa del Lago taken after the fire but before work began. A headline read: "We're burned up, not burnt out." On the back of the card was a photo of the club taken before the fire. The copy read: "Good for one complimentary dessert during our

Grand Re-Opening" followed by the restaurant's address and Web site.

"I didn't have the nerve to put down a date," Mary Pat said. "Why tempt fate, huh? If everything goes according to plan, though, and the county inspectors don't mess with us, we should be up and running in two weeks. Three at the most."

I flicked the card with my finger.

"I'll be there," I said. Mary Pat smiled some more. I glanced over her shoulder at Maria. She didn't look happy at all. "In the meantime . . ."

"If I hear from Juan Carlos, you're third on my list," Mary Pat said.

"Third?"

"Right behind Riley and the Hennepin County Sheriff's Department."

I sat in my Jeep Cherokee for a few minutes, unsure where to go next. Navarre was still out there. I could have rented a boat, I suppose, and searched Lake Minnetonka, but if the county deputies couldn't find him, I doubted my chances. Mrs. R's killer was out there, too. I had no idea where to look for him. I searched the parking lot and the area around Casa del Lago, thinking he might have staked out the place the way wannabe gangster Arnaldo Nunez had. He wasn't there. Nor were there any other members of the 937 Mexican Mafia loitering about.

I called on my long-ago partner.

"Well, Anita," I said aloud. "What would you suggest?"

My inner voice answered, yet it was her words: *You don't know? When in doubt, you always follow the money, Rook. Who did you sleep with to get this job, anyway?*

................................Thirteen

The receptionist at the Lake Minnetonka Community Bank had green eyes that glowed like the numbers on an ancient calculator, the kind you used to be able to buy at Radio Shack. She was happy to inform me that Mr. Brodin wasn't available, yet she would not reveal where he was or when he would return. So I dropped a bomb on her.

"Mr. Muehlenhaus is anxious that I speak to him immediately."

Thirty seconds later I was walking away with Brodin's location written out in a neat and firm hand on the bank's stationery.

The sign read FUTURE HOME OF BRODIN PLAZA and featured a color illustration of a silver office tower surrounded by green grass, trees, and a glistening lake. All I saw beyond the sign was construction equipment, brown dirt, and a hole in the ground. Granted, it was a big hole . . .

I found Brodin standing at a folding table loaded with blueprints and the remains of a large fast-food meal. He was wearing an immaculate suit and a battered white hard hat that made the suit seem out of place and talking to a man, also with a white hard hat, who looked as if he dug holes for a living. Brodin smiled broadly and slapped the man on the shoulder as if they were both teammates on the same basketball team. The man didn't seem happy about it and left. Brodin bent to the blueprints and studied them while popping french fries into his mouth one at a time. It seemed awfully late for lunch or awfully early for dinner, but what did I know? It's not like I follow a standard schedule myself.

Brodin didn't see me until I was standing next to him.

"Jeezuz, McKenzie." He was visibly startled. "Where did you come from?"

"Mr. Brodin," I said, "I just came from Casa del Lago. Mary Pat Mulally said she was going to have her lawyer take a quick look at the papers you sent over before she signed them."

He shook his head. "I don't like doing business with that woman. If it weren't for Riley . . ."

I offered my hand. He shook it reluctantly.

"What do you want?" he asked.

"A few minutes of your time if you can spare them."

Brodin popped another french fry in his mouth. "I'm a busy man, McKenzie."

I thought it would be smart to move him over to my side quickly, so I waved my hand at the construction site.

"Brodin Plaza," I said. "Sounds impressive."

"Oh, it will be."

"A little late in the year to start building, though, isn't it? I mean in Minnesota."

"No, no, no. This is the best time. With a fall start, excavation and foundations can be completed before freeze-up. The aboveground building core and structure can be erected in the winter, and the skin goes up in the spring. Used to be we'd have to wait because the old masonry skins—brick, plaster, stone—they were very difficult to work with in the cold. The newer skins, though, we can put those up almost anytime. And with a mid-September start—that's when we broke ground—there's a better market for competitive bids from subcontractors that are winding down from the busy summer season and are looking for one more project to round out the year."

He ate another fry and bent to the blueprints. I bent with him. It was all pencil scratches to me, yet to Brodin it could have been the design for the tomb of Tutankhamun.

"It's going to be beautiful," he said. "Just beautiful. Six stories. Ninety-four thousand square feet. Right here—parking ramp, four hundred stalls, connected to the main building with a skyway. Lake is here; trees, park benches. I'll be moving Lake Minnetonka Community to the ground floor; the drive-through will be right here. There'll also be space for a restaurant— we're negotiating with three different national chains and an independent. Caribou has already signed on to operate a coffeehouse. In fact, we're forty-four percent occupied and the building won't even be finished for another fifteen months. It's all mine, too. Thirty-four-point-five million dollars, not counting tenant fit-out and some soft costs. Not a dime of it is Muehlenhaus money. Not a nickel."

"How about Navarre?" I asked. "Is any of his money invested?"

Brodin's head came up. His eyelids blinked at me like the shutter of a camera.

"What's that supposed to mean?" he asked. He grabbed a few more french fries and washed them down with soda.

"Just curious," I said.

"I resent your manner."

That's all right, I don't mind, my inner voice said. Fortunately, I was smart enough to keep it to myself (and that hasn't always been the case). I needed information; I needed the man to talk, and antagonizing him wasn't going to get it done.

"Mr. Brodin, I don't mean to be rude," I said.

"You're a serious man and serious things are happening. I need your help."

"What things?"

"Have you heard about Mrs. Rogers?"

"Yes. Tragic."

"Did you hear that Anne Rehmann was assaulted in her real estate office?"

Brodin reached for what I assumed was a chicken tender, dipped it in barbecue sauce, and took a bite.

"I don't think I know her," he said.

"The man who attacked them was seen outside Riley's building this morning."

His eyes grew wide.

"It was just dumb luck that I was there to stop him from attacking your daughter."

He took another bite of chicken, and it occurred to me that Brodin was compulsive in the same way an alcoholic was compulsive. The difference was that instead of trying to drink his troubles away, he ate them.

"This person is definitely looking for Navarre," I said. "I hope you can help me find him first, find him before any more damage is done."

Brodin set down the remains of the chicken and wiped his large hands with a napkin.

"Juan Carlos Navarre." He pronounced the name slowly and carefully like a child identifying the thing he disliked most. "Mrs. Rogers introduced us at the club. He told me he was a Spanish national, that he was moving to Minnesota. He said he wanted to transfer funds from his bank. He asked if I could accommodate him and I did."

"A bank in Madrid?"

"I'm not at liberty to say."

"How much?"

"I have a duty of confidentiality to my customers."

"I have five million dollars. Can you at least tell me if it's more or less than that?"

"Confidentiality is not just confined to account transactions. It extends to all the information the bank has about the customer. And McKenzie, you're worth four-point-two million dollars."

"I am?"

"Don't you keep track?"

"I have people for that," I said. Actually, I had a person—H. B. Sutton, who was a financial genius even if she did live on a houseboat. She's been chiding me for months now because I can't be bothered to come in and review my portfolio.

Four-point-two million? my inner voice said. *Better set up an appointment.*

"You seem to know a lot about my finances, yet you won't tell me about Navarre's," I said aloud.

Brodin ate the rest of the chicken tender.

"Can you at least tell me if he's tried to access his accounts in the past week?" I asked.

"No."

"Following the money might be the only way to find him."

"That can't be my concern."

"The police—"

"If the police come to me with a warrant, I'll give them whatever information the court orders me to give them. Beyond that—I will not breach client confidentiality. Stop asking. If I won't break the rules for that old man on the lake, I sure as hell won't do it for you."

"Mr. Muehlenhaus asked you to violate confidentiality?"

"Many times. That's why I'm not welcome at the Pointe, why he works so hard to turn my daughter against me. One reason, anyway. If you don't jump when Muehlenhaus says, he jumps on you. You of all people should know that. Fucking McKenzie."

"When I first learned Mr. Muehlenhaus called me that, I was kinda honored. Now it just pisses me off."

"Try living with 'deadbeat son-in-law' for twenty-eight years."

Brodin raised his cup of soda as if toasting me and drank from it. He was a man of halves, I decided. Half handsome, half smart, half ambitious, half brave, half spoiled. The toes of his expensive Italian shoes were brightly polished, yet the heels were scuffed.

"You told Riley that Navarre was a con man

who was only after her money," I said. "That makes sense if he doesn't have any. If he does . . ."

"He can't be trusted."

"Why not?"

Brodin waved his hand as if that explained everything.

"Besides," he said, "there's no comparison between his wealth and hers, none. Wait, you want a comparison? He can afford to buy a luxury suite at Target Field to watch the Twins play baseball. She can buy the goddamn team."

"Is Riley really worth that much?"

"The old man has been slowly transferring his assets into her name, been doing it for years, so when he dies she won't have to pay taxes on his estate. The death tax, they call it. The old man can't cheat death. He sure as hell can cheat the tax man."

"Does Navarre know this?"

"I have no idea what he knows, what Riley might have told him. I should never have introduced the two of them at the club's Fourth of July party."

"You introduced them?"

That's not the way Riley told you it happened, my inner voice reminded me. *Or at least that's not the way she remembers it.*

"I was chatting with Navarre," Brodin said. "He saw Riley and asked, who is that girl with the white hair? What else could I do?"

216

Another french fry. Another sip of soda.

"Riley was always a wild girl," Brodin said. "She takes after her mother."

"I didn't get that impression."

"Wild might be a bit harsh. Willful? Tell her to do one thing and she'll do the opposite out of spite. That's why Sheila married me, because her family told her not to. It's also the reason why she won't divorce me. Because that's what her family wants."

He chuckled.

"Sheila can be as mean as she is pretty," he said. "Damn if she isn't very, very pretty."

"I met your wife. You're right. She's very pretty."

"I won't give you a dissertation on our marriage, McKenzie. It wasn't a happy one. People say—old man Muehlenhaus says—I married her for money and position. They're wrong. I loved her. Truly, I did. Sheila was oh, so beautiful and exciting, and I loved her. She didn't love me, though. She was getting older and she thought she should marry and have children because that's what we teach women they should do. That's what the Muehlenhauses expected her to do. I just happened to be standing there at the time. Some people shouldn't get married, though. They don't have the disposition for it. Sheila is one of them. Doesn't mean they're selfish or self-centered. Doesn't mean they're bad people.

217

Sheila isn't a bad person no matter how hard she works at it. Just a lousy wife. I only regret . . . I just wish we could have done better for Riley's sake."

I left Brodin to his fast food and returned to the Jeep Cherokee feeling no further ahead than when I started. I wondered if Lieutenant Pelzer was doing any better and gave him a call. He informed me that his deputies had painstakingly searched Lake Minnetonka yet were still unable to find the *Soñadora*.

"How is that possible?" I asked.

He didn't know.

That's when I suggested that he get a warrant to access Navarre's accounts at Lake Minnetonka Community Bank since it was clear Brodin wasn't going to give them up willingly.

"That might give us an idea where he is," I said.

"What will I tell the judge?" Pelzer said.

"That you're acting on the personal observations of a credible confidential informant who has provided reliable information in the past."

"What observations are those?"

"Whatever observations you need, LT."

"Did you play fast and loose with the law when you were in harness, too, McKenzie?"

"On occasion."

"I'll think about it. In the meantime, this should

make you happy. We found blood at the crime scene this morning. Apparently you hit your target."

"How much blood?" I asked.

"Enough that we're checking every hospital and health-care clinic in the Cities."

"You're right, that does make me happy."

We promised each other to keep in touch, and I ended the call.

Now what? It was my inner voice speaking, yet I heard Anita Pollack.

When I slipped the cell back into my jacket pocket, my fingers found the card Mary Pat Mulally had given me. Looking at it made me smile. The woman was a true optimist, and of all the people I had met in the past week, I liked her best.

Think it through.

Think what through? I asked my former partner as I stared at the photograph of the burnt-out restaurant.

The fire.

What about the fire?

When was it set?

According to the South Lake Minnetonka PD, at approximately 4:30 a.m. Thursday. Dammit!

You see it now, don't you?

Mrs. R's killer had her for twelve hours—9:00 p.m. to 9:00 a.m. He couldn't have set the fire. It certainly wasn't Navarre. He had been with Anne Rehmann at the time. Besides, he had no motive.

So who did it?

Two Twelve Medical Center in Chaska was new. From the intersection of Highways 212 and 41 just south of Lake Minnetonka, it resembled one of those business motels that promised travelers a clean room, continental breakfast, and free Wi-Fi. The wide-open lobby, complete with a Subway sandwich shop, gave off the same vibe. It wasn't until you noticed the sick and injured waiting God knows how long for assistance from people who seemed too busy to help them that you knew it for what it was.

A nurse gave me the room number for Arnaldo Nunez without asking why I wanted it, and I took the elevator to the fourth floor. I didn't trouble the medical personnel at the nurse's station. I simply hung a left and followed the carpeted corridor until I found the room. The door was open, so I didn't bother to knock. Nunez was lying fully clothed on top of the bed, his hands behind his head, and staring at the ceiling. His left pant leg had been scissored off six inches above the knee to accommodate the cast he was wearing. A pair of crutches was leaning against the bed.

He turned his head and looked expectant when I entered, and it occurred to me that he was waiting to be discharged. When he saw I wasn't a doctor, his face clouded and his eyes became fierce.

"What are you doing here?" he wanted to know.

"Just checking up on you. How's the leg?"

"Broken in four places. They had to put in a steel rod."

I whistled low as if I were impressed, but I really wasn't. I stepped closer to the bed and gave his head the once-over.

"I was told you had a concussion, too. Doesn't look like there's any permanent damage, though," I said.

"Fuck you," Nunez said. "I got headaches. I've been nauseous for two days."

"Whose fault is that?"

"Yours."

"How is it my fault?"

"You wrecked my car."

"I had nothing to do with that."

"You did. You must have."

"Why would you say . . . you don't remember what happened, do you?"

He didn't answer, yet for a moment his eyes seemed to reach for a memory that was just beyond his grasp.

"Amnesia about the events that cause a head injury is pretty common," I said. "I've had a couple of concussions myself, so I know."

"You don't know nuthin'."

"I know you tried to burn down the Casa del Lago the other night."

"I already told the cops. I ain't had nothing to do with that."

"No, not you personally. I meant your play-mates in the New! Improved! Nine-Thirty-Seven Mexican Mafia. The guy in the red Sentra or the one who was driving the black Cadillac DTS, probably. Nice T-shirts, by the way. Does your mother know you're wearing those T-shirts? How 'bout your brother?"

"Fuck you."

"I'm sure the boys and girls in West St. Paul are very impressed."

"You just an asshole. You don't know nuthin' about it."

"I know this much, Arnaldo—what do your friends call you? Arnie? I know this much, Arnie. I know you're looking for someone. You set fire to the restaurant to draw him out."

"You police? If you police you have to say."

No, you don't have to say, my inner voice told me. *Where do criminals get that idea from, anyway?*

"No, I'm not police," I said aloud. "Arnie . . ."

"Don't call me that."

"Arnaldo. I'm not a policeman, and the ones who questioned you yesterday, they're nothing to worry about, either. If you don't help me, though,

I can arrange for you to meet some *real* cops, like the ones who put Cesar away."

He told me to get out, and he kept telling me in a loud, screeching voice until a couple of nurses and an orderly appeared. So I left.

I returned to the elevator, stepped inside the car, hit the button for the first floor, and stood facing out. I saw her just as the doors closed—an attractive young woman with long black hair. I hit the OPEN DOOR button, but it was too late, so I pressed the button for the third floor and the elevator stopped. I got out of the car, found the staircase, and climbed it to the fourth floor. No one noticed me as I walked quickly back down the corridor to Nunez's room. I stopped outside the door and listened.

"That fucking McKenzie," Nunez said.

God, that's getting old, my inner voice said.

"What does he know?" a woman's voice asked.

"He don't know nuthin'."

"He must know something or he wouldn't have come here."

"Look, you going to give me a ride home? I've been waiting all day. You gonna give me a ride?"

"McKenzie could ruin everything."

"Fuck 'im."

"This is your fault, Arnaldo."

"My fault? I didn't do nothing."

"You and your little friends. You're so stupid."

"I am your brother. You do not talk to me that way."

"*Estúpido.* Mary Pat is good to me. She is a friend. She gave me a job; said she'd make me an assistant manager as soon as I finish a college course that she's paying for. There was no reason for what you did. I would have told you if he showed up again. It was just a matter of time."

"Got tired of waiting."

"What if Mary Pat finds out?"

I walked into the hospital room.

"Good question," I said. "What if Mary Pat does find out?"

Maria spun to face me. Her mouth hung open, and her beautiful eyes exploded with a fearful light.

"*Buenas noches*, Maria," I said.

I had knocked her off balance by my abrupt appearance, yet her equilibrium quickly returned.

"It is too early for *noches*," she said. "It is still afternoon."

"*Buenas tardes*," I said.

"*Buenas tardes.*"

"At the risk of sounding racist, you got a lot of 'splainin' t' do."

Maria turned toward her brother. He was standing now, a crutch under each arm.

"Tell him nothing," he said.

"In a minute your brother is going to start screaming for me to get out of here," I said.

"This time I won't leave until the police arrive."

"Say nothing."

"Maria?"

She was standing between her brother and me, turning her head back and forth as if she were at a tennis match.

"I'm not here to jam you up," I told her. "You or your brother. I like Mary Pat, and I don't want her to be upset any more than she already is."

"Maria," Nunez said. She turned her head to look at him. "We do not talk about our business."

"I don't care about your business." Maria's head turned again. "I don't care about the fire. I care only about Navarre."

"This is a family matter, Maria." Her head turned once more. *"La familia."*

"No, it's not. Someone else is after Navarre, too. Someone who hurt friends of mine in an attempt to find him. Who killed friends of mine. Who might hurt or kill Mary Pat. Or even you." Maria pivoted so that she was facing me. "Help me. Please."

"You do not say anything. Maria." She spun to face her brother. "You know the rules."

"Please," I said again. "I just need to know why you're looking for Navarre."

Maria looked me directly in the eye.

"He is not Navarre," she said.

"Maria," her brother said. "Do not say anything more."

"Who is he?" I asked. "Maria, who is he?"

She put her hands over her ears and shouted. "Stop it. Stop it, both of you."

"Maria," I said.

"McKenzie, it is not for me to say. You must speak to my brother." I glanced at Nunez. She shook her head. "My brother Cesar. It is for him to say."

Fourteen

The face of Cesar Nunez bore all the marks of a trouble-prone life. Despite that—and the tattoos that peeked out from around the collar of his white T-shirt and up and down his arms—he had the forlorn expression of a businessman who fought all the way to the top only to discover it hadn't been worth the effort. He yawned at me, and I wondered what kind of hours he kept and whether he had any choice in the matter. Probably not.

Since both Maria and Arnaldo refused to provide any more information to me, I decided to go to the top.

After all, my inner voice told me, *if you want someone to break the rules, go see the people who actually make the rules, because they do it all the time.*

Unfortunately, visiting hours for the Minnesota Correctional Facility in Stillwater had already expired by the time I left Chaska late Friday afternoon. My first chance to see Cesar was at eight fifteen Saturday morning in the prison's noncontact visiting room. So that's where I was, sitting on a stool attached to the wall that resembled a toilet seat. Cesar was sitting on a molded chair inside a tiled room the size of a closet. A brick wall, iron bars, and reinforced glass separated the two of us.

I picked up the black telephone receiver so I could speak to him, yet he did not pick up his. Instead, he merely gazed at me through half-closed eyes, his expression as vague as the dark side of the moon.

I returned the receiver to the cradle and found my cell phone. I called up the photograph of Navarre that Riley had sent me and pressed the phone to the glass. Cesar glanced at it and yawned some more. I called up the photo of an angry-looking Arnaldo, the one where he was wearing a 937 Mexican Mafia T-shirt, and pressed that against the glass. Cesar took one look at it and snatched his telephone receiver off the wall. I quickly grabbed mine.

"Where did that come from?" he asked.

"I took it in the parking lot of a restaurant that your brother and his Mexican Mafia friends set on fire Wednesday night."

"Nine-Thirty-Seven don't exist no more. It's gone."

"Arnaldo seems to be reviving it. Both he and Maria."

I used the names of Cesar's brother and sister on purpose to see what kind of reaction it would provoke. Yet Cesar gave me nothing but a blank stare. I recalled the photograph of Navarre and pressed it against the glass again.

"He calls himself Juan Carlos Navarre," I said. "Who is he really?"

"You a cop?"

"No, I'm not."

"Who are you then?"

"My name is McKenzie. Look, you're not the only one searching for Navarre. There are a couple of others, too. One of them raped and murdered a friend of mine to get information. That's who I want."

"I don't care about you or your friend."

"You do care about Navarre. Help me find him."

Cesar leaned back and prepared to hang up his phone. I rapped on the glass with my receiver.

"You dumb jerk," I shouted.

Cesar brought the receiver up to his mouth as if he wanted to give me a few choice words before hanging up. I beat him to it.

"Hey, asshole. Do you want Arnaldo to join you in here? He's looking at an arson rap. Maybe you can share a cell with him. And Maria? Pretty girl. Why don't you just punch her ticket to the women's prison in Shakopee as an accomplice? We'll see how long she stays pretty. You fucked up your life; you want them to fuck up theirs?" I found Arnaldo's pic again and showed it to Cesar. "He's wearing a fucking gang sign on a T-shirt. How long do you think he's going to last before the cops grab him up?"

Cesar stared at the photograph of his little brother.

"Arnaldo is trying hard to find Navarre—for you. Only he and his crew haven't got the smarts for it. I do. Give me something to work with. Once I find Navarre your people can do whatever you want with him. I don't care. He means nothing to me."

"You give him up?"

"In a heartbeat," I said, wondering at the same time if it was true.

Cesar stared at the pic of his brother some more and leaned forward. He whispered into the receiver.

"Jax Abana."

"Who is he?" I asked.

"*Traidor.*"

"*Traidor*? Traitor? Did you say traitor?"

Cesar hung up the phone without answering, left the visiting room, and made his way back to his prison cell.

I called Bobby Dunston from the prison parking lot.

"I need a favor," I said.

"It's nine o'clock," he told me. "At nine thirty I'm leaving the house. I'm taking Shelby and the girls to TCF Stadium to watch the alma mater play Ohio State."

"The Gophers are going to get crushed."

"You are the most negative person I know, McKenzie. How do you even get through the day?"

"I need a favor."

"So you said. I'm saying if I can't do it in the next thirty minutes, it's not going to get done."

"Can you reach out to someone for me?"

"Who?"

"Anyone involved with the Nine-Thirty-Seven Mexican Mafia thing that's still around."

"Everyone's still around, McKenzie. You're the only one who quit."

"Yeah, yeah, yeah."

Like you haven't heard that before, my inner voice said.

"There's a detective in West St. Paul that worked the case," Bobby told me. "He's the guy I spoke to Thursday morning—the one who gave me the intel I passed on to you."

"Can you ask him to meet with me?"

"I can ask, but he'll want to know what the meeting's about."

"Tell him the confidential informant that burned the Nine-Thirty-Seven to the ground is back in town."

"Jax Abana," the detective said. "Now that's a name I haven't heard in a good long time."

"Seven years," I said.

"Closer to eight."

I met Ted Ihns for an early lunch at Boca Chica Restaurante on Cesar Chavez Street in an area we call District del Sol on St. Paul's west side—which was not to be confused with the City of West St. Paul a mile down the road, where Ihns worked as a police detective. West St. Paul, in fact, was actually located due south of downtown St. Paul. It got its name because it happened to be on the west side of the Mississippi River. Don't ask me why they didn't call it something else, I only live here.

Boca Chica might have been the oldest Mexican restaurant in the Twin Cities. It was also one of the finest. Ihns ordered Mole Poblano con Pollo—chicken served on a bed of Spanish rice with a chile ancho and Mexican chocolate sauce poured over the top—and I had Pescado ala Boca Chica, a broiled walleye fillet smothered with the owner's renowned poblano sauce. The meals were so good that neither of us spoke until we were nearly finished eating.

"Where did you hear the name?" Ihns asked.

"Cesar Nunez."

"He does have reason to remember it. How's he look, Cesar?"

"Like he wishes he were somewhere else."

"Ain't gonna get out of the jug for quite a while yet."

"Because of Jax Abana?"

"Exactly because of Abana."

"He was a traitor, then."

"Oh, yes. Indeed he was. He served up the Nine-Thirty-Seven on a platter, gave us everything. We thought, at first, that he was putting us on. He had no reason to turn, no reason to make a deal. We had nothing on Abana. All I knew, all I heard was that he was an up-and-comer in the gang. I could have ID'd most of the Nine-Thirty-Seven by sight back then. Not him."

"Just came forward like a good little citizen, did he?"

"Yeah, right. Turned out that Abana was the gang's CFO. Eighteen and right out of high school and he was handling all of the Nine-Thirty-Seven's finances."

"So why did he turn?"

"For the money. Why else?"

"Did you pay him?"

"Of course not. What happened, Abana gave us the drugs, the guns, the prostitutes, the gamblers, an annotated list of all the Nine-Thirty-Seven's customers, and, of course, all the leaders. What he didn't give us was two hundred and sixty-seven thousand dollars in cash, pretty much the Nine-Thirty-Seven's entire treasury. He neglected to share that with us. We wouldn't have even known it existed except Nunez and some others accused us of stealing it. We didn't steal it, by the way."

"Never thought you did."

"Others aren't so sure. I blame TV. Have you ever seen a cop show where half the force wasn't dirty?"

"*Barney Miller*?"

"I mean in the last forty years."

Nothing came to mind.

"What happened to Abana?" I asked.

Ihns brought his closed fingers to his mouth, blew on them, and let his fingers fly open.

"Poof," he said.

"Poof?"

"Gone, baby, gone. Disappeared with all that cash. Which explained a lot."

"Explain it to me."

"Abana was happy to give us information on the Nine-Thirty-Seven, yet he refused to go on the record. He refused to testify. We told him we could put him in Witsec, give him a new identity, give him protection if he took the stand. He wouldn't even consider it. The feds pushed hard, too. I didn't know why he was so adamant until I heard about the money. If he had entered the Witness Security Program, he would have had to give it up."

"Did you look for him?"

"No, why would I?"

"To get the money back," I said.

"Yeah, well, it was a small price to pay to take so many assholes off the street at one time, you know?"

"It was a good bust."

"Best of my career. Now you say he's back." I showed Ihns the photograph Riley had sent to my smartphone.

"He cleans up real good, doesn't he?"

"Abana didn't have short hair and a polo shirt when he was Mexican Mafia?" I asked.

"Hardly. He was also trying to grow a mustache. Pitiful thing. You say he calls himself Juan Carlos Navarre now?"

"That's what the passport says."

"Passport?"

"Spanish. Apparently he's a lot wealthier than two hundred and sixty-seven Gs, too."

"Well, good for him. What you need to understand, McKenzie, I have no interest in Abana. There's no paper on him. He's not wanted. As far as I know, he's just another law-abiding citizen."

"Where did he get his millions? His passport?"

"Maybe he invested in hog futures. Maybe he moved to Spain. All I know, McKenzie, what I knew about him from the moment he opened his mouth—Abana is ungodly smart. We're talking genius smart."

"Not so smart," I said. "He came back home, didn't he?"

"West St. Paul is home. Compared to this place, Lake Minnetonka is some mythical kingdom beyond the sea."

"Hardly."

"I'm just saying it's pure dumb luck that he bought into the same restaurant where Cesar Nunez's little sister worked. I mean, what are the odds?"

"They would have been a lot better if he had stayed away."

"Like I said, Abana's smart. If he came back, there's a reason."

"Does he have family here?"

"A mother. A sister."

"Think he might have been in contact with them?"

"Now that wouldn't have been very smart at all, would it?"

I found Delfina Abana sitting on the top of three concrete steps that had sunk several inches below their original forms, her back to the screen door of her small house. The steps ended at a chipped sidewalk that divided her spotty front lawn in half, a lawn about the size of the paper napkins you find in fast-food joints. Her sidewalk intersected the city's sidewalk, although the way the concrete slabs rose, fell, and tilted this way and that, I didn't think West St. Paul took much pride in it. The kids playing up and down the street didn't seem to notice, though. They just went about their business as if everything was exactly as it should be.

You don't see that much anymore, I told myself—kids running around a neighborhood on an early Saturday afternoon as if they owned the place. These days you're considered a poor parent if you allow your children freedom of movement, if you don't carefully arrange their playdates and chaperone every outdoor excursion. Which was unfortunate. I thought about how I had been raised, how Bobby Dunston and I spent our days roaming hither and yon without a care in the world and without adult supervision. Kids today are missing out on a lot, I told myself.

I found a place to park and locked the SUV, thankful that I hadn't embarrassed the neighborhood by driving my Audi into it. Delfina watched every movement intently from her stoop, and it occurred to me as I crossed the street that I had been mistaken. The kids were being supervised, not by their parents perhaps, but by people like her who watched out for people like me. They just didn't know it.

"Who you?" she asked.

I stopped on the boulevard, a three-foot-wide strip of packed dirt between the sidewalk and the broken asphalt street, and introduced myself.

"You police? I got nothing to say to police."

"No, ma'am," I said. "I'm not the police."

She waved me forward. At the same time she glanced up and down the street as if she were concerned that someone might be watching. I had no doubt that someone was. The houses were set only a few feet apart. Residents standing at their windows could look through their neighbor's window and read the label on the jar of pasta sauce Mom was pouring over the spaghetti. There were few secrets in a neighborhood like that.

I stopped at the foot of the steps.

"What you want?" she asked.

"I'm looking for Jax."

"You said you weren't police."

"I'm not."

"Why you asking questions 'bout Jax, then, if you ain't police? Jax gone a long time now."

"Have you heard from him?"

"Haven't spoken to my Jax since he was forced to run away. Why you come here talking about my baby I ain't seen for so long? You go 'way."

I pulled my cell from my pocket and called up Abana's photograph, the one where he was pretending to be Juan Carlos Navarre. I held it up for Delfina to see.

"Is this Jax?" I asked.

She stared at the pic, blinking several times as if she couldn't believe what she was seeing. She stood slowly and extended her hands. I climbed a step so she could reach the cell easily. She took it in both hands, caressing it the way a fortune-teller might caress a crystal ball. Her head came up. Instead of the joy I had expected to see in her eyes, there was fear.

"You come inside," Delfina said. "Come inside now."

She stood and opened the screen door. I stepped into her living room and she followed, closing first the screen and then the interior door. The living room was awash in blue except for a broad water stain on the wall behind the couch that was gray. Forest green drapes that were fading to a color that matched the stain framed the windows. She waved the cell at me.

"Where is my baby? Where is Jax?"

"I don't know. That's why I came to see you."

Delfina shook her head as if she were having trouble comprehending what I was telling her.

"He is here?" she asked. "In the Cities? He's not in West St. Paul. If he was in West St. Paul people would know. People would tell me."

"He was," I said. "In the Cities, I mean. I don't know where he is now."

"He is okay? My Jax is okay?"

"I don't know."

Her eyes became moist and her expression tightened. She took a fist and beat it against her breast, and for a moment I thought she might start weeping. She didn't, though.

"He can't be here. Jax. Bad people looking for him. Bad men. Do you know about the bad men?"

"Yes."

"They want to hurt him."

"The Nine-Thirty-Seven Mexican Mafia."

"They say he was one of them. Say he betrayed them. It's not so. He was never one of them. He was a good boy. A good boy. Good in school. Look. Look."

Delfina left the room quickly. When she returned she was carrying a box that originally held a pair of boots. She waved me toward the kitchen—the walls were painted a sickly yellow and the dirty white linoleum on the floor had been worn through in spots. She set the box on a table made of metal and covered with a thick white lacquer trimmed with red.

"Here, here," she said. "Jax is a good boy. An honor student. Look."

Delfina took a certificate from the box and handed it to me. It stated that the President's Award for Educational Excellence had been presented to Jax Abana. Another certificate said Abana won an AP Scholar Award. Another boasted that he was an AP Literature and Composition Class MVP. Delfina produced a faded clipping taken from the *St. Paul Pioneer Press* that cataloged the top students in every high school graduation class in the area. By virtue of his name, Abana was listed first among the honor students at Henry Sibley Senior High School. Under "Favorite Quote" he'd written: *Winning isn't everything, it's the only thing— Vince Lombardi.* Under "College" he'd designated *Undecided.*

"Here, here," she said again. She handed me a heavy medal attached to a ribbon. The medal was engraved with images of a book, star, Olympic torch, globe, and what looked like a magic lamp. "The lieutenant governor of the state of Minnesota put this around his neck at the graduation ceremony. The lieutenant governor. It means he graduated, my baby graduated, in the top one percent of his class. Number one."

After that there was an 8½ × 11 glossy photograph of six students standing together on a stage, each dressed in a black graduation gown and mortarboard, each with a medal draped around their neck, each smiling brightly. Jax was the only male.

I have to admit I was impressed. The closest I came to the top one percent of my high school graduating class was passing them in the hallway.

Delfina reached into the box and retrieved a college-lined notebook. She opened the notebook and showed me what Abana had written on the first page.

Daily Schedule
6:30 AM—Exercise
7:00 AM—Shower and dress
7:30 AM—Breakfast (most important meal of the day)
8:10 AM—School bus
8:30 AM—Period one

241

9:22 AM—Period two
10:14 AM—Period three
11:06 AM—Period four
11:59 AM—Lunch
12:34 PM—Period five
1:24 PM—Period six
2:16 PM—Period seven
3:30 PM (time approx.)—Home from school/quick snack
4 PM—Work at car wash
6:30 PM—Home for dinner
7 PM—Homework/study
9:30 PM (if time permits)—Read for pleasure
10:30 PM—Sleep

Off to the side of the page Abana had written, *Only children play video games,* underlining the sentence several times. It was an opinion I shared. Beneath that he'd written another word that he'd drawn a thick circle around. The word was *Muffie.*

"Jax was not what they said," Delfina said. "A gangster. He was never that. He was a good boy. I don't know why they say those things about him. He had to run away because they said those things."

"He came back," I said.

Delfina stared at the pic on my smartphone some more.

"You have seen him?" she asked.

"No," I said. "We've never met."

She turned to me, her large eyes filled with questions. I answered the most obvious.

"I don't know where he went," I said. "I only know he disappeared and his girlfriend asked me to help find him."

"Jax has a girlfriend?"

"Yes."

"Is she pretty?"

"Yes, I think so. Very pretty."

"She come from a good family, this pretty girl?"

I didn't know how to answer that question, so I just nodded my head. That made her smile for the first time since we met.

We both heard the front door open, and we turned to face it. A woman, dark like her brother and not much older than Riley Brodin, stepped inside the house. She called absent-mindedly while she wrestled with a white shopping bag adorned with a bunch of red targets.

"Mama, I'm home," she said.

She saw us standing in the kitchen. Her eyes locked on my face, and her head cocked to one side.

"Who are you?" she asked.

Delfina moved quickly toward her, letting my cell phone lead the way.

"Abril," she said. "Jax. Jax is home. He's seen him."

"What are you talking about?" the young woman asked. She set the bag down and took the cell from Delfina's hands, examining it closely. After a moment, her head came up and she started walking toward me.

"Who are you?" she asked. "What are you doing here?"

I explained.

"Get out," she said.

I tried to argue with her.

"What right do you have coming here, putting us at risk again?" she said. "Do you know how many people around here were hurt by what Jax did? How many went to jail? I could point to houses up and down this street where they lived, where their families still live. Even today some of them spit on the sidewalk when we walk by. Now you say he's back. He's back! Damn him."

"No, no," Delfina said. "It's a lie. Jax didn't do anything wrong. He's a good boy. Now he's come home."

"He can't come home," Abril said.

"He has."

"Mama, he was one of them . . ."

"No."

"If he came home . . ."

"No. It is not true."

Abril threw her arms around her mother and drew her close.

"Maybe you're right, Mama," she said. "Maybe you're right."

At the same time she fixed her eyes on my face

and jerked with her head toward the door. I stepped outside and waited. A few moments later, she joined me.

Abril returned my cell phone.

"Mama thinks Jax is the one who got away," she said. "The one who escaped when so many in the neighborhood were jailed. She'll die thinking that. To her he'll always be *a good boy.* She refuses to see him the way he really is."

"What way is he?" I asked. "Really."

"A selfish opportunist. He took off and left us holding the bag."

"Why?"

"The gang life, there's no future in it, and Jax was always about the future. His future."

I told Abril that I'd seen all of her brother's academic awards. She told me that Jax had been accepted at every college he applied to, all nine of them. The University of Minnesota had always been keen on keeping the state's best students at home and offered him a half-ride academic scholarship. So did Wisconsin and Notre Dame. Northwestern, Boston University, and the others offered only low-interest loan packages.

"Minnesota, Wisconsin—tuition is about twenty-five thousand dollars for residents, counting room and board," Abril said. "All the others are sixty thousand or more. A year. After everything, Jax couldn't afford to go to college."

"Why not apply for financial aid? The government has a program. I have a friend whose daughter is in college. I'm told there's a lot of scholarship money to be had if you know where to look."

"What was Jax going to put on the applications? That he was a poor Hispanic with no father and a mother who's in the country illegally, who has never even paid taxes?"

"There are organizations he could talk to. Programs . . ."

"Not for Jax. I hated that he became Nine-Thirty-Seven. I understand it, though. He had nowhere else to go."

I wasn't so sure, a kid that smart. Maybe smarter than anyone gave him credit for.

"Is it possible that he joined the Mexican Mafia with the sole purpose of eventually stealing its money so he could pay for his education?" I asked.

Abril stared as if she had just seen me saw my assistant in half and wondered how I had managed it.

"I don't know if he planned it," she said. "Maybe he did. I only know when he had the opportunity, he took the money and ran, leaving Mama and me to face the neighborhood alone."

"If he did do it to pay for school, which school would he have gone to?"

"I don't know. Why don't you ask his Anglo whore?"

●●●

Mary Gabler née Walker was not a whore, Anglo or otherwise. She was a very pretty twenty-six-year-old community relations manager for Wells Fargo Bank, who lived in Mendota Heights with her husband of fifteen months, and who agreed to meet me at a coffeehouse not far from the Mendakota Country Club—but only if I promised to call her "Muffie."

"That's what they called me all through grade school," she said. "High school, too. Probably my mother just started calling me that when I was an infant and it stuck. She still calls me that. So does my family, some old friends, too. Only the people I've met since I went to Notre Dame call me Mary."

"Did Jax Abana call you Muffie?"

"Yes, he did. Jax—I haven't spoken to him since, what? A week after graduation?"

It was when she said "graduation" that I remembered where I had seen her before. In the photograph that Delfina Abana showed me. She was the blonde third from the left.

"You dated," I reminded her.

"He was my bad boy. A girl has to date at least one bad boy in her lifetime. At least that's what I told myself afterward."

"How bad was he?"

"Up until the end, he wasn't bad at all. At least, he was good to me. People, my friends, they told me I was crazy for getting involved with him, but I never knew if that was because he couldn't be trusted or because he was Hispanic."

"Could he be trusted?"

"Turned out no, he couldn't. It was fun while it lasted, though. Exciting. He took me places where a white Catholic girl from the suburbs is rarely found. Kinda opened my eyes to the world a little bit. Heckuva lot more than Notre Dame did, I can tell you that."

"They say he was a member of a street gang called the Nine-Thirty-Seven Mexican Mafia," I told her.

"I asked him about that. He said it wasn't true, although he had friends in the gang. I actually met a few of them."

"You believed him, then?"

"Well, yeah. How many four-point-oh honor students do you know who are in street gangs?"

Just the one, my inner voice answered.

I thought that Muffie must be very good at her job because she spoke easily in a way that made the listener feel comfortable. Plus, she never stopped smiling—until I said, "You stopped seeing him after graduation."

"It's an old story, Mr. McKenzie. Boy meets girl. Boy tires of girl. Boy never calls girl again and he refuses to answer when the girl calls him. After a while girl knows that she's been . . . discarded. She is upset, the girl. After a while, she gets over it. She vows from that moment forward to share herself only with gentlemen, who, to her great surprise and happiness, are actually quite numerous."

"Jax didn't go to Notre Dame, then?" I asked.

"No. We talked about it when the acceptance letters started rolling in, but I didn't think that was going to happen even before we broke up. I just couldn't picture Jax in South Bend, Indiana. Could you?"

"Where did he go to school?"

"I don't know. Why don't you ask his whore?"

There's that word again, my inner voice told me.

"What whore would that be?" I asked.

"Right before I left for college my freshman year, my friends and I went shopping up and down Grand Avenue in St. Paul. We ended up at a Dunn Bros coffeehouse. This was early afternoon in late August, maybe the beginning of September. The place was nearly deserted, yet there was Jax Abana at a table with a woman sitting in his lap that was old enough to be his mother, for God's sake, and they were playing tongue-hockey in front of everyone. I saw Jax and Jax saw me and there was an expression on his face like he was afraid I was going to go over there and start beating on him or something in front of his mom. Seriously, though, life is way too short for that. So I gave him one of these . . ."

Muffie blew me a kiss and smiled. "Afterward, I turned around and walked out."

"Did you ever find out who the woman was?"

"The whore? A friend, one of the friends that were with me, found out a couple of weeks later and posted it on my Facebook page. You'll never guess who it was."

Patricia Castlerock was not a whore, either. She was an associate professor of English at Macalester College in St. Paul who taught undergrads all about the Harlem Renaissance, American Modernism, and Anglophone-Caribbean Literature, as well as race and film study. Macalester did not keep faculty hours on Saturdays, so I was lucky to find her grading papers in her office on the second floor of Old Main, the first building built on campus when the college was established in 1885. She was startled when I rapped on her open door. Her head came up and she whipped off her cheaters, and my first thought was that Muffie Gabler was mistaken. Big sister perhaps, yet there was no chance the woman was old enough to be Jax Abana's mother.

"I apologize if I startled you," I said.

"That's quite all right," she said. "I'm afraid we don't keep office hours on the weekends."

"I apologize for that, too. If I could have just a few minutes of your time—it's important."

Castlerock set down her red pen.

"What does this involve?" she asked.

"It concerns one of your former students. A man named Jax Abana."

She thought it over for a few moments and shook her head. "I don't believe I know a student by that name. This would have been when?"

"Seven or eight years ago."

Again she thought about it; again she shook her head.

"I don't think so," she said. "I could check. However, I am pretty good at remembering the names of my students."

Now it was my turn to do some thinking. Finally I said, "He might have called himself Juan Carlos Navarre."

"No . . . no, that doesn't ring any bells, either. Are you sure he was one of my students? Perhaps you should check with the registrar's office. It opens at eight Monday morning."

"Like I said, it's important. Would you be so kind . . ." I fished my cell from my pocket and called up Navarre's pic. "If you could take a look at this . . ."

Castlerock sighed her impatience and took the smartphone from my hand. She stared at the photo for a good ten seconds. When she finished her face was pale and her upper lip trembled just so.

"What is your name?" she asked.

"McKenzie."

"Mr. McKenzie, there's a coffee shop on Grand and Snelling. Do you know it?"

"Dunn Bros," I said.

"Meet me in twenty minutes."

Yes, it was *that* Dunn Bros, kitty-corner to the Macalester campus. I found a table more or less in the center of the room, and while I waited, I wondered if I was in the same chair where Muffie Gabler's ex-boyfriend sat while making out with Professor Patricia Castlerock. I might have asked, except the way the lady blew in through the door and marched on my position, I didn't think she would have appreciated the question.

"May I get you something?" I asked.

"No," Castlerock said. "I don't want to be here that long."

I motioned toward the chair opposite where I sat. She took it.

"He was not a student when I knew him," Castlerock said. She spoke almost breathlessly, as if she had prepared her remarks in advance and was desperate to get them out. "It's important that you understand that I did nothing unethical. Our relationship was not in violation of any college rule or regulation. If you wish to question my judgment, feel free. My moral principles remain intact."

A lot of questions came to mind at that moment.

Unfortunately, I didn't get a chance to ask any of them before a young woman wearing a white bib apron that seemed too big for her approached.

"What'll ya have, Prof?" she asked. "The usual?"

Castlerock's demeanor changed abruptly. Her voice softened and she smiled demurely.

"Good afternoon, Casey," she said. "Yes, perhaps I will stay a bit longer. How about—I think a small café mocha today with plenty of whipped cream."

"For you, sir?"

"Coffee," I said. "Black."

"Ahh, old school."

I liked that she said that, although I had a sneaking suspicion she was making fun of me.

"How's your paper coming?" Castlerock asked. There was genuine concern in her voice.

"It's really hard," Casey said.

"It's meant to be, dear."

I don't know why, but the girl seemed cheered by the remark. Both she and Castlerock were smiling, yet as soon as Casey turned her back to the table, the professor's expression became troubled again and her voice hardened.

"Who are you exactly?" she asked. "What do you want?"

"You're getting a little ahead of me, Professor," I said. "I'm not here to put you into the jackpot." Her expression changed to one of curiosity.

"It's police slang. It means trouble, get you in trouble."

"Oh." She spoke as if she had just learned something and was happy about it. I liked her for that.

"As I said earlier, my name is McKenzie, and I'm looking for the man in the photograph I showed you."

"David Maurell?"

"Is that what he called himself?"

"Are you saying that isn't his real name?"

"No, it's not."

"What is his name?"

"That, Professor, is a long story. I'll be happy to tell it, if you tell me yours."

She agreed, so I explained about Jax Abana—but not Juan Carlos Navarre—right up to the point where Muffie Gabler saw her and Abana at Dunn Bros. I even used the term Muffie had employed, tongue-hockey.

When I finished, Professor Castlerock glanced around the coffeehouse as if it suddenly contained bad memories. By then Casey had delivered our beverages. Castlerock took a sip from the mug and came away with a dollop of whipped cream on her nose. She brushed it away with the back of her hand.

"David seemed so much older than the boy you describe," she said. "Certainly he pretended to be older. Twenty-four, twenty-five. I spend a great deal of time with postadolescents, McKenzie. The way David behaved around me, I believed he was that mature. I met him here. It might have been at this very table. He approached me; used the book I was reading as his hook. The book was about the Harlem Renaissance, and David said he had opinions on the subject that he would be happy to share if only I allowed him to buy a dessert to go with my coffee. I was flattered, to be honest. A lot of very pretty coeds spend time here, yet he was interested in me. So, in exchange for a double chocolate brownie, I offered him a seat at my table."

"Did he know anything about the Renaissance?" I asked.

"He knew enough to quote Claude McKay, Langston Hughes, even Duke Ellington."

"Hell, I can do that."

"Mr. McKenzie, he knew me. He knew the papers I wrote on the subject. He knew my book."

The man does his homework, doesn't he? my inner voice said.

"What did he want?" I asked aloud.

"Eventually he told me he wanted to go to college. He said he was employed in the construction industry, yet it was becoming increasingly difficult to find work because of the housing crisis. He claimed he wasn't bitter about it. He said it only encouraged him to finally pursue his dream to become a writer."

"The man you knew as David Maurell said he wanted to attend Macalester College to become a writer?"

"It's been done before, McKenzie. Probably I was naive. Or unduly smitten, if you prefer. This is an international school. We draw the best students from all around the world. I said I would help him get in. He said tuition wouldn't be a problem. His parents left him enough in their wills to pay it. It was his high school transcripts that concerned him. There are ways to get around that, however. In the meantime, I allowed him to audit a couple of my classes. He fit in well. He and one of my students became very close friends. Collin Baird."

All of my internal alarm bells and sirens flared at once. It was so loud in my head I could barely hear my own thoughts—CBE were the initials on the bag I found inside Navarre's closet.

Collin Baird, Esquire? my inner voice said.

"What happened?" I asked.

"David stopped coming to class. Stopped coming here. He never called and never returned my calls. I thought it was me, that he had grown weary of our relationship and wished nothing more to do with me. I guess I still do. There was a young woman in the class. I never saw David speak to her, but the way he watched her—I saw the breakup coming, McKenzie. That doesn't mean it hurt any less."

"The young woman—do you remember her name?"

She looked up as if she expected to see the name written on the ceiling. I didn't wait.

"Riley Brodin?" I asked.

"Yes. How did you know?"

It was all starting to make sense to me.

"What about Baird?" I asked.

"Collin dropped out, too. I didn't think much about it at the time. Students drop classes, don't they? They quit school. You'd be surprised at how many go home during Christmas and spring breaks and never return. In Collin's case, he wasn't much of a student to begin with; certainly he was struggling in my class. I suspected his high school transcripts did not match his true intellectual abilities. We get a lot of that these days—grade inflation.

"Eventually the police came around," Castlerock added. "They told me David and Collin had driven to Collin's home in Illinois, but apparently disappeared on their way back here. It was very worrisome to me even though I was told there were no indications of foul play and the police were treating it as a simple missing persons case. Since then I've discovered that twenty-five thousand men go missing every year in this country, and one out of five is Latino, like David. However, only a tiny fraction is the result of kidnapping or murder. The vast majority go missing because they want to go missing."

"Do you believe that Maurell and his very good friend Collin Baird went away together?" I asked.

"It was easier to believe that than the alternative. It turns out I was right, too." Castlerock gestured more or less at the pocket where I kept my cell. "The photograph that you showed me. It was taken recently, wasn't it?"

"Sometime in July."

"David is back."

"So it would seem."

"What about Collin?"

"I don't know."

"Why?"

"Why what?"

"Why did David come back after all this time?"

"Your guess is as good as mine, Professor."

Professor Castlerock left the coffeehouse first; I stayed to settle the bill. Before she left, she asked if I should find David, to have him call her. I said I would. I was lying. I liked her. I liked Muffie Gabler, Abril and Delfina Nunez, Anne Rehmann, and Riley Brodin, too. The more I learned about Jax Abana–David Maurell–Juan Carlos Navarre, the less I wanted him around the people I liked.

I stepped outside and immediately began searching for the red Sentra. I had picked it up outside the Nunez residence in West St. Paul and let it follow me first to the coffeehouse in Mendota Heights and then to Macalester College. It was now parked in the customer lot of the Stoltz Dry Cleaners and Shirt Launderers across Grand Avenue from Dunn Bros. I waited for the traffic to clear and crossed the thoroughfare. I walked up to the driver's-side window and peered inside. The window had been rolled down. The driver gripped the steering wheel with both hands and stared straight ahead. Arnaldo Nunez was sitting in the passenger seat and looking uncomfortable in his heavy cast. He leaned forward to look at me.

"Fuck," he said.

"Hello to you, too," I said.

"How long you know we be here?"

"Since I took a right off the street where Mrs. Nunez lives."

Arnaldo stared at the driver, who continued to stare straight ahead.

"Don't feel too bad," I said. "A one-car tail is damn near impossible to pull off if you don't know what you're doing. If you want, I could give you lessons."

"Fuck," Arnaldo said.

"Why exactly are you following me, anyway?"

"Cesar says you're after Jax. He says you're gonna give him up once you find him. We're supposed to watch you, make sure you keep your promise."

"Fair enough. So, Arnaldo, have you learned anything interesting so far?"

"Only that you really like your coffee, man. And you meet lots of good-looking women."

"You're going to love the next place we go. Can't promise any babes, though. Try to keep up."

I hung a right onto Snelling Avenue and went north until I caught the I-94 entrance ramp. From there I headed east until I found I-35E and went north again. I signaled my turn well in advance so that the red Sentra was on my bumper when I exited onto Pennsylvania Avenue, hung a right onto Phalen Boulevard, hung another on Mississippi Street, and went east again on Grove Street. I turned left into the large parking lot. The Sentra kept going straight. I don't know if it was all the cop cars that spooked them or the sign on the red brick wall—ST. PAUL POLICE DEPART-MENT. The idea that Arnaldo and his driver would keep heading east until they reached the Wisconsin border made me chuckle.

Sergeant Billy Turner was one of the few friends I still had in the St. Paul Police Department; one of the few cops who didn't think I sold my badge when I resigned to collect the reward on the embezzler. He was an African American living in Minnesota who played hockey, which made him a true minority in my book. I met him in his office on the first floor of the Griffin Building. The Missing Persons Unit shared space with the Juvenile Unit because—Professor Castlerock's math notwithstanding—approximately seven hundred thousand persons go missing each year and all but fifty thousand are kids. Well over half are runaways who eventually return home, and another two hundred thousand are family abductions related to domestic and custody disputes, leaving approximately sixty thousand boys and girls seventeen years or younger that the police consider "endangered." Billy was a busy man.

"I can give you ten minutes, McKenzie," he said. "You're lucky to get that, because it's Saturday and I want to go home. Me and the missus are going to my sister-in-law's for dinner."

"Your sister-in-law a good cook, is she?"

The question slowed him down.

"Okay, make it fifteen minutes," he said. "What do you need?"

"What do you remember about a missing persons involving two young adult males named David Maurell and Collin Baird?"

"Help me out."

"Macalester College about eight years ago?"

"Yeah, yeah, yeah. College kids coming back from some bumfuck town in Indiana. They never made it. Hang on a sec."

Billy sat in a swivel chair, spun until he faced his computer, and typed in a few commands.

"Yeah, yeah, yeah," he said. "Baird is from Galena, Illinois, not Indiana. My mistake. This wasn't our case, McKenzie. Jo Daviess County in Illinois had jurisdiction since the kids were last seen in Galena. What I have, kid never called his family and his family couldn't get a hold of him. Family became worried and checked with the school. Macalester had no record of the kid returning to campus after spring break. Jo Daviess asked for an assist. We made inquiries. All we discovered was that this Maurell kid didn't seem to exist. He wasn't enrolled at the school. Didn't have a permanent address. No driver's license. No Social Security number. Spoke to a woman who knew him, what's her name, ahhhh . . . Professor Patricia Castlerock. All she had was a cell phone number. Forwarded what little intel we generated to Jo Daviess. They sent out bulletins—you know the drill. If anything came of it, they didn't bother to tell us." Billy spun in his chair to face me. "This is getting to be a long time ago, McKenzie. What's your interest?"

"Maurell has apparently resurfaced using a different name."

"Should I care?"

"I don't think so. Hennepin County might, though."

"Now the important question—is this going to get me in trouble with Bobby D upstairs? You know the bosses don't like us doing favors for civvies like you."

I was pleased to hear how he referred to Bobby. If Billy had called him by the proper title, Commander Robert Dunston of the Major Crimes Division, it would have been a sign of disrespect or at least disagreement.

"Bobby should be cool with this one," I said. "Although, if you'd rather keep it to yourself . . ."

"Uh-huh."

"Do you have the name of someone I could reach out to in Galena?"

"Hang on."

Billy swiveled back in front of the computer screen, found a name and phone number, scribbled them down on a sheet of paper, and gave it to me.

"Time's up, my man," he said.

I called the Galena Police Department from the parking lot and asked for Officer Lori Hasselback. *Chief* Hasselback took the call and said she remembered the Baird case vividly. She was intrigued by what I had to tell her and agreed to meet me. She said she would review her notes before I arrived. I asked if Baird's family would also consent to an interview.

"You can ask," she said.

• • •

My next call was to Nina Truhler.

"Hey," she said.

"Road trip," I said.

"When?"

"Right now. I'll pick you up at your place."

"Fun. Where are we going this time?"

"Galena, Illinois."

"Never heard of it."

"River town. Lots of antique stores. General Grant used to live there. You'll like it."

"I will?"

"We'll spend the night in Winona and arrive early tomorrow afternoon."

"No, no, no, wait a sec, McKenzie. I've gone on these impromptu road trips with you before, and they've always been a great time. In the past, though, it was let's go catch the Cash Box Kings at Buddy Guy's place in Chicago and since we're there, we might as well take the Red Line to Cellular Field to see the White Sox. Or the time you said we just had to fly down to Kansas City and decide once and for all who served the best barbecue in town . . ."

"It's Oklahoma Joe's."

"No, it's Arthur Bryant's. Anyway, we ended up at Kauffman Stadium watching the Royals play Detroit. San Francisco . . ."

"San Francisco was your idea."

"Yes, but it was your idea to get tickets to watch

the Giants at AT&T Park. My point being, there is no professional baseball in Galena, Illinois. Is there?"

"No."

"Then why are we going?"

"It's kind of a long story."

"Involving Riley Brodin?"

"Yes."

"You can tell me on the way."

Fifteen..............................

Nina must have been watching for me, because she came out the front door of her house just as I pulled into her driveway. She was carrying one bag and pulling another, both of which were bigger than my single suitcase. When I exited the Jeep Cherokee she asked, "Where's the Audi?"

"It's in the shop."

"What's wrong with it?"

"Catalytic converter," I said.

"We're not driving all that way in this thing, are we?"

It sounded like a question, yet it really wasn't. I was about to protest—what's wrong with my SUV?—only she said, "We'll take my car," and tossed me the keys before I could. "You drive."

Truth be told, I liked driving her Lexus even though it was an automatic, so I said nothing while she punched a code into the keypad next to the garage door. The door opened, we swapped vehicles, and a short time later we were on Wisconsin Highway 35, also known as the Great River Road, heading south. The plan was to drive the east side of the Mississippi down to Galena and then take Highway 61 on the west side back home.

I suppose it was possible to fly, but if you didn't

have to, why would you? Flying used to be fun, at least for me. Now it was one long exercise in personal humiliation and tedium, starting with the officious and mostly ceremonial TSA and including flight attendants that oh-so-prettily forbade you from using your cell phone yet were happy to rent you one of theirs.

The thing about Nina's Lexus, though, was that it was old—built without a voice-activated navigation system, Bluetooth mobile phone, backup camera, remote ignition starter, seat warmers, or even an MP3 port. At least she didn't pay extra for those options. I complained. Nina said that some people buy cars simply to get from Point A to Point B in relative comfort.

"We don't need gadgets that rival the starship *Enterprise*," she said.

I complained some more.

"If my rich boyfriend decides to buy me a new car, I'll get all the thingamajigs he wants," she said.

"Actually, I'm not as rich as I thought I was. I've been telling people I'm worth five million dollars, but it's closer to four million."

"Poor baby."

"I'm just saying."

The truth was, I didn't care all that much. I had everything that money could buy, or rather I had everything I wanted that money could buy, which, I suppose, isn't the same thing. My needs were small and easily fulfilled by the $140,000 or so in income that my admittedly medium- to low-risk investments realized each year. The folks who lived on Lake Minnetonka, on the other hand, to them money was a magic lamp. They rubbed it to make their wishes come true.

The Lexus had a six-CD player, and Nina fed it from a cache that she kept in a shoebox on the floor. The first CD belonged to an artist I had not heard before, Sophia Shorai, channeling Oscar Brown Jr. with a startling clear and vibrant voice—*"Sample and savor all of life's flavor."* She was backed only by Tommy Barbarella's solo piano.

"Why don't you play the piano anymore?" I asked.

Nina's eyes seemed fixed on something in the sideview mirror.

"I never seem to have the time," she said. "Switch lanes, will you?"

I signaled and moved from the left lane to the right.

"I remember when you played the blues at the governor's charity thing a couple of years ago," I said. "That was beautiful."

"It was only fair. Truth is, I'm not very good. Switch lanes again."

I did.

"I thought you were sensational," I said.

"You're prejudiced. You do know that we're

being followed, right? A black car behind the pickup?"

"Cadillac DTS."

"What's the DTS stand for?"

"Deluxe Touring Sedan. I was hoping you wouldn't notice. Nina, we need to talk."

She revolved in her seat so she could get a good look at me.

"The Caddy must have picked me up at my place when I went home to pack, only I missed it," I said. "Which means he followed me to your house. They know where you live."

"Who're they?"

I explained about the Nine-Thirty-Seven Mexican Mafia.

"So?" Nina said.

"Not only that—I wasn't going to tell you this, but the man who raped and murdered Irene Rogers probably broke into my house Thursday night. He had waited for me, but I didn't show. I was at your place. If we had been living together, though . . ."

"Don't do that."

"The Audi isn't in the shop because of car trouble. It's in the shop because he shot it full of holes."

"I knew it. I just knew it."

"Knew what?"

"The moment I said we should live together I knew you would try to find a way to get out of it.

Shelby is right. You do have commitment issues."

"I don't have . . . Nina. That's not it at all."

"What is it, then?"

"I'm worried about you. I can't ask you to move in with me. I can't put you at risk. I just can't."

"Bullshit."

The word stung like a slap. Nina almost never cursed, and when she did, you had better pay attention.

"First of all, you're not asking me. I'm asking you. And since you brought it up, I've been at risk since the day I met you. How 'bout the time a man broke into *my* house and put a gun to *my* head, for God's sake, and then kept me there, prisoner, until you came over so he could shoot you?"

"That's what I mean."

"How 'bout the time those guys rammed the back of *my* car, *my* Lexus—this Lexus—and threw a couple of shots at us for good measure?"

"That's my nightmare. I don't know what I would do if something happened to you. Especially if it happened to you because of me."

"McKenzie, I told those stories for months afterward; told them to anyone who would care to listen. It gave me great pleasure to do so. Hasn't it occurred to you even once after all these years, after all the nuttiness we've been through together, that I might actually like living the devil-may-care life?"

No, my inner voice said. *It hadn't.*

We drove in silence for a few more miles. By then we were near Lake Pepin, about sixty miles downstream from St. Paul. Villa Bellezza Winery and Vineyards came up on our left and Nina told me to pull in. She said she wanted to get a bottle of Cinque Figilie and Sangua Della Pantera—she recited the names the way the rest of us might order a Dr Pepper. I suspected, though, that she just wanted to get out of the car and away from me for a few minutes.

I parked in the lot near the door and she went inside the villa. A few minutes later, I said, "screw it" and followed her.

"Just in time," she said when I approached the counter. She handed me the bottles without another word and went back outside while I stayed to pay for them. A couple of minutes later, I stepped into the bright sunshine. I couldn't find Nina at first, and then I did. The black Cadillac DTS was parked at the far end of the lot. Nina was using the roof to balance herself as she leaned toward the driver's window and spoke to whoever was inside.

"Sonuvabitch," I said.

I set the wine bottles on the asphalt and reached for the Beretta holstered behind my right hip and moved toward the car. At the same time, Nina beat a quick rhythm on the roof of the Caddie, threw a wave to those inside, and started walking back toward where the Lexus was parked. She was smiling.

"What the hell do you think you're doing?" I asked her.

"Chatting with the boys," she answered in a cheerful voice. "Did you know, Arnaldo's leg was broken in four places, poor thing. I told them that we weren't actually looking for Juan Carlos just now, but if they wanted to keep following us to Illinois that was fine, too. I told them we would be staying at the AmericInn in Winona tonight, the one overlooking the river, if they should get lost. Hope you don't mind."

I did mind and told her so in no uncertain terms.

"Don't ever do that again," I said.

She shrugged as if she would think about it, but not too hard.

A few minutes later we were in the Lexus heading south and not talking. Apparently the Cadillac DTS had turned around and gone home.

Prudence Johnson, one of my favorites, was on the CD player. She and a handful of composers had collaborated to turn fourteen poems by Edna St. Vincent Millay into a stunning jazz album called *A Girl Named Vincent*. One of the composers, Laura Caviani, played piano on most of the tracks.

"I'm going to buy you a piano," I said. "A baby grand. A good one. Wherever we live, you and I, there has to be room for a piano."

"Well," Nina said. "It's not a new car. Still . . ."

• • •

There was nothing particularly special about the AmericInn in Winona except for the view. It was on the Minnesota side of the Mississippi, and from our balcony we could see the sun dapple the river as it curved slowly around the bend and glisten off the steel girders of Main Channel Bridge—a cantilever bridge so old that it qualified for the National Register of Historic Places.

The parking lot stretched out between the hotel and the river, and I also had a good view of the comings and goings of the guests. There were no red Sentras or black Cadillac DTSs in the lot and no one sitting in a different make or model of vehicle that I could see.

Nina, what were you trying to prove? I asked myself silently.

I sat on the balcony and sipped some of her Cinque Figlie from one of the plastic cups the hotel provided. After a while Nina joined me. She was wearing a silk nightgown beneath a silk robe cinched at the waist, her hair still damp from the shower. Her eyes—those riveting silver-blue eyes that captured my heart so long ago—caught the fading sunlight and held it.

"We need to talk," I said.

"Again?"

"We need to have rules, you and I."

"What rules?"

"Rule Number One—never try to prove how

brave you are. Never. Fear is God's way of telling us to think before we do something stupid."

"Like walk up to a car filled with gang-bangers?"

"Exactly like that."

"Okay. What else?"

"The rest we'll make up as we go along."

We remained on the balcony not speaking until the sun was down and ribbons of light outlined the bridge. From the darkness I heard Nina's voice.

"Come to bed."

Galena was a sparkling gem of a town located along the Mississippi River at the bottom of a steep hill. At one time it had been bigger than Chicago. However, the collapse of the lead-mining industry and the advent of a nationwide railroad system rendered the river port irrelevant until it reinvented itself as a tourist town mostly around the exploits of General Ulysses Simpson Grant, who actually lived there for only a couple of years.

We checked into the DeSoto House, the city's oldest operating hotel, where $250 rented us a Parlor Suite with a sitting room and gas fireplace for the night. While we checked in, a young man bounded down the winding staircase as if he were in a dreadful hurry. When he reached the bottom, he looked up to see his girl descending slowly, dragging her hand along the banister.

"What are you doing?" he asked her. His voice dripped with impatience.

"General Grant touched this banister," she said. "So did Abraham Lincoln, Mark Twain, Herman Melville, Stephen Douglas, who else?"

"Teddy Roosevelt," the desk clerk said.

"Teddy Roosevelt," the girl repeated.

"So what?" asked the boyfriend. "Do you think all that greatness will rub off on you? I bet they polished the banister since those guys touched it."

"You're such an idiot," the girl said as she brushed past him and walked out the front door.

"He is an idiot," Nina repeated after the boyfriend followed the girl outside.

It never occurred to me to argue with her.

After we claimed the room and unpacked our bags, Nina said, "What do we do first?"

"What do you mean, we?"

"You don't really believe I drove all this way just to sit in a hotel room while you go out and enjoy yourself, do you? This is a nice suite, by the way."

"Nina, you and I are not Nick and Nora Charles, okay?"

"Okay, but what do we do first?"

I sighed dramatically and called the Galena Police Department. That's when I discovered that Chief Hasselback was out and wouldn't return until Monday morning—why she hadn't told me that when I spoke to her earlier I didn't know.

Still, it gave us plenty of time to explore the town and its many century-old buildings. I found a store called the Root Beer Revelry that sold nearly ninety different varieties of root beer. I bought two cases of assorted brands with names like Iron Horse, Gale's, Jack Black's Dead Red, Sea Dog, and Frostie with the idea that I would gather a group of trusted and discerning confidantes for a taste testing to determine the world's greatest root beer. Nina told me to let her know how that worked out.

Meanwhile, she discovered Old Blacksmith Shop Mercantile, an 1894 blacksmith shop where, under the guidance of the resident smithy, she fashioned an ornate fireplace poker. I mentioned that neither she nor I had a fireplace. She told me that our new home would have one—it was a prerequisite. Again, who was I to argue?

We found a former movie theater where they filmed scenes for *Field of Dreams* that was now an antique store, and a former firehouse that was now a theater that was supposed to be haunted. And then there was the bar where I was told that the recipe for Red Stripe beer was actually developed in Galena and sold to an Englishman, who turned it into one of Jamaica's better-known exports. I drank a bottle; suddenly it didn't taste quite the same.

Eventually we ended up at the Perry Street Brasserie for dinner. Throughout the meal—hell, throughout the day—I had the distinct impression that we were being watched. It whispered at me like a buzzing mosquito that I was unable to swat. Yet I couldn't identify the watchers.

Either you're being unduly paranoid, my inner voice warned me, *or these guys are very, very good.*

Chief Lori Hasselback was lovely in the way you'd expect a former high school homecoming queen to be lovely, with soft blue eyes and shoulder-length blond hair that she twirled around her finger as she spoke. She didn't look like a police officer. She looked like an actress pretending to be a police officer—think Emily Procter in *CSI: Miami.* That she had somehow managed to rise from beat cop to chief of the Galena PD in seven years impressed the hell out of me—until I learned the entire department consisted of herself, two lieutenants, one investigator, six officers and two meter maids that only worked from 8:00 a.m. to 4:30 p.m. The Jo Daviess County Sheriff's Department answered calls after hours and on weekends and holidays. That's why I had to wait until Monday to meet with her. I had never heard of a part-time police department before.

We met the chief Monday morning on the first floor of a gray brick building on Main Street that the cops shared with the other city departments.

The only building in downtown that seemed to have been built in the past half century, it was located between Fritz and Frites, a German and French restaurant, and Little Tokyo, a restaurant serving Japanese cuisine. She suggested that we chat where it was more comfortable and led us across the street to Kaladi's 925 Coffee Bar. After buying coffee, Nina and I sat on a black leather sofa beneath a colorful mural that I couldn't describe if I wanted to. Hasselback sat in a matching chair to our left. She dragged a lock of hair across her mouth, then let it fall as she began speaking.

"I remember Collin Baird," she said. "Didn't need to review my notes, either. He was an asshole. Bully in a letterman's jacket. You know the type. He had good grades, but I suspect that had more to do with his ability to throw a tight spiral than his study habits. Some women had accused him of peeping their windows, but we never caught him at it. The deputies did catch him the summer after he graduated from high school with a fourteen-year-old girl. They were drinking in the cemetery around midnight; the deputies came along before things went too far with the girl. Probably they should have busted 'em both for trespassing or at least given 'em minors, but it's a small town and everybody knows everybody and the deputies didn't want to ruin the girl's rep, so they were let off with a warning."

The way Hasselback spoke, especially the way she said "minor"—a citation for underage drinking that comes with a hundred-dollar fine and attaches to an eighteen-year-old's permanent record—made me think she was more of a cop than I had given her credit for.

"I was a rookie when he went missing. Caught the case. Good riddance, some might say, good riddance to bad rubbish—you hear that a lot from the old folks around here. Only you can't choose the vic, am I right? One of the first things you learn on the job. I worked the case with the county deputies. Interviewed the mother; the old man had taken off years earlier, and it was just her and the kid. She gave us diddly-squat. The college and the cops in St. Paul, they didn't give us anything to work with, either. My first thought: like father, like son—the kid simply took off just like the old man had. The fact that we couldn't get a handle on this David Maurell character was what made me think there was fuckery afoot."

"Wait," I said. "What did you say?"

Hasselback's head jerked slightly as if she were surprised to be interrupted.

"I said . . . I apologize for my language," she said.

"No, not at all. I had an old friend in St. Paul homicide named Anita who used to say that."

"Oh, yeah?"

"Was she pretty, too?" Nina asked.

Hasselback's head jerked again, and she looked at Nina as if it were the oddest question she had ever heard. Nina pulled at the hem of her black skirt and the cuff of her blue shirt as if she were wishing she had worn something else.

"Anyway, we sent out bulletins," the chief said. "I didn't expect much; the boss told me not to expect much. Then we got a hit. Laredo, Texas. The PD there spotted Collin Baird's car parked in a shopping mall lot near the Juárez-Lincoln International Bridge that crosses the Rio Grande. Car was clean. Nothing to indicate"—the chief quoted the air—"foul play. Took a chance and contacted Mexican Customs, who are a helluva lot more cooperative than we give them credit for. Turns out they dinged Collin Baird's passport a week earlier. That told us the little SOB went to Mexico."

"What about Maurell?" I asked.

"Nothing on him—whoever he is. You say he's the one who turned up in the Twin Cities?"

"He's the one."

"I'd like to speak to him."

"You and me both, Chief."

"What I don't get—why park the car?" Nina asked. "McKenzie, you and I have driven across the border, why not him? Why not just drive across the bridge into—what's the city on the other side of Laredo, Texas?"

"Nuevo Laredo," Hasselback said. "Maybe he wanted the cops to find the car, wanted his mother to know he wasn't lying dead in a ditch somewhere."

"He could have done that by picking up a phone," I said.

"Yeah, he coulda."

"Maybe he did," Nina said.

We agreed to visit Collin Baird's mother together. Chief Hasselback warned that she didn't expect anything would come of it.

"I've spoken to her on and off over the years, mostly about her son," she said. "The woman's a walking ten-ninety-six."

"What's that?" Nina asked.

"Mental case," I told her.

The chief gave us directions to Mrs. Baird's house and then told us to follow her. Nina and I were sitting in the Lexus waiting for her to pull out of her parking space when I decided I could no longer hold it in.

"What was that all about before?" I asked. " 'Is she pretty, too?' Where the hell did that come from?"

"Chief Hasselback is an attractive woman," Nina told me.

"What does that have to do with anything?"

"I was just wondering if you noticed."

"Nina, she's a cop."

"I thought you'd like that about her."

"I don't believe it. Are you jealous? You need to tell me, because I've never seen you jealous and I'm not sure what it looks like."

"I'm not jealous."

"It kinda sounds like you are."

"I'm sorry. I've never been a sidekick before. I don't know how to behave."

"You're not a sidekick. What do you think, that we're Batman and Robin?"

"I was thinking more like Sam Spade and Effie Perine."

"Sam didn't sleep with Effie. She was his secretary."

"We don't know what they did after hours."

"All right, all right, Rule Number Two—"

"Should I write this down?"

"You are forbidden to be jealous and we must never have a conversation like this again."

"Is that two rules, or one rule with two parts?"

"This is why couples should never work together. What?"

Nina leaned across the seat and buzzed my cheek.

"I like that you said couple," she said.

"Couple, not partners."

"We'll see."

Mrs. Baird lived in a small two-story house in a heavily wooded area on top of the hill, not terribly far from Galena's senior high school, home of the Pirates. She met us on her front stoop, and I immediately noticed her nervousness. I marked it down as a consequence of Chief Hasselback's presence. When I was a cop, I used to make people nervous, too, especially when I appeared unannounced on their doorsteps.

Mrs. Baird demanded to know why we were there. The chief told her we wanted to talk about her son. She brought her hand to her throat and moved backward until she bumped into her closed screen door. The words came out in a rush.

"I don't know where he is," she said. "I haven't seen him. Why are you coming here now? I haven't seen him, I tell you."

Chief Hasselback set a hand on the woman's shoulder. It was meant to be a gesture of comfort, yet Mrs. Baird flinched just the same.

"These are the investigators from Minnesota I told you about," the chief said. Nina brightened at the word "investigators." I was more interested in the phrase "I told you about."

"They're the ones who found David Maurell in Minneapolis," Hasselback added. "They want to ask a few questions about him."

Mrs. Baird stared at me with such intensity that I found myself cautiously reaching behind my right hip and patting the Beretta beneath my sports coat.

"You're McKenzie," she said.

"Yes." I offered my hand. She refused to accept it. Her eyes had the obstinacy that comes from seeing too many changes in life and not being able to change with them.

"David," she said. "Yes. We want to talk about David. Let's go inside and talk about David."

She turned her head and gazed through the screen door inside her house. After a moment, she stepped back and opened the door. "Please, come inside."

I was last across the threshold. There was a wooden staircase to my left that led upstairs. What caught my eye and held it, though, was the pictures on the wall, all of them religious, and so many that I thought they must be her first line of defense against the world.

Mrs. Baird led us away from the staircase to the corner of her living room that she had reserved as a sitting area. There were books stacked on a coffee table and next to the chairs; books with titles like *God Has a Dream*, *Fasting and Prayer*, and *Reading the Bible Again for the First Time*, as well as *Mysterious Ways* and *Give Us This Day* magazines. She sat facing the staircase. We fanned out on either side of her.

"Tell us about David," she said.

Us? my inner voice asked.

I reached inside my pocket and produced the

smartphone. I called up Navarre's photo and showed it to her.

"Mrs. Baird," I said, "is this the man you know as David Maurell?"

Her mouth formed a sneer and through it she said, "That's him. That's the man who . . ."

"Who what?"

"Who ruined my son's life."

Chief Hasselback leaned back in her chair and made herself comfortable as if she expected a long story. Nina hunched forward, resting her forearms on her knees, as if she expected the same thing.

"How did he do that?" I asked.

"Ask him. David's up in Minnesota, isn't he? Do you know where?"

"He was in Minnesota. I don't know where he is now."

Mrs. Baird snorted. "Oh, he's still there. We know that much."

We?

"How do you know that?" I asked.

"We just do."

"What do you know about Maurell?"

"When he came to visit that one time, he seemed very shy. Very polite. I remember that Collin kept teasing him because of a classmate they had at Macalester. A girl. David thought she was the most beautiful girl he had ever seen, only he was afraid to speak to her. I thought it might be

285

because of David's accent. Collin said it was because the girl's family was extremely wealthy and David's was poor.

"Perhaps not poor, exactly. David's people had escaped from Cuba when Castro took over. They became American citizens and started a company that sold sugarcane, but they weren't rich by any means—at least that's what David said. He said his family's dream was to return to their native land. David didn't want to go to Cuba. He was born in America. Cuba was a foreign country to him. So he and his family were at odds. That's why he came here with Collin on break instead of going home."

Oh, he's good, my inner voice told me.

"He and Collin were great friends," Mrs. Baird said. "They met in college, you see. David would buy him gifts—and me, too. David seemed always to have plenty of money on hand. I said, put the money in a bank. Only Castro confiscated everything, all of their money and property, so his family didn't trust banks. This was America; the banks can be trusted here, I told him. Then the financial crisis hit and we found out, no, we can't trust our banks, either."

Very, very good.

"But he was a liar," Mrs. Baird said. "He lied about everything."

"What do you mean?"

Mrs. Baird rose abruptly from her chair and

crossed the room to what could only be described as a knickknack shelf. At the same time, I heard a creaking sound on the staircase. So did Nina. She rotated her head to see. She turned back when Mrs. Baird said, "Look." Mrs. Baird found a photograph of a young man dressed in black high school graduation robes not unlike the ones Jax Abana had worn and carried it back to where I was sitting. She thrust it at me.

"Look," she repeated. "Collin was a good boy. He never did anything to anybody. He never did anything wrong." Mrs. Baird was looking at Chief Hasselback when she said that last part. "People said he did things, but that wasn't true. He was a good boy. A good student and athlete. People were jealous of him."

I took the photograph and stared at it for a moment. It might have been taken eight years earlier, yet I recognized the young man instantly.

Sonuvabitch.

"David, David was such a liar," Mrs. Baird said. "He lied to Collin. He showed Collin money that he had, thousands of dollars, and he said he and Collin would go to Iraq and invest the money. He said that Iraq was the new land of opportunity because the people there needed so much help to rebuild after the war. He said that they could invest the money and Collin would help and they would become rich and split the money fifty-fifty."

"Iraq?" Chief Hasselback said.

Sonuvabitch.

Chief Hasselback shifted her position in her chair so that she could look into Mrs. Baird's eyes.

"How do you know this, Mrs. Baird?" she asked. "How did you know they went to Iraq? When I called Saturday, and all the times we talked before that, you thought Collin had gone to Mexico. We all did."

There was another creak from the staircase.

"What is that noise?" Nina said. She stood and moved toward it.

"Where did this information come from, Mrs. Baird?" Hasselback asked.

"Nina, wait," I said.

Nina cocked her head in an effort to see around the corner at the top of the staircase.

I stood, letting the photograph of the man who had assaulted Anne Rehmann, the man who had raped and murdered Mrs. Rogers, slip from my fingers. It bounced against a book on the coffee table and rattled to the floor.

That's when I saw him.

On the staircase.

I reached for the Beretta. My hand closed around the butt and I yanked it from the holster.

Collin Baird gripped the banister with his left hand and leapt over it.

Nina gasped and brought her hand to her

mouth the way someone might when startled during a horror movie.

Baird had an automatic in his right hand. As he jumped, he swung the gun in a high arc. It crashed against Nina's temple just as his feet hit the floor.

The force of the blow spun her body. Nina caromed off the wall and slid to the floor.

Baird pressed his free hand against his ribs and grimaced as if the jump had hurt him, and I wondered if that was where he had been hit during our shootout.

He waved his gun at us.

I brought the Beretta up.

"Not again," Mrs. Baird said.

She shoved at me.

"Police," Hasselback shouted. "Don't move."

Collin Baird threw a wild shot in our direction and ran for the door.

I shoved Mrs. Baird away and took off after him.

I paused for a beat when I reached Nina's side. Her eyes were closed and her mouth was twisted in an ugly grin. She had brought her hand up and was covering the wound on her head. Blood seeped between her fingers.

"Nuts," she said.

I left her there.

I hit the screen door with my shoulder. It flew open and I dove across the lawn, landed on my shoulder, and rolled into a crouch. I brought the Beretta up with both hands and swept the muzzle over the front yard and street and surrounding houses. Collin Baird was not there.

I thought I heard running behind me and turned toward the noise. I moved quickly to Mrs. Baird's house and began to move cautiously around it. The two sides of my brain were shouting at each other. "He's getting away," said one. "Go slow," said the other.

The backyard opened up onto a wooded area. I took cover at the corner of the house. I waited. I listened. I saw and heard nothing.

I dashed across the yard into the woods and paused again.

Training and experience had quieted the shouting. I told myself, this was his ground. He grew up here. Following him into the woods would be a fatal mistake.

Rule Number One, my inner voice said.

I slowly backed out.

Sonuvabitch!

I listened to the sound of sirens approaching, sirens that almost always came too late. I didn't want to be the one standing there with a gun in my hand when the cops arrived, so I holstered the Beretta and made my way back into the house. I found Nina sitting in a chair near the door. She was pressing a folded handkerchief to her temple.

A trickle of blood ran down her hand and wrist and spotted her blue shirt and black skirt. Her eyes were wet with tears, yet she made no sound. I knelt before her.

"Let me see," I said.

She shook her head and gestured toward the sitting area. Chief Hasselback was kneeling next to Mrs. Baird. She had doubled up her hands and was applying pressure to an area just above the woman's breasts—standard procedure for treating a sucking chest wound. Her hands and wrists and shirt were soaked with blood.

"Stay with me, Mrs. Baird," the chief said. "It'll be all right. Help is on the way. Help will be here soon. Stay with me."

I moved to the chief's side and looked over her shoulder. Mrs. Baird's eyes were closed, and if she was breathing, I didn't notice.

"Stay with me," the chief said. "Just for a few more minutes. Help is coming."

The front door opened and paramedics filled the room. They relieved the chief. She stood and watched them work. Blood dripped off of her hands onto the floor. She didn't seem to notice the blood until the paramedics confirmed what we already knew.

"She's gone."

Sixteen ....

I felt like a kite baffled by the changing winds. At any moment I could come crashing down. I tried not to let Nina know it, though.

They separated us as soon as the Jo Daviess County sheriff deputies arrived. They took her to the Midwest Medical Center, where they gave her three stitches just to the left of her eyebrow and a neurological exam to test for concussion symptoms. Fortunately, her memory and concentration, strength and sensation, vision, hearing, balance, coordination, and reflexes were just fine.

They brought me to the Public Safety Building just behind the courthouse in Galena. The chief deputy was furious that I had the audacity to bring a concealed weapon into his county. I reminded him that I had a permit to carry. He reminded me that "this is Illinois, not goddamn Minnesota."

The questions came fast and furious, and it took a while before I was able to explain that Collin Baird was the "unidentified suspect" wanted in Hennepin County for the rape and murder of Irene Rogers and the criminal sexual assault of Anne Rehmann. By then he could have easily slipped into Iowa or Wisconsin, which would have made quick capture that much more unlikely. The deputies sent out their alerts and bulletins just the same.

"Why didn't you tell me about Baird?" Chief Hasselback asked.

"I didn't realize it was him until I saw the photograph," I said. "I think that's why he came out of hiding, because he knew his mother was showing me the photograph. Otherwise, who knows . . ."

"What was he doing down here?"

"The Hennepin County deputies think I might have shot him the other day, but not bad enough to knock him down. Where do you go when you're hurt?"

"You're a guy who likes playing with guns, is that what you're telling me?" the chief deputy wanted to know. "Some kinda poster child for the NRA?"

I suggested a way the chief deputy could entertain himself. He told me that a few days in county jail on a weapons charge would give me plenty of time to show him how it was done. By then the assistant county attorney had arrived. He didn't like me any better than the chief deputy, yet he was more inclined to send me home than send me to jail since I never actually fired said weapon. In the end, it was Chief Hasselback who tipped the scales in my favor. Just the same, the chief deputy confiscated my Beretta. He told me if I didn't like it I could sue to get it back. We both knew that wasn't going to happen, though. Cops don't sue cops, ex or otherwise.

"Why are you busting my chops?" I asked him.

"Because we haven't had a killing in this county in over eight years."

Several hours passed before Nina was transported from the hospital to the Public Safety Building. I had no doubt they had already asked her the same questions they had asked me and compared the answers. They kept us apart just the same.

Calls were made to Lieutenant Pelzer. I don't know if he vouched for me or not. I do know that he thanked the chief deputy for his efforts in identifying Collin Baird and promised cooperation since they both were now looking for the same suspect. The chief deputy seemed pleased by that.

The ACA wanted to know if Baird killed his mother by accident or on purpose. Chief Hasselback wondered what difference it made. The ACA said it was the difference between a second-degree murder charge and first-degree manslaughter. The Chief thought it was a straight-up accident.

"He was shooting at McKenzie, and Mrs. Baird stepped in the way," she said.

I wasn't so sure.

"In just a few minutes she gave us a lot of

information that Baird didn't want us to have," I said. "Who knows what she might have given us had she lived?"

"Do you actually believe he murdered his own mother?" Hasselback asked.

"He wouldn't be the first."

The chief deputy suggested I was just saying that because I didn't want to take responsibility for what happened. He wasn't entirely wrong, although, damn, how was this my fault?

Eventually Nina and I were reunited. We were told we could return to our hotel. The chief deputy said he wanted us to stay in town because he might have more questions. I told him that I was driving home to Minnesota the first thing in the morning. The chief deputy said, in that case, I could spend the night in lockup. I told him if that happened I would lawyer up and then he knew what he could do with his questions. Once again Chief Hasselback came between me and a bad outcome. I thanked her when the three of us were in the parking lot.

"Are you always this hard to get along with?" she asked me.

"I thought Collin Baird was just another one of Jax Abana's victims like all the others," I told her. "It hadn't occurred to me that he might be involved somehow in what was happening until I saw the photograph. If it had . . ."

"If it had, Mrs. Baird might still be alive."

"Something like that."

"It really isn't your fault."

"Feels like it, though."

"Good-bye, McKenzie."

I offered to shake her hand. She pulled it back. She had washed—several times—yet there were still bloodstains beneath her fingernails. I took both of her hands in mine just the same and gave them a squeeze.

"Take care, Chief."

"You, too." And then, "Ms. Truhler? You did real good."

Nina was standing on the passenger side of the Lexus.

"All I did was stay out of the way," she said.

"Without a whimper or a curse," Hasselback said. "You did good."

A few minutes later, we were in the parking lot of the DeSoto House. Night had fallen, and most of the shops up and down Main Street were closed—Monday night in downtown Galena. There were plenty of streetlamps, though, and the light they cast reflected off the pale pink bandage covering Nina's stitches.

"Does it hurt?" I asked.

"Yes, it hurts. So does childbirth and stepping on a Lego with your bare foot."

"We'll get you some ice."

"Get me a drink."

"That, too."

"The emergency room doctor was very kind. Very careful with the stitches. She told me when she was done that if anyone could see the scar without a magnifying glass she'd go back to medical school."

"That's good. How do you feel?"

"Tired. Drained. How do you feel?"

"Okay." What else was I going to say? That even while carrying the burden of what happened at Mrs. Baird's house I felt elated, I felt jazzed? A psychologist I dated once accused me of being an adrenaline junky. That wasn't true—I didn't jump out of planes or hang from mountain ledges by my fingertips. Yet Nina wasn't too far wrong when she said, "You're an adventurer. You do what you do for fun . . ." I just didn't know how to admit to it without sounding like a jerk.

We completed the short walk to the front door of the hotel. I held it open, and Nina stepped inside the brightly lit lobby. She had been wearing the bloodstained shirt and skirt most of the day without complaint, yet the expression on the faces of the clerk and the young couple standing in front of his desk brought home how disheveled she appeared. She turned to me.

"I look like crap," she said.

It was because of the turning that she saw them first—a man and a woman—both in suits. He wore a tie; she didn't.

They rose up behind us from chairs flanking each side of the doorway.

"McKenzie," the man said.

He reached into his jacket pocket.

"McKenzie," Nina shouted.

She slipped around me and kicked him swiftly in the groin with the point of her shoe.

He cupped his genitals with both hands and fell to his knees as if he had been downed by a surface-to-air missile. The words he cried were not fit for small children.

The woman stepped backward and went into a defensive stance.

Nina pivoted to face her.

The woman dipped her hand into the open bag that hung from her shoulder.

Nina took a step forward, fists clenched.

I jumped between them and waved my hands like a referee stopping a heavyweight bout.

"Wait, wait, wait," I chanted. I spun toward the woman and pointed at her bag. "Don't. Don't do it. Please don't. It's not necessary."

She brought her hand out of her bag. It was empty.

Nina took another step forward. I caught her by the shoulders and held her.

"Nina, it's okay," I said. "It's all right. Everything is all right."

"They were attacking us," she said.

"No, they weren't."

"But, McKenzie—"

"Sweetie, we're in a well-lit hotel lobby surrounded by witnesses and security cameras."

Nina cocked her head so she could get a good look at the trio standing at the registration desk. If they had been disconcerted by Nina's bloody clothes, their expressions now suggested they were all stunned to the point of paralysis.

"It's okay," I told them. I continued to hold Nina by her shoulders. "No problems here."

"Speak for yourself," the man muttered from his knees.

The young man at the desk began to move— slowly—as if he were coming out of a trance.

"It's all right," I said.

He drifted to his computer and began working the keyboard as if performing a familiar task would somehow return everything to normal. The young couple turned to watch him. A moment later he looked up and smiled. They smiled back.

The man remained on his knees. I offered a hand to help him up, only he waved it away.

"I'm fine just where I am for now," he said.

"Oh, get up, you big baby," the woman said.

"Who are you?" I asked.

He reached into his pocket. I heard Nina take a deep breath behind me. He removed a thin leather wallet, opened it, and held it up for me to see. It contained a government-issued identification card.

"Special Agent Matthew Cooper, Department of Justice," he said.

"Oh, no," Nina whispered to me. "What did I do?"

"You assaulted a federal officer," I told her. I started to laugh, which she didn't appreciate at all.

"Am I in trouble?" Nina asked.

Cooper rose slowly to his feet.

"I didn't see anything if you didn't see anything," he said.

"Don't worry about it," the woman said. "He'd be too embarrassed to write it up, how a woman half his size kicked his ass."

"That's not what she kicked," Cooper said. He gestured with his thumb. "My partner."

Nina turned toward her. I thought she might offer to shake hands, but she didn't.

"Special Agent Zo' Marin," the woman said.

"That's Greek," Nina said.

"So it is."

"Means 'life of the sea.' "

"So it does."

"I'm tired."

Nina moved to the winding staircase and started to climb it. The rest of us followed.

The moment Nina entered the hotel suite, she tossed her bag on the bed, kicked off her shoes, and pulled her shirt out of her skirt. She moved to the bureau where she kept her Sangua Della Pantera. She grabbed the wine bottle by the neck, scooped up a corkscrew, and padded toward the bathroom.

"I'm going to take a bath," she said.

She stepped inside the bathroom and closed the door behind her. I went to the door and rapped gently with a knuckle.

"Are you okay, sweetie?" I asked.

"Leave me alone."

I stepped away from the door.

"Trouble in paradise?" Marin asked.

"She's had a long day."

"Yeah, that's what we heard," Cooper said. "Like to talk to you about that, if we might."

I directed them to the sitting area. The agents took the love seat, and I sat in the chair opposite them. The gas fireplace was between us. I thought about turning it on, yet decided not to.

"All I can offer you is root beer," I said.

"Root beer?" asked Cooper.

"I have forty-eight bottles."

"Oh God, not another one," Marin said.

"You discovered the Root Beer Revelry, too?" Cooper said. "I love that place. When this is over I'm going to have them ship a bottle of every variety they have to our field office in Chicago."

"In the meantime . . . ," Marin said. "Mr. McKenzie, what do you know about Collin Baird?"

"Almost nothing. What do you know about him?"

"We know he shot his mother today," Cooper said. "Some say he was trying to shoot you."

"That's what some say. Look, guys, I'm not trying to play with you. I know very little about Baird. I came here trying to get a handle on someone else—"

"David Maurell," Marin said.

"The fact that Baird was here came as a great surprise to me," I added.

"Fine," Cooper said. "Let's talk about David Maurell."

"Let's." I settled back against the chair. "You first."

The two agents glanced at each other. Marin grinned.

"He's just like you," she said. "Goddamned cowboy. All right. The first thing you should know, McKenzie, is that Coop and I are in the Investigations Division. We've been assigned to the Office of the Special Inspector General for Iraq Reconstruction—"

Cooper interrupted to say, "The Office of the Special Inspector General is an independent entity working out of the Department of Justice whose mission is to detect and deter waste, fraud, abuse, and misconduct in DOJ programs and personnel."

"Do you mind?" Marin asked.

"No, go 'head."

"The amount of fraud perpetrated in Iraq following the war is almost incomprehensible," Marin told me. "It's anywhere between sixty and one hundred billion dollars, depending on who you're listening to."

"That's billion with a *B,*" Cooper said.

"Half this money came from Iraq, its cash and oil reserves," Marin said. "The rest came from Uncle Sam. The IG for Iraq Reconstruction was put in place to get a handle on it. So far we're talking over two hundred prosecutions of one type or another. Which isn't to say that a lot of people are going to jail. Most contractors are merely being bumped off the approved list of vendors, you know?"

"Which brings us to Maurell," Cooper said.

"Which brings us to Collin Baird," Marin said. "Baird was listed as the president and CEO of a company based in Laredo, Texas, called CB Enterprises, Inc. This company seemed to be legitimate. Incorporation papers proved it was three years old by the time it opened an office in Baghdad. What's more, CBE had enough money and connections to—how shall I say this?—*impress* the army into awarding it an eighty-million-dollar contract under its Logistics Civil Augmentation Program. The contract required CBE to replace the tents of our soldiers with housing trailers within a calendar year. To perform this task, CBE hired a Kuwaiti-based company as a subcontractor. The subcontract required the Kuwaitis to supply two thousand, two hundred and fifty-two trailers to the army's Camp Anaconda. However, they were able to supply only half that many by the deadline.

"The army asked, where's the rest of our trailers? The Kuwaitis put them off for a few days by claiming that the delay in delivery was caused by the army's failure to have military escorts available for the trucking convoys that carried the trailers. Eventually the army said screw it, and sent a detachment to pick them up. Only there were no more trailers. There had never been as many trailers as CBE had promised, and CBE and the Kuwaitis knew it going in. The army went to have a talk with Baird. Unfortunately, he had disappeared at approximately the same time as the army sent its detachment to Kuwait, disappeared along with forty-eight-point-seven million dollars."

"Wow," I said.

"McKenzie, he's not even in the Top Twenty of the crooks who ripped us off in Iraq," Cooper said. "It was a massive clusterfuck."

"In any case, the DOJ has been looking for him ever since," Marin said. "No luck. We've been unable to find Baird. More to the point, we've been unable to find the money. We still can't figure out how he or the money got out of Iraq.

Which isn't to say that Baird is some kind of criminal mastermind. There was so much chaos over there . . ."

"But then we got a break," Cooper said.

"Yes," Marin agreed. "We got a break. McKenzie, have you ever heard of the Financial Crimes Enforcement Network?"

"No," I said.

"FinCEN operates out of the U.S. Treasury Department. It's their job to generate data on suspicious financial transactions, including cash deposits of ten thousand dollars or more, and pass it on to the appropriate law enforcement agencies. It's how we detect money laundering and such."

"I knew somebody did that."

"Now you know who. It turned out that a lieutenant colonel in the Army National Guard out of Alabama deposited forty thousand dollars in cash into his checking account the day after he returned from Iraq. He had carried it home in a duffel bag. It was the same lieutenant colonel who was supposed to have been monitoring the contract with CB Enterprises. He turned a blind eye to what CBE was doing in exchange for the cash and an all-expense-paid vacation to Thailand. He confessed to all this about five minutes after our guys knocked on his door. He is now an ex–lieutenant colonel doing time in Talladega on fraud charges."

"He was the one who put us onto David Maurell," Cooper said. "The colonel said Maurell was introduced to him as the company's CFO, yet it was clear to him that he ran the show, that Baird was just a figurehead. The colonel thought it was arranged that way because Maurell was of Cuban descent and the U.S. Army preferred to work with true-blue white Anglo-Saxon Protestant Americans. Anyway, according to the colonel, Maurell disappeared before Baird did—along with all of Uncle's Sam's money. Baird had no idea where Maurell had gone. So when he ran, he ran alone."

"It was Maurell who engineered everything," Marin said. "Unfortunately, the DOJ knows nothing about him. The man's a ghost. No valid passport, no Social Security number—we were able to trace him only as far back as Laredo. That's where his trail evaporated. We've been hoping to grab Baird so he could fill in the blanks.

"Two and a half years, McKenzie," Marin added. "Over two and a half years the DOJ has been working this case one way or another and we've been getting nowhere—until we heard that you were coming down to Galena."

"Wait, wait, wait," I said. "You have a tap on Chief Hasselback's phone?"

"Of course not," Cooper said. "What do you take us for?"

"We have a tap on Mrs. Baird's phone," Marin

said. "We're watching everyone who had ever known Baird; you can't possibly be surprised by that."

"No, I guess I'm not."

"When the chief called Mrs. Baird to tell her that you were coming down to talk about Maurell and her son's disappearance, we felt we should listen, too. We didn't know Baird was in Galena, either. We figure he must have slipped into town sometime Saturday night after the chief called his mother."

"Or Sunday," Cooper said. "While we were watching you."

So it wasn't just your imagination, my inner voice suggested. *You really were being followed.*

"Now it's your turn," Cooper told me.

I started with Jax Abana and the Nine-Thirty-Seven Mexican Mafia, filling in the blanks as I went.

"The two of them never did run to Mexico," I said. "Baird must have crossed the border just to see what was what. The fact the Laredo PD found his car—if they had gone into the shopping mall, they might have found him, too. Meanwhile, Maurell used the money he stole from the Nine-Thirty-Seven as seed to create his fake corporation, and after a few years he found a way to sneak into Iraq to make his play."

"Where is he now?" Marin asked.

"Somewhere in Minnesota, I'm guessing,

living under the name Juan Carlos Navarre."

"Why would he go back to Minnesota?" Marin asked.

"There's a girl named Riley Brodin. She was in the class he audited at Macalester College seven years ago. He went back to Minnesota for her."

"That's crazy," Cooper said.

"I've known men who have done crazier things for a woman," Marin said.

"Anyway, Navarre or Maurell or whoever he is is still in Minnesota. I know it." I pointed at Cooper. "So is Collin Baird. He wants his share of the loot. He wants his revenge, too, and he'll do anything to get them."

"Okay," said Marin. "We're going to Minnesota. We're going tonight. Give me the name of your contact."

"Lieutenant Pelzer, Hennepin County Sheriff's Department."

"This isn't just about Maurell and Baird, McKenzie. It's also about the money. We want it back. I don't suppose you know where it is."

"Try the Lake Minnetonka Community Bank," I said.

Shortly after the agents left, I went to the closed bathroom door and knocked.

"Are they gone?" Nina asked.

"Yes. Can I come in?"

"No."

"Okay."

I slid to the floor and sat with my back against the door frame.

"What are you doing?" she asked.

"Just sitting here feeling sorry that I involved you in all of this."

"It's what I wanted, isn't it?"

"No, what you wanted was the fun and games, and I had hoped to give them to you. What happened with Mrs. Baird, that should never have happened."

I heard the splashing of water, but no words. Finally Nina asked, "What did the Department of Justice want?"

"Information. Turns out that Jax Abana alias David Maurell alias Juan Carlos Navarre scammed the army out of forty-nine million bucks in Iraq a couple of years ago."

"You're kidding."

"Now we know where he got his money."

My cell phone started playing "Summertime."

"Just a sec," I said and answered it.

"McKenzie," Greg Schroeder said, "where are you?"

"Galena, Illinois."

"Why?"

"What do you want, Greg?"

"Old man Muehlenhaus is going crazy. So crazy that he said to call you."

"What's happened?"

"Riley Brodin is missing."

"Define missing."

"I lost her, or rather I should say she lost me."

"Butterfingers."

"She received a phone call. Said it was from her BFF Mary Pat Mulally. Next time I looked, she was gone."

"Have you spoken to Mulally?"

"She says she hasn't heard from Riley for two days."

"Navarre," I said. "He finally contacted her."

"That's my guess."

"Did the old man call the county sheriff?"

"To tell him what? That his sound-of-mind twenty-five-year-old granddaughter has voluntarily run off with the multimillionaire Spanish entrepreneur she's been sleeping with?"

"Greg, this is way more complicated than either of us thought."

I gave him the Reader's Digest Condensed Books version of my Monday so far.

"Christ," he said. "I gotta go."

"Call Lieutenant Pelzer," I said.

"Yeah, yeah, yeah . . ."

After he hung up, Nina called to me. "What's going on?"

"Riley Brodin is missing. They think she ran off with Navarre."

I heard the water splash as Nina got out of the tub. A moment later she opened the door. She had pulled on a white cotton shift without bothering to dry off. It clung to her body and in some areas seemed almost transparent, revealing to me all the things it was meant to conceal.

"We have to go home," she said.

"It's two hundred and eighty miles. Even if we take Highway 52 instead of 61, it's still a five-hour trip."

"We can take turns driving."

"No. It's too late. You lost a lot of blood and you're tired. So am I. Tomorrow morning will be better."

Nina slid to the floor next to me, her back against the opposite doorjamb. I changed positions so I could reach out and stroke her calf beneath the hem of her shift.

"I'm worried," she said.

"Me, too."

"You have a way of dealing with it, though—emotionally, I mean. You don't panic. You don't waste time or energy."

"I practice a lot when I'm alone."

"That's why you left me this morning. After Baird pistol-whipped me. I'm sitting on the floor, bleeding all over the place. You took one look and left me. Didn't even hesitate. You were off to get Baird."

I removed my hand from her leg.

"I knew you were going to be all right," I said. "I'm sorry if it seemed as if I didn't care."

"Put your hand back."

I did.

"I'm not complaining, McKenzie. I'm just saying, I couldn't have done that. I see everything as a whole and how it affects me personally. You break it down into component parts and never let any of it bother you. That's why you can do this and I can't."

"I don't know, sweetie. The way you took on Special Agent Matthew Cooper of the U.S. Department of Justice . . ."

"I was tired and I was angry and I was scared and—"

"I will remember it always with great pleasure."

"Stop it."

"Wait until I tell Bobby," I said. "Harry and Chopper and all the other guys, too."

"They'll think I'm a jerk."

"No, honey, they think I'm a jerk. They adore you. My friends have always liked you more than they've liked me. It's something I've learned to live with."

"You're joking."

"I'm really not. Come on, now. Get up. Take this off."

"I need to tell you, McKenzie, if you're thinking what I think you're thinking . . ."

"I'm thinking we need to dry you off and wrap you in a blanket and sit in front of the fire and cuddle."

"Cuddle? Oh my God, what's happening?"

"Do you have any wine left?"

"Yes, but I dropped the bottle in the tub. It's half bathwater."

"That's okay. I have plenty of root beer."

"The perfect end to a perfect day."

Seventeen ....

Connie Evingson was my favorite jazz diva after Ella, Sarah, Billie, Etta, and maybe Shirley, and she was singing "The Girl from Ipanema" from the CD player as the Lexus crossed into Minnesota. So many lesser talents have covered the song over the decades that it has been transformed into the blandest of elevator music clichés. Yet she somehow managed to infuse it with the same sensuality, melancholy, and longing that could be heard in the original 1964 recording by Antônio Carlos Jobim, Astrud Gilberto, and Stan Getz. Which is why I was miffed when my cell phone interrupted the song.

I answered it the way I always do. "McKenzie."

"McKenzie," Victoria said in reply.

"Hey, sweetie."

Nina mouthed, "Who is it?" and I told her.

"Put it on speakerphone."

I did, raising my voice so I could be easily heard over the traffic. "What's going on, Vic?"

"I found him," she said.

"Found who?"

"Juan Carlos Navarre, who do you think?"

"What do you mean, you found him?"

Nina leaned forward as she listened to the conversation.

"Remember," Victoria said, "you told me to see if I could find out who shot up the kidnappers that grabbed whoever it was that Felipe Navarre paid ransom for that one time?"

"Vaguely," I said.

"They were killed in ambush by the Guardia Civil. It's Spain's military-style police force, okay?"

"Okay."

"While looking for that, though, I found something else. What do they call that? There's a word . . ."

"Serendipity," Nina said.

"Oh, hi, Nina."

"Hi. How's your parents?"

"Better, now that Mom's cutting me some slack."

"Victoria," I said.

"Oh, yeah. Serendipitously, I found an article printed seven years ago in *El Mundo*, *El Mundo del Siglo Veintiuno*—The World of the Twenty-first Century. Anyway, these guys are like *Sixty Minutes*; they have a reputation for investigative reporting. One of their more frequent targets is the Guardia Civil. They busted the commander for embezzling, among other things.

"About nine years ago, *El Mundo* printed a story that accused members of the Guardia Civil of acting as mercenaries in the employ of Felipe Navarre, who, it claimed, had paid them a reward for hunting down and killing the ETA guys that supposedly kidnapped his son—Juan Carlos Navarre."

"You're kidding."

"No, no, no—now listen. According to *El Mundo*, it was all one big giant hoax. The ETA had nothing to do with the kidnapping. Instead, the paper claimed that Juan Carlos had staged the kidnapping to rip off the old man, and the old man used the Guardia Civil to kill the co-conspirators."

"You're kidding," I repeated.

"I'm really not."

"What happened to Juan Carlos?"

Nina was listening so intently that she moved across the seat, straining against her shoulder harness.

"He disappeared," Victoria said. "The paper said that Felipe disowned Juan Carlos when he learned the truth about the kidnapping. Cut him off, cut him out—never spoke about him after that; wouldn't even acknowledge that he had a son. There was speculation—at least a columnist at *El Mundo* speculated—that Felipe might have had his son killed, too. I don't believe it, though."

"Why not?"

"The ransom money was never recovered. I think Juan Carlos took the cash and ran like hell and Felipe let him. Just let him go."

"How much was the ransom?"

"Ten million euros."

"How much is that in real money?"

"I looked it up—just over thirteen million dollars. McKenzie, what if he came to America?"

"Victoria—please tell me that you have a photograph."

"I'm sorry, I don't."

"Find one."

"You already owe me one hundred dollars."

"Find a photograph and I'll pay your college tuition."

"Whoa, Harvard, here I come."

Nina leaned back in her seat after Victoria hung up. She smiled brightly.

"There might be a happy ending after all," she said.

"What are you talking about?"

"For Riley and Juan Carlos."

"No."

"Why not? If he really is Juan Carlos . . ."

"He's not."

"If he really is . . ."

"Not a chance. Nina, the man who's stalking Riley—"

"Stalking?"

"He rented the house across the bay so he could stare at the purple flag at the end of her dock through a telescope, for God's sake. He's not Juan Carlos Navarre, the real Juan Carlos Navarre. He can't be. He has to be Jax Abana. I showed his photograph to his mother, to his sister, to Collin Baird's mother, to two of his former lovers, to Cesar Nunez, to the police detective who worked the case—they all identified him. Jax Abana."

"They identified a man they hadn't seen in seven, eight years from an image on a cell phone." Nina pointed her finger at me. "You told them what to expect before they actually saw the picture."

"That's not entirely true."

"Confirmation bias, I think they call it—you see what you expect to see, what you want to see. You also told me that what'sisname, the detective, Ihns—he said that Abana looked different back then. He had a mustache."

"So what?"

"He doesn't now. McKenzie, you're the one who's told me many times that eyewitness testimony is notoriously unreliable."

"His mother would know who he is, his sister would know, don't you think?"

"Maybe Navarre looks just like Abana. Maybe they're doppelgängers."

"Impossible."

Nina cleared her throat and gave her voice a professorial tone. "When you have eliminated the impossible, whatever remains, however improbable, must be the truth," she said.

"You're quoting Sherlock Holmes now? Nina, there is no doubt in my mind that Jax Abana alias David Maurell is pretending to be Juan Carlos Navarre. I believed it when I was sure there was no such person. Now that I know there is, I believe it even more. The only question is— what happened to the real Juan Carlos?"

"Confirmation bias."

"Stop it."

"There's only one way to settle the argument."

"Find the sonuvabitch, I get it."

We were on Highway 52 in Inver Grove Heights and fast approaching St. Paul when my cell phone started playing "Summertime" again.

"Don't you think it's time you found a new ringtone?" Nina asked.

I pulled the phone from my pocket and handed it to her. "Answer that for me."

She did.

"Bebe's Peanut Shop, Bebe speaking," she said.

Serves you right, my inner voice told me.

I'm guessing the caller must have apologized for dialing the wrong number, because Nina quickly said, "Not necessarily," and added, "Who's calling, please?" When she had an answer, she told me, "Lieutenant Pelzer?"

"Put it on speakerphone," I said. After she did, I raised my voice again. "LT?"

"Bebe's Peanut Shop?"

"Little something I have on the side. What can I do for you?"

"There are a couple of things I want to talk about. Meet me at the Casa del Lago."

"Any particular reason you want me at the restaurant?"

"That's where we found the *Soñadora* this morning."

"It might take me ninety minutes to get there from where I am."

"Sooner would be better."

"I'm on my way."

Nina deactivated my smartphone.

"The entrance ramp to Interstate 494 is just up a ways," she told me. "This time of day, traffic will be light. We can be in Lake Minnetonka in forty-five minutes."

"I'm taking you home first."

"Oh, c'mon, McKenzie."

"How's your temple? A little sore? A little puffy? I must say, that's a becoming shade of purple. Really sets off the stitches."

"Don't be like that."

"Besides, I like Pelzer. He's been very good to me so far. I don't want you beating him up."

Nina folded her arms across her chest, and for a moment she looked just like her daughter when Erica was young—and she was pouting.

"I promise to call and tell you everything that happens," I said.

"It'll be quicker if you take me to the club. You can borrow my car if you want."

"Thank you."

"You break it, you buy it."

The hull of the *Soñadora* was white with a thin flaming-red racing stripe running from the bow to the stern. Its cockpit upholstery and carpet were white, and so was the sundeck pad. Inside, a white 32-inch LED TV, two-burner stove, micro-wave oven, refrigerator, and stereo system were surrounded by white handcrafted cabinetry, white leather upholstery, and birch floors. Even the innerspring mattress inside the private stateroom was hidden beneath crisp white covers. It was so clean it looked as if it had just come from the showroom.

"I don't suppose you found anything when you searched it," I said.

Lieutenant Pelzer's brow knitted as if he were considering the many different ways he could respond to the question and finally said, "No signs of life, if that's what you mean."

"The wastebaskets weren't just empty," Special Agent Matthew Cooper said, "they were polished."

We stood watching as the boat strained gently against the springlines that secured it to the pier that accommodated customers of the Casa del Lago. Three thoughts came to mind—first, this is a damn expensive toy, and second, I should get one. The thought I gave voice to, however, was "Who reported it?"

"Ms. Mulally," Pelzer said. "She said it was here when she arrived this morning to let the workers in. She seems upset."

"Why?"

"She won't tell me. Maybe she'll tell you."

"I'll talk to her."

Pelzer had been carrying a small package that he switched from one hand to the other. I didn't ask what was inside.

"While you're at it, old man Muehlenhaus won't answer my questions, either, with or without an attorney present," he said.

"I'll try to talk to him, too."

"Good, since that's the only reason you're not sitting in jail right now." He raised and lowered his eyebrows Groucho Marx–style like he wanted to tell me something without actually speaking the words.

"I did thank you for that, right?" I asked.

"I don't remember."

We left the dock and started moving toward the restaurant's patio. We could hear the noise of construction inside the restaurant yet couldn't see what was being built. Special Agent Zo' Marin intercepted us.

"You boys get it figured out yet?" she asked.

"We were hoping you would explain it to us," Cooper said. "Feminine intuition and all that."

She grinned as if she had heard it before.

"I just got off the phone." To prove it, she slipped a smartphone into the pocket of her black jacket. I don't know if she and Cooper intended to dress like Men in Black, yet they did. "A federal judge has agreed to temporarily freeze all of Navarre's assets in the Lake Minnetonka Community Bank under Title Eighteen, Section Nineteen Fifty-seven."

"Section Nineteen Fifty-seven?" I asked.

"It's illegal for anyone to move the proceeds of a specified unlawful activity through a financial institution—or a merchant such as a boat dealership, for that matter—in an amount greater than ten thousand dollars. Navarre could appeal. He would probably win, too. This is a blatant violation of his rights; the man has yet to be formally charged with a crime. To appeal, though, would require that he appear in a federal court of law, and that would give us the chance to prove he's actually David Maurell. In the meantime, FinCEN is backtracking the deposits. So far, we know they came from Banco Central de España in Madrid. Beyond that . . ."

"How much of Navarre's money is in Minnetonka Community?" I asked.

"Thirteen million."

"That's ten million euros."

"So it is."

For a moment I felt a thrill of panic that started below my heart and spread outward.

"Jeezus," I said. "What if we're wrong? What if he really is Juan Carlos Navarre?"

"Then the United States government will apologize profusely."

"Yeah, well, that's your problem," I said. "Right now my big concern is Riley Brodin. If she's with Navarre, then she's in danger."

"What are you talking about?" Pelzer said.

"Didn't Greg Schroeder call you?"

"I don't know him."

"Dammit. Schroeder's a PI who works for Mr. Muehlenhaus. He was supposed to tell you—I don't believe it."

I explained what Schroeder was supposed to tell Pelzer.

"Now I know why Muehlenhaus won't answer my questions," he said. "He thinks he's protecting his granddaughter."

"His granddaughter or the Muehlenhaus legacy?"

"What's that mean?"

"It's complicated. Listen, we need to assume that Baird is still after Navarre and that Navarre is now traveling with Riley."

"Legally," Pelzer said. "They're traveling legally, so you know there's nothing we can do about it."

"I know," I said, and for a moment I felt the frustration of all those people who had asked for help when I was police, only to be told that "nothing could be done," that we couldn't search for someone unless there was clear evidence that a crime had been committed.

"We've sent out e-briefs on Baird," Pelzer said. "But . . ."

"Yeah, I know."

"What?" Cooper asked.

"There's no system set in place that we can use to alert law enforcement statewide, let alone nationally," Pelzer said. "We have a system called the e-brief to spread information, which is just that—e-mail briefings that target specific local and county police in the areas where we think the suspect might be. Any suggestions on where Baird might be?"

"What about the FBI?" I said. "They must have a better system."

Marin chuckled at that.

"We've had an FBI Crime Alert on Baird for thirty-one months now," she said. "We wouldn't even have known for sure he was in the country if not for McKenzie."

There was some communal headshaking.

Pelzer said, "You'd think we could do better."

Cooper said, "You'd think."

Pelzer handed me the package.

"This is yours, by the way," he said.

I peeked inside. It was my SIG Sauer. I left it in the bag.

"Thank you," I said.

"You're welcome."

"Listen, I want you all to know that I appreciate it very much that you guys have allowed me to stay involved in this."

"Why not?" Marin said. "So far you've done most of the work."

"Speaking of which . . ." Pelzer threw a thumb at the restaurant.

I locked the bag inside Nina's Lexus before I went inside.

Mary Pat Mulally was drinking. I found her sitting alone on a stool at her own bar, a glass and a half-filled bottle of Grey Goose vodka in front of her. I wondered if the bottle had been half full when she started, but the glassy look I saw in her eyes when I sat next to her told me that it hadn't.

"Hey," I said.

Mary Pat's response was to stand on the rung of the stool, lean over the bar, grab a glass, place it in front of me, and slide the Grey Goose in my direction. I caught the bottle and poured a shot just to be polite.

"I promised the deputies I would call if Navarre showed up, and he must have because there's his goddamn boat," she said. "The *Soña*-fucking-*dora*."

"No sign of Riley?"

"Screw Riley. She's where she wants to be."

"Where's that?"

"With Navarre, where do you think?"

Mary Pat drained her glass of vodka and poured some more. At the rate she was going, I knew she wouldn't last much longer, and I wanted to speak to her while she was still coherent. I took the bottle, poured a little more vodka into my glass, and set the bottle where she'd have to reach across me to get to it. If she noticed, she didn't let on.

"You gave me the impression that Riley was getting ready to kick Navarre to the curb," I reminded her.

Mary Pat snorted at the remark.

"That's the impression she gave me," she said. "Riley's such a . . ."

"Such a what?"

"Confused woman. One day she wants one thing. The next she wants something else. She can be so smart, so mature, so understanding of the world and her place in it. Then she behaves like an eight-year-old."

"The girl can be infuriating."

"Don't insult her," Mary Pat said. "Who are you to insult her? She's not a girl. She's a woman."

The rebuke should have told me something, yet it didn't.

"I'm so frightened," Mary Pat added. "Riley can take care of herself better than most people except—except when she can't."

"Where would Riley go if she was in trouble?"

"She used to come to me. I've called her, McKenzie—sent texts. She won't pick them up. What the hell do you want?"

I didn't see Maria approach until Mary Pat called her out.

"The carpenter wants to know—" the young woman began.

"Can't you make one goddamn decision on your own? What do I pay you for?" Mary Pat raised her hands as if she were surrendering. "You know what? Who gives a damn?" She slid off the stool, reached past me to grab the Grey Goose by the neck, and stumbled toward her office.

"What's wrong with her?" I asked.

"You really have no idea, do you?" Maria said.

"If I knew . . ."

"She's in love with Riley."

"Oh."

How the hell did you miss that? my inner voice wanted to know.

"Oh? Is that all you have to say, McKenzie? For a minute there I actually thought you were smart."

"I can't imagine what gave you that impression."

"Me, neither."

I took a pull of the vodka, hoping it would restore my powers of observation. I don't think it did. Maria sat next to me.

"Will you do me a favor?" I asked the young woman. "Will you keep an eye on Mary Pat for me?"

"I'd do that anyway."

"Let me know if she hears from Riley?"

"Why not? McKenzie—thank you for not telling her about the fire; for not telling Mary Pat about Arnaldo and the rest of them."

"Don't worry about it."

"Everything is all messed up. Cesar is furious with Arnaldo about the T-shirts and trying to bring back the Nine-Thirty-Seven. He says if he was here, he'd beat Arnaldo's ass. At the same time, he despises Jax Abana and wants to see him dead. I don't know what's going to happen. Nothing good, probably."

"Whatever happens, you need to stay out of it."

"That's what Cesar said."

Good for him, my inner voice said.

"Does Arnaldo know where Navarre is?" I asked aloud.

Maria shook her head slowly.

"He's waiting for you to tell him," she said.

I found Lieutenant Pelzer leaning against his car when I left the restaurant. Greg Schroeder was arguing with him, waving his hands as he spoke. Pelzer didn't look too happy about it. In fact, he looked like he was *this*close to expressing his displeasure when he saw me crossing the parking lot.

"So you two have finally met," I said. "Are you besties now? Going to have matching bracelets made up?"

"No," Pelzer replied in a voice that made me believe that he didn't appreciate the joke. "Not even close. Did you get anything?"

I shook my head.

"Keep in touch," he said. He made to open his car door. Schroeder stopped him.

"Wait a sec, LT," the detective said.

Pelzer pointed at him yet looked at me. "Is this shamus a pal of yours?" he asked.

"I never saw him before in my life," I said.

"Then you won't mind if I jail his ass for obstruction if he opens his mouth one more time."

"Not even a little bit."

"Lieutenant." Schroeder's voice was low and calm. "Look at it from my point of view."

"No," Pelzer said. "You look at it from my point of view, because that's the one that matters."

With that, the lieutenant slid into his car, started it up, and drove off.

"What a hard-ass," Schroeder said.

"Yeah, I'm liking him more and more, too. So what did you do, Greg? Draw Muehlenhaus's name and point it at him like a gun?"

"Something like that."

"You could always go over his head—Major Kampa runs Hennepin County's Investigative Division."

Schroeder stared at me for a moment, maybe wondering if I was joking, and then began to chuckle. "That could only be good for me," he said. "I know Kampa and he is so much more reasonable." He laughed again.

"What did you want to know that Pelzer wouldn't tell you?" I asked.

"Everything."

"What did you offer Pelzer in return?"

"Nothing."

"Yet you two can't get along. I just don't understand it."

"McKenzie . . ."

"Cops work on a strict quid pro quo basis. You know that even better than I do. If you want this, you have to give 'em that and plenty of it."

"I'm just following instructions."

"I bet."

"What can you tell me?"

"What do I get in exchange?"

"My undying gratitude."

"Greg, everything is about the same as it was yesterday when we spoke on the phone."

"Does Pelzer know that Riley is probably traveling with Navarre?"

"Yes."

"Did you tell him?"

"I did."

"Do me a favor—explain that to Mr. Muehlenhaus."

"Why don't you?"

"I'd rather you tell him."

"All right, I will."

"Come with me—in my car."

"Excuse me?"

"Probably I should tell you—the old man's orders were to bring you to the Pointe. Forcibly, if necessary."

"I'll meet you there."

Schroeder paused a moment before he said, "You don't think I can bring you—forcibly?"

"No, I don't. Even if you could, though, the price would be too high."

"How high?"

"No more free drinks at Rickie's."

"That would be a tragedy."

"I think so, too."

I wanted to follow Schroeder, but he obviously wanted to follow me, so we sat in the parking lot of the Casa del Lago staring at each other through the windshields of our vehicles for about five minutes before he finally flipped me the bird and drove off. I gave him a healthy head start.

Eventually I found myself on Shadywood Road going north through the tiny town of Navarre and wondering, not for the first time, if it had just been a coincidence that Juan Carlos chose that name. I hung a right at the intersection of Shadywood and North Shore Drive and drove east across the bridge. It was another place on the lake where the road came between the homes and their docks. It's also where Arnaldo and the Nine-Thirty-Seven wannabees made their move.

I admit they caught me by surprise. The black Cadillac came up hard on my rear bumper and blew its horn before I knew it was there. I kept driving and the horn kept blowing—I was startled, yet not particularly afraid. I just wanted a moment to think it through before I did anything rash.

I took my foot off the accelerator and let the Lexus slow on its own. The Caddy pulled around me. I could see Arnaldo's face through the passenger window. He didn't look happy. On the other hand, I'd never seen him look happy. He jabbed his finger more or less toward the shoulder of the road as the Caddy sped past.

We weren't terribly far from the house where Juan Carlos Navarre had lived, where Mrs. Rogers had lived, and it occurred to me that Arnaldo had staked it out in case Navarre returned. He wasn't actually following me; he merely saw me driving past and jumped on my tail—he must have recognized Nina's Lexus from when he saw it during our trip to Galena. None of this was important, of course, yet knowing it somehow made me feel better.

When the Caddy slid in front of me and slowed down, I followed its lead and pulled onto the shoulder. On one side of the road was a brown house with huge windows that was built to resemble a Swiss chalet. On the other side was a long wooden dock. A blue and white canvas canopy had been erected at the tip. There was a boat beneath it.

I sat in the Lexus for a moment before deciding it would be rude of me to wait for Arnaldo since he had the broken leg and all. So I left the vehicle—after first checking the load in the SIG Sauer and shoving it between my jeans and the small of my back. I slipped my sports jacket on as I exited the car, walked around the back bumper, and approached the Caddy from the passenger side. The window had been rolled down. I noticed that Arnaldo wasn't wearing his seat belt and the door was unlocked—facts that I kept to myself.

Arnaldo gestured toward the driver. It was the same man who had been driving when they had followed me to Dunn Bros.

"We're getting better," Arnaldo said.

"So you are," I said.

The driver grinned at the compliment.

"To what do I owe the pleasure this time?" I asked.

"You made promises . . ."

"We've had this conversation before, Arnaldo."

"We're having it again. We're gonna keep having it until you do what you said you were going to do. You think you can make promises to the Nine-Thirty-Seven and not keep 'em, McKenzie? Is that what you think?"

"It's not what I think."

"Why didn't you call us, then? Huh? Navarre, whatever Abana calls himself, his boat was docked at the restaurant, wasn't it? When were you gonna tell us about that? Huh? Huh? We hadda find out on our own."

Maria, my inner voice said. *Remember what Cesar told you—don't get involved.*

"I promised to find Navarre, not his boat," I spoke aloud.

"Don't fuck with me, McKenzie. You think you can fuck with me? I will cut off your balls and feed 'em to you."

"Arnaldo, when you say real stupid shit like that you ought to smile so a guy knows you're joking, otherwise bad things could happen," I said, although the man had a legitimate point. It would be dangerous to break my word to the Nine-Thirty-Seven. Arnaldo was as frightening as a summer cold. If Cesar should take offense, though . . .

One problem at a time.

"Where is he?" Arnaldo asked. "Where is Jax

Abana? You said you'd deliver him up. Where the fuck is he?"

"I don't know."

"You don't know? You don't know? It's been three fucking days."

"How long have you been looking for him? Hmm? Back off, Arnaldo."

"You fucking telling me what to do?"

"Arnaldo . . ."

"No one fucking tells me what to do. 'Specially some white-ass motherfucker. I'm tired of waiting. I am fucking tired of you. You know what I'm gonna do? You don't deliver Abana right fucking now, I'm going to pay your woman a visit. Yeah, that's right, Nina Truhler. Think I don't know her name? Think I don't know where she lives? Lives in fucking Mahtomedi. Yeah, I'll go pay her a visit. She'll love a visit from us. Won't she?"

Arnaldo glanced at his driver and hit him playfully on the arm. The driver didn't appear happy. I think he realized that his buddy had gone too far over the line, even if Arnaldo did not.

"Yeah, she would," he added. "Give her some dark meat . . ."

You did warn him, my inner voice said.

I yanked open the Caddy door and grabbed Arnaldo by the throat.

I dragged him from the car and threw him into the ditch between the road and the shoreline.

He hit the ground and rolled down the modest hill, the cast on his leg bouncing off the rocks, dirt, and tuffs of grass.

I slammed the car door shut and pulled the SIG Sauer out from under my sports jacket. I pointed it through the open window at the driver.

"Get out of here," I said.

The driver stared at the gun as if he had never seen one before.

I put a round through the driver's-side window. The safety glass shattered into a thousand tiny shards that flew all around him.

The driver quickly started the Caddy and drove off.

I turned toward Arnaldo. He was trying to stand but was having a tough time managing it with the cast.

I used my shoe to push him back down onto the ground.

He cursed me until I pressed the barrel of the SIG Sauer against his cheek. The muzzle was still hot and burned a small circle into his flesh that I knew would probably disappear in a few days. He whimpered at the pain just the same.

"I'm going to say this slowly in words that you'll understand," I told him. "If you go near Nina I will kill you. I will kill your sister. I will kill your driver and every one of you Nine-Thirty-Seven pukes. I will kill your mother. I will kill your father. When your brother gets out of stir, I'll be standing on Pickett Street waiting, and then I'll kill him, too. You go tell Cesar I said so. Be goddamn sure you tell him *why* I said so. Go 'head, Arnaldo. Make him proud."

I stood over him. Arnaldo looked frightened, yet not nearly frightened enough as far as I was concerned. I fired two rounds, one on each side of his head. He screamed as if the bullets had hit him. Dirt exploded upward, soiling his face and throwing debris into his eyes. He covered his face with his hands and screamed some more.

I returned to the Lexus. I set the SIG on the seat and started the car. My hands were shaking as I drove away.

Greg Schroeder was waiting in his car at the mouth of the long narrow road that led to Mr. Muehlenhaus's estate. He started it up and fell in behind the Lexus when I drove past, making it look as if he had been escorting me all along. We drove to the end of the driveway. There was an enormous amount of room, yet Schroeder insisted on parking at an angle on my rear bumper so that it would be difficult for me to drive away without him first moving his vehicle. He left his car in a hurry and approached mine. I watched him in the mirror. By then the jitters from my confrontation with Arnaldo had mostly subsided, and I was calm enough to be amused by his behavior.

"Vanity of vanities, all is vanity," I said, quoting Rembrandt. Or was it King Solomon?

He opened my door and gestured for me to get out.

"Really, Greg?" I said.

"This is where I remind you that I saved your life. Twice. C'mon, play along."

I let him pull me out of the Lexus by my arm and give me a shove toward the colossal house. Muehlenhaus was standing between the white columns that held up his porch. He descended the steps as we approached, the massa greeting his field hands. We stopped when we reached him. Schroeder released my arm and took a step backward.

"Here he is, Mr. Muehlenhaus," Schroeder said.

"Thank you, Gregory," Muehlenhaus said.

I found it all sort of entertaining. I turned my head and looked at Schroeder to see how he was taking it. That's why I didn't notice Muehlenhaus raise his hand.

He slapped me.

It wasn't a particularly hard slap. I had been hit harder by teammates who were congratulating me for scoring a goal in a hockey game, an admittedly uncommon occurrence—and I was reminded that despite his robust health, Muehlenhaus was an eighty-something-year-old man. Yet none of that registered until later. What flashed in my brain at the moment of impact like a lightning strike was Arnaldo Nunez and his threats against Nina.

I slapped him back.

I regretted it immediately. I was angry with Arnaldo, not him. Only there was no way to take it back.

Muehlenhaus reeled at the blow and brought his hand up to cover his mouth.

Schroeder dashed past me and grabbed the old man by the shoulders to keep him from falling.

"He hit me," Muehlenhaus said.

"I saw that," Schroeder replied.

"Do something."

"What do you want me to do, Mr. Muehlen-haus? Do you want me to shoot him?"

The way that Muehlenhaus's eyes grew wide, I realized that was exactly what he wanted done.

"If you want me to shoot McKenzie for not taking your bitch-slap like some kind of inden-tured servant, I will. That's what you would have done, right, Mr. Muehlenhaus? You would have just stood there and taken it." Muehlenhaus's eyes narrowed slightly. "Just say the word. You're my employer and my friend. If you want me to kill him, I will."

"No," Muehlenhaus said. He pushed Schroeder away and stood on his own two feet. He glowered at me. "There are other ways to deal with some-one like McKenzie."

"No, there really aren't," Schroeder said. "There's nothing that he needs . . ."

Except Nina, my inner voice said.

"Nothing you can take from him that he can't do without. We've already talked about this."

You did?

"We agreed that's what made him useful to you," Schroeder added. "So let's decide right now what to do about this. Do you want me to kill him?"

"No," Muehlenhaus said.

"Hire a couple of guys to beat on him?"

"No."

"Well, then . . ."

Muehlenhaus muttered the words under his breath, yet I heard them just the same—"Fucking McKenzie."

"What exactly do you want from me, Mr. Muehlenhaus?" I asked. "You didn't really bring me here to slap me around, did you?"

"I told you to stay out of my family's business."

"You didn't really believe I would, did you?"

"Riley has run away."

"I had nothing to do with that."

"I want my granddaughter back safe and sound."

"I agree with the safe and sound part, but—"

"But what?"

"She did leave with Navarre voluntarily."

Muehlenhaus stepped in close, and for a moment I thought he might take another poke at me. I clasped my hands behind my back so he could have a clean shot.

"Navarre is a criminal," he told me. The way he said it, Muehlenhaus could have substituted the most vicious personal slur and he would have meant the same thing. "Riley does not have enough pertinent information to make a sound judgment about the man."

That was probably true, I told myself.

"It is up to us to decide what's best for her," Muehlenhaus added.

I wasn't entirely sure about that. Out loud I said, "For what it's worth, I don't believe Navarre is a danger to her."

"We have to do something."

"I've already alerted detectives throughout the area to be on the lookout," Schroeder said. "They have descriptions of Riley, Navarre, and Riley's Infiniti. I think we should expand the search to the whole Midwest, if not the entire country. Of course, that would cost a great deal of money."

Muehlenhaus waved his hand as if he were shooing away a fly. "It doesn't matter," he said. "Can it be done quietly?"

"Quietly takes longer," Schroeder said.

"What are the police doing?"

"The police are looking for Collin Baird. Legally, they have no reason to look for Navarre or your granddaughter."

Again he waved his hand. "A mere technicality," Muehlenhaus said. "I can deal with that with a phone call."

"So much for quiet," I said.

"Do you have something to say, McKenzie?"

I recalled what Riley's mother told me—*She deserves her chance.*

"If you make your granddaughter the subject of a nationwide manhunt simply because you don't like her choice in men—"

"He's a criminal."

"Riley might not see it that way. She might see it as you trying to control her life, like you did her mother's."

"What do you know about it?"

"Only what I've been told."

"By Sheila?"

"Yes."

Muehlenhaus glared at me, yet it wasn't personal. He felt he had to glare at something while he thought it over, and my face was closest. A moment later, his eyes refocused.

"I don't know what my daughter told you, or how much of it is true. The fact remains that my granddaughter—whom I love dearly—is behaving foolishly, whether you agree with that assessment or not. The fact remains that her relationship with Navarre has put her in danger."

"Perhaps."

"I want her home," Muehlenhaus said. "I want her safe."

"So do I."

"See to it."

Muehlenhaus spun around and made his way back toward the house. I called to him.

"I'm sorry about the slap."

"Just bring her home, damn you."

I waited until he was inside the house, the front door slammed shut behind him, before I said, "That went well."

"This is the third time I saved your life," Schroeder said.

"This doesn't count. You weren't really going to shoot me."

"Muehlenhaus knows people who are a helluva lot scarier than I am."

"Girl Scouts selling cookies on the corner are scarier than you are."

"What I'm saying."

We made our way back to our cars.

"I don't know how to find these kids, Greg—no idea where to even begin looking for them. Do you?"

"The feds could issue a hotwatch order, try to trace their movements through credit card transactions or cell phone use."

"If they do, they'll have to do it off the books. I doubt a judge would issue a warrant. Neither of them has actually been accused of a crime. Freezing Navarre's assets is already pushing it."

"One good thing. If we can't find them, Collin Baird won't be able to, either."

"I would feel a whole lot better if I believed that."

"You don't?"

"Do you?"

"No."

Nina was sitting at her desk and finishing dinner when I arrived at Rickie's. I watched her eat— Atlantic salmon roasted in a cherry-bacon crust with lemon butter sauce, braised vegetables, and heirloom potatoes. It was Monica Meyer's Chef Special for the day. Meanwhile, she watched me drink.

"Are you sure you don't want some food to go along with all that Scotch?" Nina asked.

"I'll grab a cheeseburger later."

"Don't let Monica hear you say that."

"Why? Is she going to yell at me, too? Do you know three of your employees stopped me on the way to your office to ream me out? Jenness wasn't even going to pour me a drink, and I promised to pay for it this time."

"They all think you're a bad influence on me." Nina dabbed at her stitches with her fingertips as if she wanted to make sure they were still there. The bruise had already changed from deep purple to an almost pretty blue-green. "It's possible I might have embellished the story somewhat. You know, for dramatic effect."

"Did you tell them you assaulted a federal officer, too?"

"The man reached for a gun. I did what I had to do."

"You told them that?"

"At the time I thought Agent Cooper was reaching for a gun, so—yes."

"Nina, forget the saloon business. You oughta go into politics."

"Are you sure you don't want anything to eat? I bet I could get Monica to make you a cheeseburger."

"I'm good."

"You're just going to sit there and brood. And drink. Is that it?"

"That depends. Who's playing upstairs, tonight?"

"The Willie August Project."

"I love those guys—'Empire at Twilight,' great song."

"So your plan is to sit, brood, drink, and listen to modern jazz."

"I'm a multitasker."

"Give me back the keys to my Lexus, since you won't be driving home."

"Are you going to tuck me into bed, too? What a wonderful woman you are, Nina Truhler."

"Yes. Yes, I am. By the way, I was thinking I might take your advice and start playing the piano again. This place practically runs itself now . . ."

There was more—something about a trio and taking up where Blossom Dearie left off. I wasn't listening, though. Instead, my head was filled with thoughts of Riley Brodin and my inability to find her, much less look out for her, as I had promised. Did she love Navarre so deeply that she was willing to risk her life to be with him? Would she turn her back on her family, on the Muehlenhaus name and all that it meant—not to mention the money? I couldn't think of anything more foolish, and yet people have done that sort of thing before, haven't they? Many times. With tragic consequences. Shakespeare wrote about it.

So did Leo Tolstoy and Alexandre Dumas. I was sure Nina would find it very romantic. 'Course, she had always been a glass-half-full kind of gal, while I prided myself on being a realist—on seeing a glass that's neither half full nor half empty, but rather one that's twice as big as it needed to be. I heard her mention a piano teacher and refresher courses . . .

"Are you listening?" she asked.

"Sorry. Guess I'm a little preoccupied."

"You have to give him credit."

"Give who credit?"

"Juan Carlos."

"Why?"

"He did get the girl, didn't he?"

"I doubt he'll keep her long."

"You're just being cynical."

"Says the women with three stitches in her head. I thought you were voting that Juan Carlos Navarre was legitimate?"

"Yeah, well, the more I think about it, the more implausible it sounds. I think now what happened was that David Maurell—"

"You mean Jax Albana."

"Whoever. I think he saw Riley in college, fell hopelessly in love, and spent the past seven years changing his life so he could come back here and win her hand. Don't you think that's romantic?"

"I would if he had actually changed his life, but he didn't. Navarre didn't go to school. He didn't become a doctor or engineer or someone of consequence so he could impress the lady. He used the money he stole from the Nine-Thirty-Seven to steal even more money from the U.S. government. Change his life—all he did was change his name."

"Boo."

"Nina, you can't possibly be on this guy's side. Listen, he didn't even know Riley when he masterminded the destruction of the Nine-Thirty-Seven. He didn't know her when he tried to seduce his way into Macalester College. None of that was for her. Nothing he ever did was for her. It was for himself. Think of the women he's used along the way. Navarre is a very selfish man."

"Yet he came back for Riley," Nina said. "He could have gone anywhere, done anything with the money he stole. Yet when all was said and done he came back for her. He risked everything to come back for her."

"Yes, he did. Now what?"

"I suppose living happily ever after is out of the question."

"Navarre knows about Collin Baird. That's why he's in hiding. Baird must have remembered his obsession with Riley—for lack of a better word—and cornered him here. Navarre must also assume, because of the heat generated by Baird, that the feds are hot on his trail by now, too. Not to mention the Nine-Thirty-Seven Mexican

Mafia, or what's left of it. So he'll run again. Which might have been his intention from the very beginning—get in, get the girl, get out. He rented Mrs. R's house instead of buying, after all, and he never did put the cash down for a membership at Club Versailles."

"Will Riley run with him, do you think?"

"You're the hopeless romantic, sweetie. You tell me."

"I'm asking you."

"I believe Riley is such a contentious young lady because she hasn't quite figured out who she is yet."

"And?"

"Now we're all going to find out. Dammit. Where can they be? I don't know where to look. It'll be easier after a period of time, after they've had a chance to settle in somewhere. Then there are all kinds of tricks you can use—everything from chasing Social Security numbers to reviewing the mailing lists of the magazines they read. Right now, though . . ."

"Have you spoken to Riley's mother? After Collin Baird was shot, he drove two hundred and eighty miles to see his mom. If I were in trouble, I'd probably do the same thing. Mothers—even after everything Abana and Baird did, their mothers still love them, still want to protect them."

I wagged my finger at Nina.

"That's a good idea," I said. "Sheila would protect Riley, too. And Navarre. There's no way she would rat them out to Mr. Muehlenhaus."

When I said, "Let's go," Nina thought I was bringing her along with me. She was annoyed when I drove back to her place in Mahtomedi so I could swap her Lexus for my Jeep Cherokee. Call me cheap, but if it came to it, I'd much rather buy myself a new SUV than buy Nina a new luxury car.

"Leaving me behind," she told me. "This isn't going to happen when we move in together."

That's an argument for another time, my inner voice said.

Sheila Muehlenhaus Brodin lived on a cul-de-sac in Lake Elmo, an outer-ring suburb of St. Paul, which put her about as far away from Lake Minnetonka as physically possible while still being considered a resident of the Twin Cities. There were two cars parked in the driveway. I thought I recognized one, yet couldn't place it. The mystery was cleared up, though, when I ranged the doorbell and Alex Brodin answered.

"Who is it?" a woman's voice bellowed from deep inside the house.

"That fucking McKenzie," Brodin replied.

"Stop calling me that," I said.

Brodin stepped away from the door without saying if he would or wouldn't.

"You might as well come in," he said.

"I'm surprised to see you here."

"Sheila and I visit frequently. Misery loves company."

I crossed the threshold. Brodin led me into a spacious living room. The thing I noticed first—couldn't help but notice—was an enormous painting of an alluring woman with lustrous eyes and deep red hair that matched her gown. There was nothing else on the walls and nothing nearby to compete with the painting. It was as if the entire room had been built solely to accommodate it.

"She's beautiful, isn't she?" Brodin said.

"Yes," I said.

"Thank you," Sheila Brodin said as she entered the room. Of course, the painting was of her. "I was eighteen when I sat for it." She placed a hand on her stomach. " 'Course, that was before childbirth."

"You haven't changed a bit," Brodin said.

Sheila bowed her head at the compliment and then turned it my way as if she were expecting me to repeat it. When she got bored waiting, she drifted to a bar complete with stools located in the corner. A full wine rack was on display, as well as assorted liquor bottles, ice bucket, and glasses. I had seen temporary bars set up in the homes of friends and acquaintances during parties, yet none that were permanent. Sheila's bar was as much a fixture of her house as the painting.

"I'm drinking bourbon," she said. "Alex?"

"I'll have the same."

"McKenzie?"

"I came because—"

"I know why you came here," Sheila said. "Riley and her Prince Charming have escaped the clutches of the evil Grand Vizier and he's dispatched his minions to bring them back."

She held up a bottle of Maker's Mark for me to see.

"Over ice," I said.

I was partly raised by a man who insisted that good Kentucky bourbon was meant to be taken straight—"the way God intended." He would have rolled over in his grave if he knew I was diluting it with ice. On the other hand, I had already consumed several alcoholic beverages, and I thought it best to keep my wits about me—whatever of those I still had left, anyway.

Sheila fixed the drinks, gave one to Brodin and one to me. She raised her own glass and said, "To true love."

"Hear, hear," Brodin said.

"Why not?" I said.

After we finished drinking, Sheila said, "I thought we had an understanding, McKenzie—you were going to look out for Riley."

"I'm trying, God knows."

"Then what are you doing here? Let the girl have her chance."

"Things have happened since we last spoke. Do you want to hear about them?"

"Does it involve the Department of Justice freezing Navarre's assets?" Brodin asked.

"Yes."

"Then I want to hear."

Sheila found a chair and sat, folding her legs beneath her. She waved her drink at me.

"You have the floor," she said.

I explained as succinctly as I could. I was surprised that neither of them interrupted to ask questions.

When I finished, Sheila said, "I don't believe you."

"You think I'm lying?"

"If you're working for the old man, yes I do."

"I'm not. How many times do I have to say it?"

"What McKenzie said about the DOJ freezing Navarre's money this morning—that's true," Brodin said. "I told you how I'm screwed because of it. Brodin Plaza. If something isn't done by the end of the month, if I don't get additional funding, I'm going to have to halt construction. I went to the old man. He blew me off. I told him I wasn't interested in his money, just in help talking to the government. He said *a real man* solves his own problems."

"That's what I mean," Sheila said. "It's all just

another elaborate ploy so he can get his way. Be a big man on the lake."

"I don't believe this," I said.

"I've been dealing with his crap all my life, McKenzie. You have no idea, you really don't."

"I've been getting it, too," said Brodin. "Ever since I married Sheila. The man's a monster."

"You people," I said. "Brodin, did it ever occur to you that Mr. Muehlenhaus said no to your request because he was unable to say yes, that he didn't have any juice with the Department of Justice, that he didn't have contacts who did, and he was afraid for you to find out? The first time I met her, Riley told me Mr. Muehlenhaus's strength came from the perception people have that whatever it is, he can fix it, break it, build it, or make it go away. *The perception.* She understands it, how come you don't? In the right light and at the right angle, even the tiniest object can throw an immense shadow onto the wall. But it's an optical illusion. The shadow only makes the object *appear* bigger than it really is. Which raises the question—have you two been spending your lives doing exactly what that old man told you to do, living under his thumb, because you're afraid of his shadow?"

Neither of them seemed to have anything to say, so I kept going.

"Listen, I don't care," I said. "This is none of my business. All I care about is Riley. I'm not trying to bring her back to Mr. Muehlenhaus. I'm not trying to keep her away from Navarre, whoever he turns out to be. I'm trying to protect her from a man who's already murdered two people and assaulted another to get at Navarre. Now, dammit, where the hell is she?"

Sheila unfolded her legs and rose slowly from her chair. She crossed the carpet and stood in front of me. For a moment, I had the feeling she was going to spit in my face. Instead, she sighed deeply like someone giving in to unpleasant news.

"Promise you won't tell the old man," she said. "Promise that you're just going to make sure she's safe."

"I promise."

"The family has a place on the lake up north. Beautiful place. It was once featured in *Minnesota Monthly* magazine. They're going to spend the night there before driving to Canada."

Nineteen

In the language of Minnesota, "a place on the lake up north" could be damn near anywhere. Start with "a place." That suggested anything from a clearing where you pitched your tent or parked your trailer to a rustic cabin or palatial lake home. "The lake" was whichever one of our eleven-thousand-plus bodies of water where you owned or had access to "a place." And the phrase "up north" referred more or less to the entire region a half-hour's drive beyond the Cities—roughly two-thirds of the state. To the Muehlenhaus clan, it was a family compound consisting of a large main house surrounded by six small cabins located on the north shore of *the* lake—Lake Superior—near Lutsen, about four hours away by car assuming you obeyed the speed limit, which I seldom did.

8:34 p.m. and I was already on my way when I called to tell Nina about it.

"You're not going to swing by and pick me up, are you?" she asked.

"No, I'm not."

"Is it because you're afraid I'll get hurt or because you think I'll be in the way?"

"Yes."

"Here I thought you'd be happy I was showing an interest in your work."

"Next time I need to drive two hundred and forty miles in search of a crazed killer, I'll save you a seat."

"You say that, but you don't really mean it. Can you at least do me a favor? Stop at Betty's Pies and get me a blackberry peach crunch."

"Are you serious?"

"You might as well. Driving along the north shore, it's on your way."

"Nina, I'm not stopping to buy a pie."

"Ohhhh," she moaned.

"What?"

"Where Baird hit me with the gun—it's really starting to ache. Don't worry about me, though. I'll just take an aspirin."

"Fine. Blackberry crunch."

"Blackberry peach crunch. Oh, while you're at it, get a five-layer chocolate pie, too."

"This is why I didn't take you with me. You don't have the right mindset for this sort of thing."

10:17 p.m. and I was fast approaching the bright lights of Duluth when it occurred to me that instead of worrying, I should reach out to the Cook County Sheriff's Department. I thumbed 9-1-1 into my cell phone keypad and asked the operator to transfer my call to the county's nonemergency line. From there I was connected to dispatch. I gave the woman my name and requested a "welfare check" on Ms. Riley Muehlenhaus Brodin.

"Is there an issue we should be aware of?" she asked.

I explained that Riley had been linked to a murder that took place in Hennepin County and I was concerned for her safety. I gave the woman the names of Lieutenant Pelzer and Collin Baird, as well as Riley's address and the license plate number of her Infiniti sports car.

Dispatch told me Cook County had a deputy patrolling near the area and would request that he knock on Riley's door. I thanked her and hung up the smartphone.

I didn't stop worrying, though.

10:52 p.m. and I was driving at speeds that invited arrest. I-35 was all torn up in downtown Duluth, and I had a helluva time working my way through the construction area before connecting with Highway 61 and following it north along the shore of the big lake. I nearly cracked up while dialing Riley's cell phone. She didn't pick up then anymore than she had the first three times I called.

11:25 p.m. and I was a few miles north of Two Harbors and rolling past Betty's Pies, the iconic tourist stop located midway between Duluth and my destination. It was closed.

"Gee, sorry about that, Nina," I said.

I still had an hour's drive in front of me.

Lutsen was a small tourist town built on a high bluff overlooking Lake Superior and flanked by four mountains and a dozen ski resorts. Some people liked it better than Aspen. Since I had never spent time in either place, I was happy to go along with their assessment.

I slowed before I reached the edge of town and began scanning the shoulder of the highway for the unmarked road Sheila told me about. I found it at 12:17 a.m. and followed it downward toward the lake. I stopped near the bottom when my headlamps illuminated the rear bumper of a Cook County Sheriff's Department cruiser. It was parked directly behind a Honda Civic. I put the Jeep Cherokee in park and engaged the emergency brake, yet I did not turn off the engine or the lights. I slowly walked to the cruiser and looked inside. It was empty. I rested a hand on the hood. It was still warm.

Next I proceeded to the Civic. Its engine was cold. I looked inside. There was a copy of *Minnesota Monthly* on the front seat.

"Dammit," I said,

From where I stood, I could look down the rest of the driveway. It led to the main house and the six cabins. The buildings were huddled together beneath the slanting bluff as if for protection from the enormous, temperamental lake, although it was calm enough when I arrived, the tide out. There were no other vehicles that I could see. All the cabins were dark, but there were lights shining through the windows on the ground floor of the main house.

I watched them for a moment from a distance. A bright moon shone overhead, and the sky was filled with a billion stars. I quickly returned to the Cherokee, extinguished the headlamps, and shut off the engine. I was alarmed by how quiet the world became. I could hear no noise at all, not even the sound of surf rolling up on the shore of the lake.

I pulled the SIG Sauer and moved toward the lights, a moth to a flame.

It was just a few degrees above freezing and I could see my breath as I negotiated the driveway and crossed the lawn; I could feel the cold air nipping at my bare hands as I gripped the gun.

There was movement in the back of the house. I squatted in the shadows and watched. It was Collin Baird—I recognized him immediately. He was standing in a well-appointed kitchen and eating ice cream directly from the carton, not a care in the world.

I edged closer.

The lights inside were bright enough that I knew they were reflecting off the glass in the kitchen windows like a mirror. Baird would be unable to see me, I was sure, yet I zealously avoided the shafts of light pouring from the windows onto the grounds anyway as I closed on the house and began moving along its walls.

The windows were high up, so I was forced to stand on my toes. Through one I could see a handsome living room with arched doorways and beamed ceiling. I grabbed hold of the window-sill and hoisted myself up. The furniture was elegant; a baby grand piano like the one I had vowed to buy Nina stood in the corner.

I went to another window and pulled myself up again. This time I saw a body on the floor, a man dressed in what I assumed was the uniform of the Cook County Sheriff's Department. He was lying on his stomach, his head turned away from me. I figured he must still be alive because Baird had cuffed his hands behind his back. If he were dead, why would he have bothered?

I didn't see Riley until I moved to a different window. The sight of her was like a sucker punch to the stomach. She was naked. Her hands were fastened to a chain. The chain was wrapped around a ceiling beam above her. She was suspended from the beam, her feet well off the floor, like a side of beef in a slaughterhouse. Her mouth was gagged.

I dashed to the front door. It was locked. My right brain told me to kick it open. The cooler left brain couldn't believe that Mr. Muehlenhaus would have invested in cheap locks and argued that nothing good would come from letting Baird hear me *failing* to get inside.

I circled the large house again, searching for an entry point. While I did, I saw Baird in the kitchen. He set his ice cream down and picked up something else—I couldn't see what. He passed from one window to the next as he made his way into the living room where Riley was hanging.

I didn't like shooting through windows. Glass has a way of deflecting bullets. I would have tried it anyway except for the angle. The windows were so high I could only see Baird's head and shoulders. If I missed . . .

I kept moving around the house, wondering how Baird got inside. Then I saw it—the back door was slightly ajar. I moved toward it. Baird had smashed the window and simply reached in to turn the lock.

Muehlenhaus, how careless can you be? my inner voice wanted to know.

I slipped past the door into the kitchen. Broken glass crunched beneath my feet. I hesitated for a moment, then moved forward, holding the SIG with both hands. As I approached the living room I could hear Baird's voice.

"Where should we begin?" he said. "Your tits? Nah, I'm gonna want to play with those later. How 'bout . . ."

I heard Riley's muffled cry.

"Or how 'bout here," Baird said. "Right behind your knee. I injured a knee playing football in high school once. It really hurt."

I came around the corner into the living room, the SIG leading the way. Baird was turned at an angle and didn't see me. He was holding a kitchen torch, one of those butane gas jobs that are used to melt the sugar on the top of crème brûlée. He seemed to be having a problem getting it to flame.

"Hey," I said.

He spun toward me. His eyes blinked as if they were adjusting to a bright light. Beyond that, he didn't seem frightened at all.

"You again," Baird said. "Fucking McKenzie, right?"

I moved deeper into the living room. I wanted to get close. Yet not too close.

"Ruining everything again," he said. "Who are you, anyway?"

I didn't answer. Instead, I gestured with the muzzle of the gun for him to move away from Riley. He moved a foot. I gestured again. He moved another foot. And again. Baird sighed as if bored, yet he took a third step. Riley was no longer in the line of fire. I gestured some more, just the same.

"What do you want?" Baird asked. His head turned in the direction of where I was driving him. He saw his gun sitting on the table. "Are you a friend of Navarre? He's not who he says he is, you know."

He moved closer to the table.

"His real name is Dave Maurell. He stole millions. Millions. I'm just trying to get my share."

He was still holding the kitchen torch, and I knew what he was thinking; I could read it in his face. He was wondering if he dared throw the torch at me and try diving for the gun while I was distracted.

At the same time, I could see Riley out of the corner of my eye. She was hanging perfectly still. Whatever terror, whatever discomfort she was feeling had been momentarily forgotten while she watched the scene unfold.

"I'll split it with you. There's enough for everyone. If Dave hadn't been so greedy . . ."

Baird's knee hit the table. He looked down at it. The gun was only a few inches from his hand, no more.

My body was so tense that my hands began to tremble. I deliberately took a deep breath and let half out, forcing myself to relax. My hands became still.

Baird smiled.

"Fuck that," he said. "I know what you're trying to make me do." He dropped the torch to the floor and raised his hands above his head. "You're just gonna have to try to take me in like that asshole deputy—"

I shot him in the center of the chest.

The first bullet was probably enough to kill him.

I added four more to make sure.

The Cook County attorney was furious. The deputy had died of gunshot wounds on the way to the hospital, and he wanted to prosecute someone, anyone, and I was the anyone closest at hand. He was especially determined since the ME was willing to testify that the bullet wounds in Baird's chest were inconsistent with my official statement that he was reaching for the gun on the table when I shot him.

Once the other evidence started rolling in, though, he changed his mind. Anne Rehmann picked Baird's photo out of a six-pack, identifying him as the man who assaulted her in her office—it took her all of two seconds. DNA tests proved that it was Baird who raped and murdered Mrs. Rogers. Ballistics confirmed that the bullets that killed both Mrs. Baird and the Cook County deputy were fired from Baird's gun. (The deputy's colleagues wanted to throw me a parade for putting his killer in the ground.) The clincher was Ms. Riley Muehlenhaus Brodin, who assured the county attorney that she would not only testify on my behalf, she would spend a million dollars for my defense and another million dollars to guarantee that he never held public office again.

All that came much later, though.

Immediately after Baird's body hit the floor, I turned to the deputy. After I uncuffed his hands, I used his radio to call it in—"Officer down, officer down"—and recited the address of the Muehlenhaus estate. A flood of questions followed, but I was too busy to deal with them. The deputy's skin was a ghastly ashen color, and his breathing was so shallow that for a moment I thought he was already dead. Yet he was warm to my touch and I could detect a rapid, thready pulse. When I gently rolled him on his back he opened his eyes. They were filled with terror and confusion. I said something to him. I don't remember what. "You'll be all right." Something like that.

"I totally messed up," he said.

He closed his eyes while I examined his wound—he was shot in the left side and losing a lot of blood. I applied a tourniquet using a kitchen towel and my belt. All the while, I spoke to Riley.

"I got you, sweetie. I'll be just a few minutes. I know it's hard. You'll be all right. Hang in there."

When I said that last sentence, I turned to look up at her. I swear to God she was laughing behind her gag.

After caring for the deputy, I found a chair and used it to stand on while I freed Riley. The air was filled with sirens as I lowered her to the floor. I grabbed an afghan off the back of one of the living room sofas and wrapped her in it—I didn't want the deputies and paramedics to see her nude like that.

Riley grasped my hand and wouldn't let it go. "He was going to . . ."

"Don't think about it."

"What's going to happen now?"

So many things I couldn't even begin to tell her. I hugged her close to me and whispered into her ear.

"Just go with the flow," I said.

Riley hugged me back.

"You told me that once before," she said. "This time I'll listen."

They immediately transported the wounded deputy to Cook County North Shore Hospital in Grand Marais, about twenty minutes away. Grand Marais was one of my favorite towns, yet up until that moment I didn't know it even had a hospital. The deputies wanted to send Riley, too. She announced she wouldn't go anywhere unless I went with her. They wanted to question us both separately. She refused to let go of my hand. They tried to be considerate—Riley was the victim, after all—yet it became clear the county cops were becoming frustrated.

"Miss, this would all go so much easier if you would cooperate," the lead investigator told her.

"Give me a phone and I'll show you

cooperation you won't believe," Riley said.

"This is not going with the flow," I told her. Yet I was glad to see the combative woman I had come to know and love.

She's going to survive this, my inner voice said. *She's going to be fine.*

Still, when we had a private moment I told her, "Soon as you get home, I want you to talk to someone. A professional. I can give you a name, if you like. I know you think you're okay now, but people rarely come through something like this unscathed."

She squeezed my hand tighter. "I know," she said. "That's why I'm acting like such a bitch. I'm afraid if I think about it, if I . . ."

It was too late. The tears started to flow and her shoulders began to shake. A moment later her face was pressed against my shoulder and she was weeping loudly and nothing I said or did could console her. After that, the deputies left her alone.

The morning sun flowed through the windows, giving the low white ceiling and the white tile floor of the hospital visiting room a golden hue. The county cops had finished with us—at least for the time being—and Riley and I sat next to each other while waiting for Muehlenhaus and his minions to arrive. She was holding my hand. She had released it only sporadically through the long night and never for very long. The first time was when the paramedics wrapped her damaged wrists in gauze. The second was while the doctors were examining the rest of her after she allowed herself to be taken to the hospital, although she had insisted that I remain in the room—I did so, but I had my back turned at all times. And then again when she dressed in the jeans and sweater she was wearing now.

"Riley," I said, "where's Navarre?"

"He left. Borrowed my car about twenty minutes before that Collin Baird character showed up. How did he find us, anyway? Do you know?"

"Through *Minnesota Monthly*, I think."

"Comes from being rich and famous, I guess."

"Why did Navarre leave?"

Riley had recovered her bag as well as her suitcase before leaving the Muehlenhaus estate. She dipped into it and produced a small, square box. She gave it to me, and I opened it.

"Holy—this can't be real," I said.

"It's real, all right. Seven-carat marquise-cut diamond engagement ring."

"You could carve your name in granite walls with this thing."

"I've never been a diamond girl, McKenzie. I never saw the attraction. You have to admit, though, this is impressive."

"What happened?"

"When we reached the compound, before we even unpacked, Juan Carlos got down on one knee, gave me the ring, and asked me to marry him."

Riley paused as if she were reliving the moment. Finally she said, "My grandfather, when I was younger, told me that if I was having trouble making a difficult decision, I should flip a coin. He said that before the coin hit the ground, I would know what the decision should be. This ring—it was like a coin toss for me. The moment I saw it—I mean after I got over the shock of it— I knew exactly where I should be and with whom and it wasn't Juan Carlos. I told him so.

"What surprised me—well, the whole thing surprised me, but *one* of the things that surprised me was that Juan Carlos didn't argue. He didn't beg; he didn't try to talk me into it. I didn't actually want him to debate the issue, yet at the same time I was disappointed that he quit so easily. He simply said it was okay. 'I understand,' he said. I told him it was me, not him. I told him he was a great guy and any woman would be lucky to have him. He wasn't listening. He asked to borrow my car and that was the last I saw of him."

"You have to understand something, sweetie," I said. "A girl turns down a ring like this, the guy has to know she's serious."

"I suppose."

"Did he ever tell you his real name?"

"What do you mean? Juan Carlos isn't his real name?"

"Oh, boy."

I explained. When I finished, Riley shook her head sadly.

"That is so messed up," she said. "And you say I met him at Macalester? I don't remember. I honestly don't remember him."

She held up the ring box.

"That's even more reason why I should give this back. I don't know where he is, though. Probably somewhere in Canada. That's where we were going—to escape ETA, he said, that you tell me doesn't actually exist anymore. Geez."

"I don't think Navarre's in Canada. Maybe I'm wrong, but I'm pretty sure I know where to look."

"Will you find him for me?" Riley asked. "Will you give back the ring?"

I closed the box and stuffed it into my pocket.

She lifted my hand and pressed the back of it against her cheek. "Thank you for the loan of this," she said.

"You're welcome."

She released my hand.

By then Muehlenhaus had arrived, accompanied by Greg Schroeder and a small army of people I didn't recognize—probably lawyers—and I wondered if the old man always traveled with an entourage. He crossed the room in a hurry, stopped in front of us, and pressed his fists against his hips. He didn't ask his granddaughter if she was okay or how she was feeling; he didn't address her at all. The first words out of his mouth were "Damn you, McKenzie. You've involved yourself with my family for the last time."

Riley replied in a hard monotone. "Don't speak foolishly, Grandfather," she said. "I don't like it. For future reference, McKenzie is my friend, and not just because he saved my life. When you disrespect him, you disrespect me. You do not want to do that. I have a bad attitude. Ask anyone."

Muehlenhaus was stunned into silence. I was a little dazed myself, yet I managed to ask the woman, "Who are you?"

Riley smiled and leaned in close so only I could hear what she whispered.

"Didn't my mother tell you? I'm the Muehlenhaus Girl."

I found Navarre exactly where I thought he would be—sitting on the front steps of his mother's house in West St. Paul. It was late afternoon by the time I arrived. The streets were deserted, yet I felt the weight of a dozen eyes on me as I parked the Jeep Cherokee in front of the house and walked up the battered sidewalk.

Navarre was dressed impeccably—expensive

shoes and socks, slacks with a crease that could spread butter, a shirt that looked like it was being worn for the first time, a gold watch that reflected the sunlight. He didn't move as I approached; he didn't seem to register my presence at all. It was as if he were one of those living mannequins you sometimes see at the more fashionable depart-ment stores.

I stopped in front of him. His eyes focused on me. I reached into my pocket, found the small square box Riley had given me, and tossed it toward him. He snatched it out of the air with a quick hand and set it on the concrete step next to himself without even bothering to give it a look.

"Riley said she's sorry," I told him. "She's going to be all right, by the way."

"Of course she is," Navarre said.

"Collin Baird is dead."

"Did you kill him?"

"Yes."

"You're McKenzie, right?"

"Yes."

"Collin was my only mistake. I needed some-one to front for me, someone with a legitimate Social Security number and a clean passport. I picked Collin because he was a small-town boy who wasn't nearly as smart as he thought he was. I didn't know he enjoyed hurting people, though, especially women, until Laredo, and by then it was too late. A broken toy with no way to fix him. I'm sorry about Mrs. R. And Annie."

"Jax—"

"Call me Juan Carlos. That's the person I worked hardest to become. Almost made it, too."

"Why did you take his identity, of all people?"

"Because he was flawed. I knew Riley's people would think I was too good to be true. I knew they would check my background, well, Navarre's background. Instead of a con man, they would find a prodigal son who didn't get on well with his father—and then stop looking. They wouldn't like Juan Carlos any better, but they weren't going to like him anyway. Riley, though. Riley liked him just fine. She just didn't like him enough."

"Did you kill him?"

"Who? Navarre? Of course not. I don't kill people. What do you take me for?"

"How did you get his passport? His identity?"

"I bought it. I met him in a bar in Greece. He sold me his name for half a million euros. Said he hadn't had any use for it in years."

Then I asked him the big question. "Why did you do it?"

"Do what? Be specific."

"Everything."

"I took the money from the Nine-Thirty-Seven because I wanted a better life. I became David Maurell and tried to get into Macalester College for the same reason. Meeting Riley—meeting Riley told me *why* I wanted a better life."

"But you didn't actually meet, did you?"

"Oh, no," Navarre said. "Not back then. I wasn't worthy of her then. She would have dismissed Jax and David out of hand. I had to become someone else first."

"Where's your mother?"

"Out shopping. She's going to cook a feast for her long-lost baby boy."

"Your sister?"

"At work."

"Don't do this, man."

"I've got no moves left."

"The Department of Justice . . ."

"And go to prison for thirty years?"

"You have almost fifty million dollars of their money. Make a deal. Buy down your sentence."

"The money is in Switzerland. The account is set up so that I'd have to appear in person to get at it."

"So? Take a plane ride on the taxpayer's dime."

Navarre shook his head.

"The Nine-Thirty-Seven Mexican Mafia," I said.

"I know. Cesar's little brother—last time I saw him he was a little snot-nose punk. Probably still is. I'll find out soon enough."

"Don't do this," I repeated.

Navarre had nothing to say.

"Offer the money to Arnaldo," I said. "Buy your way out of this."

Navarre had nothing to say to that, either. Still, it's been my experience that a man who's prepared to dive into a pool will fight tooth and nail to keep from being pushed. At the last moment, Navarre might decide he had plenty of moves left. If the Cook County cops hadn't confiscated my SIG Sauer, I would have given it to him.

"Good luck, Juan Carlos," I said.

I turned and walked back to my Jeep Cherokee. Navarre called to me.

"Tell Riley . . . tell Riley I left her car at the Signal Hill Shopping Center."

I drove slowly down the street until I spied a black Cadillac DTS with silver wheels parked at the curb. I stopped. Two men were in the front seat. Arnaldo Nunez was in the back. He glanced out the window at me and nodded the way people do when they want to acknowledge your presence without actually speaking to you. I nodded back. There was nothing to be said anyway.

I drove on.

Just So You Know ....

It had been a harder winter than most. The ice didn't officially leave Lake Minnetonka until the first week of May—two days after the Twin Cities were pounded by a rogue blizzard that dropped six inches on us—and it wasn't until the middle of the month that restaurant and café owners felt confident enough to open their outdoor patios and decks to customers. It was then that Riley Muehlenhaus Brodin summoned me to Casa del Lago for lunch.

I had missed the grand reopening for reasons I don't remember, so this was my first look at the place since the fire. I was impressed to discover that Mary Pat Mulally didn't just repair the building; she remodeled to give it a more authentic look and feel. Based on the number of customers at the tables inside and out, I guessed it had recovered quite nicely.

Maria Nunez met me at the door. She seemed happy to see me; even said I was "looking good," which kind of threw me. We compliment women all the time on their appearance, yet we seldom mention it to men unless we're surprised by something.

What did she expect? my inner voice asked.

That you'd fall apart in the seven months since she last saw you?

We didn't speak about Arnaldo. What information I had suggested that Juan Carlos Navarre disappeared immediately after I left him on his mother's stoop. Whether Arnaldo killed him and hid the body or accepted the bribe I told Navarre to offer in exchange for his life remains unclear. I do know that Navarre spoke the truth—FinCEN traced his money to a bank account in Basel, Switzerland, and after some high-level finagling, the Department of Justice was able to recover it. So wherever Navarre was, alive or dead, he was broke.

Maria led me to a table near the railing of the patio with a splendid view of Gideon Bay. Riley was already waiting for me. I didn't recognize her at first. Her hair was still short, but she had allowed it to return to its natural auburn color. And she was wearing a pristine black business suit over a white silk blouse.

"Look at you, all grown up," I said.

Riley came out of her chair to hug me.

"You look great," she said.

"People keep saying that. Is it that much of a shock?"

"Given what you do for fun and games . . ."

Riley reclaimed her chair, and I sat across from her. Her eyes sparkled in the bright sunlight.

"So, what brings me here?" I asked.

Riley glanced behind her for a moment, saw no one, and turned back.

"I'll tell you in a minute," she said. "How's the lovely Ms. Truhler?"

"As lovely as ever. How's your family?"

She laughed at the question. When she finished, she said, "McKenzie, have you ever read *King Lear*?"

"Yes. I've seen it performed, too."

"What was Lear's big mistake?"

"He divided his property among his children while he was still alive."

"My grandfather put the Pointe in my name as a Christmas gift. Actually, he was trying to avoid the death tax, but still."

She laughed some more.

"Why is that funny?" I asked.

"By New Year's I had moved my parents in— both of them."

Now I was laughing, too. "How did Mr. Muehlenhaus take it?"

"How do you think?"

"You are such an evil little girl."

"Since then, my father has lost nearly sixty pounds. I helped him secure additional financing for his building—he's happy as a clam. My mother —the last time I saw her was at Club Versailles. She was drinking raspberry ice tea and dancing with my father. On the other hand, both my grandparents seem to be drinking more these days. Oh well."

"Do they talk? What do they say when they pass each other on the way to the bathroom?"

"How should I know? I don't live there."

Riley laughed some more. While she was laughing, Mary Pat appeared with a tray of margaritas. She set a drink in front of me, gave me a hug, and kissed my cheek. She must have left a smudge of lipstick, because she brushed at the spot with her fingertips.

"A toast," Riley said.

She lifted her glass with her left hand. That's when I saw it—the green eyelike gleam of an emerald set in a white gold band. I glanced at Mary Pat's left hand, third finger. She was wearing an identical ring.

"I'll be damned," I said.

"That's not the toast I was going to give," Riley said. "But it'll do."

Both she and Mary Pat sipped their drinks. I quickly joined them

"Congratulations," I said. "When's the big day?"

"I want you to mark your calendar, McKenzie," Riley said. "That's why I called you."

"You're not going to blow us off this time like you did my grand reopening," Mary Pat said.

"The wedding's going to take place the first Saturday after I get the state legislature to allow gay couples to marry," Riley added.

When you get the legislature to allow . . . ? my inner voice said.

At the same time I flashed on a headline I saw that morning in the *Minneapolis Star Tribune* newspaper—"Minnesota's same-sex marriage battle goes behind the scenes."

"I guess that means you're taking over the family business," I said.

"I think of it more as a hobby," Riley said. "Besides, I'm really busy these days. Grandfather was involved in so many different enterprises—there doesn't appear to be any synergy, any cohesion at all. It's like he invested in one thing, got bored, and invested in something else almost on a whim. Now I'm the one who's supposed to make sense of it all. The teachers at the Carlson School of Management did not prepare me for this kind of chaos."

"Nobody said it would be easy being the Muehlenhaus Girl."

"No, they didn't."

"As long as you come home at night," Mary Pat said. "That's the main thing."

The two women leaned in and kissed each other. I turned my head toward Gideon Bay to give them some privacy.

There were any number of different watercraft sharing the huge lake and I thought about Navarre's boat, the *Soñadora*, and I wondered what became of it. Did it crash and burn like its owner? Probably not. Probably it had been shrink-wrapped in blue polyethylene film and dry-docked until the next dreamer came along to claim it.

I suppose that's what Navarre was—a dreamer. But his dream was rotten at its core. Navarre believed that if he stole enough and lied enough to enough people, if he pretended hard enough, he could become the man Riley Brodin wanted to marry. Only it wasn't a man Riley had been searching for all her young life. It was love—pure and simple. And that's something that cannot be stolen or bought or faked.

In the end, Navarre thought he had almost made his dream come true. He was mistaken. The truth was, he never had a chance.

I drank my margarita and watched the boats some more. I wished them all a safe harbor.